Other Books by Alison Bass

Side Effects: A Prosecutor, a Whistleblower and a Bestselling Antidepressant on Trial
Getting Screwed: Sex Workers and the Law
Brassy Broad: How One Woman Helped Pave the Way to #MeToo

REBECCA OF IVANHOE

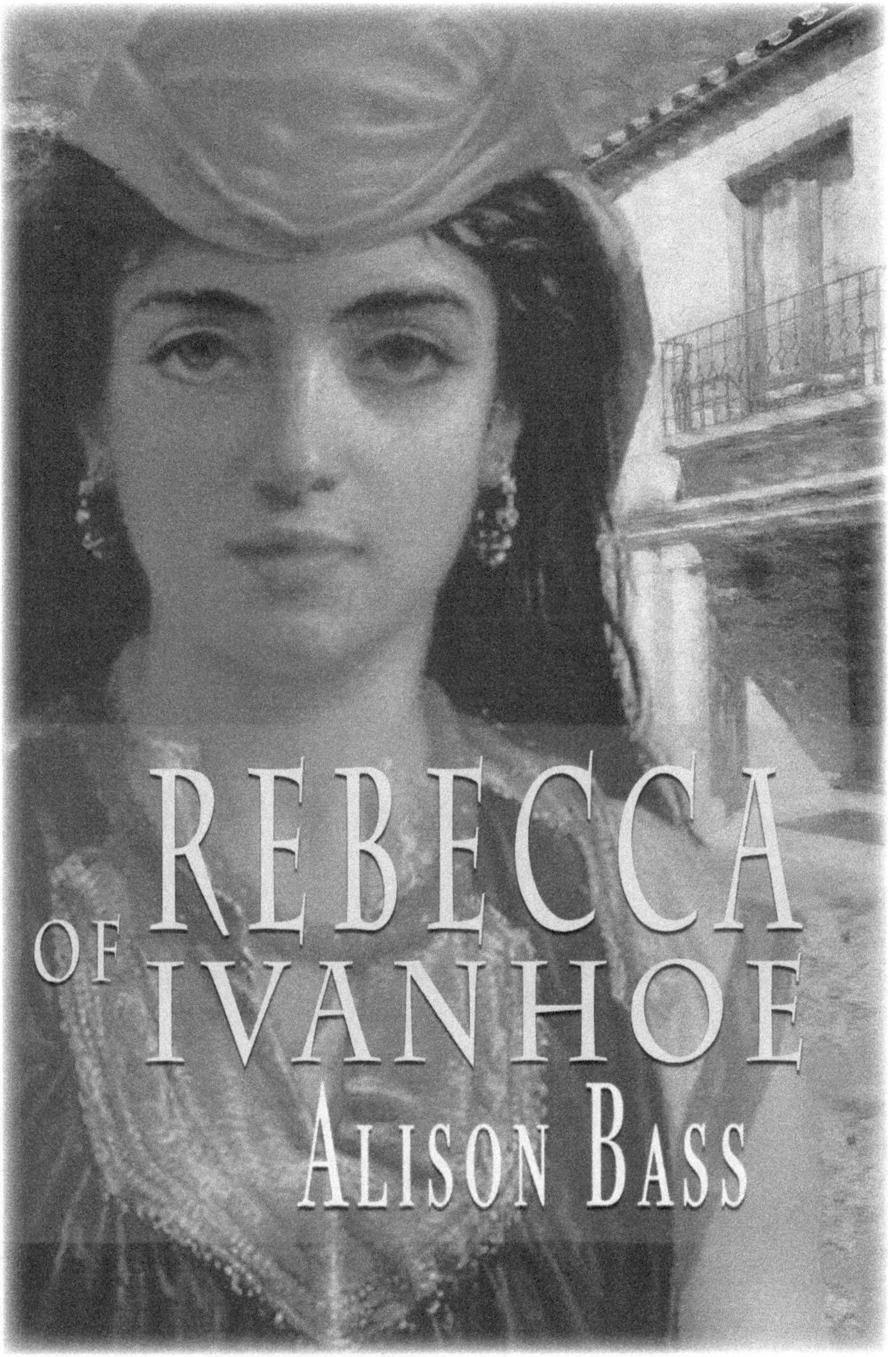

REBECCA OF IVANHOE

Alison Bass

Bink Books
Bedazzled Ink Publishing Company • Fairfield, California

© 2024 Alison Bass

All rights reserved. No part of this publication may be reproduced or transmitted in any means, electronic or mechanical, without permission in writing from the publisher.

paperback 978-1-960373-52-6

Cover Design by
Sapling Studio

Bink Books
a division of
Bedazzled Ink Publishing, LLC
Fairfield, California
http://www.bedazzledink.com

*In loving memory of my mother,
who imbued in me a love of reading*

"The beautiful Rebecca had been heedfully brought up in all the knowledge proper to her nation, which her apt and powerful mind had retained, arranged and enlarged, in the course of a progress beyond her years, her sex, and even the age in which she lived."
— *Ivanhoe: A Romance* by Sir Walter Scott

PROLOGUE
May 1194 AD

AS I SAT shivering in my cell somewhere deep in the monastery's bowels, the full horror of what was happening crashed down on me. I had once again refused Brian de Bois-Guilbert's offer to help me escape. He was prepared, he said, to incur the wrath of the Templars, the Christian military order to which he belonged, if I gave myself to him. But how could I even consider such a thing? I was a respected healer, well-known in England's Jewish community, and there was no way I was going to run off with the scoundrel who had kidnapped me, a man who readily admitted to ravaging many women while fighting in the crusades. I knew my father would understand. He would want me to stay alive at any cost, but the idea of spending my life in subservience to a ruthless blackguard who thought nothing of breaking his own vows of chastity and would not think twice about casting me off or killing me once he had tired of me. No, I could not accept that fate.

Yet it was my misfortune that the very day Bois-Guilbert brought me to this monastery in Templestowe the head of the Templars had arrived here, determined to root out venality in his order. And when this Grand Master learned that a knight of his own order was holding a maiden, a Jewish maiden no less, with the intent of having his way with her, he had exploded with fury. The preceptor of the monastery, a friend of Bois-Guilbert's, had managed to convince the Grand Master that the blame lay solely on my shoulders. I was a witch, he insisted, who had seduced a good Templar knight with my sorcery. What a distortion of reality! My insides burned with the injustice of it.

I was brought before the Grand Master and summarily tried and convicted despite my protestations of innocence. Only at the last moment was I given the opportunity to scrawl a message to my father, imploring him to find the only knight I knew that might be inclined to take up my cause: Ivanhoe. A peasant who knew my father had promised to convey the message. But that had been three days ago and neither Ivanhoe nor any other champion had arrived to fight in my name.

At night, imprisoned in my cold cell, its thick stone walls bare of any adornment, only a hard bunk to lay on, I could hear the chanting of the monks and the scrabble of rodents looking for food. I couldn't sleep for wondering what would happen to me. Was I going to suffer the same horrid fate as my beloved mentor, Miriam, a Jewish healer who had been burned at the stake a few years ago? Miriam had stepped into the void left by my mother who died when I was only four. Miriam had taught me everything I knew about healing, and her skills were known throughout the land. But that hadn't saved her. And it wouldn't be enough to save me either.

Just this morning, a Templar official had come to my cell and informed me that I would be burned alive at the end of the day if no one came forward to joust on my behalf. I couldn't imagine a more hideous, painful death. If only I had the means to kill myself first, but the Templars had taken everything from me, including the bag that contained my balsams and herbs. All they had left me with was a Bible. I tried to calm myself by reading the 23rd psalm over and over again, *Yea, though I walk through the valley of the shadow of death, I will fear no evil: for thou art with me; thy rod and thy staff they comfort me.* But then I made the mistake of going to the tiny window in my cell and looking out. And there I saw two men walking a horse-drawn cart filled with bundled sticks of wood. I moaned and would have swooned had I not at the last moment grabbed the windowsill with my hand. The wood was almost certainly bound for the deadly fire that would consume me within hours if a champion did not arrive in time.

Oh, how I wished we had left England four years ago, when the mob at York burned down the synagogue with hundreds of innocent Jewish souls cowering inside. That massacre had claimed the lives of my mother's younger brother and his family, and after that tragedy, my father and I had discussed leaving this cursed island once and for all. But I was just coming into my own as a healer and my father's business was thriving, so we decided to stay. What an enormous mistake that had been. In a matter of hours, my life might be extinguished in the most horrible way imaginable. I collapsed onto the filthy bench and thrust a hand over my mouth to stifle the scream that tore out of my parched throat.

CHAPTER ONE

September 1194 AD

IN THE DISTANCE, I could see the city of Córdoba, its shimmering white dwellings clustered around a hill with the spoke of a minaret rising above the rooftops. I reined in my horse to take in the sight. I should have been happy we were almost there, but all I felt was apprehension, a vague mounting fear. Would we be able to find my uncle and his family or be turned away at the city gates, dismissed as heathen foreigners? After five days of hard travel on horseback, I was filthy, tired, and sore. I would give anything for a hot bath and could only imagine how much more exhausted my elderly father felt, although he had not complained once during our arduous journey, first by boat from England and then on horseback from Seville, a port city near the southern edge of Spain. We had been lucky not to encounter any brigands on the road. This was a troubled time in Andalusia, and I doubted our lone armed guide could have held off a swarm of bandits.

The turbaned guide curbed his horse near mine, and I glanced with trepidation at his sheathed cutlass. It was similar to the swords my kidnappers in England had worn, only shorter and simpler in design. When we camped at night, the guide had slept an appropriate distance away from us, but I could feel his eyes burning into my body as I adjusted my robes and blankets on the hard ground. One evening when his stare was particularly pernicious, I withdrew the jeweled dagger my father had given me after my near-death experience in England. I held it up to the light of the fire as if to inspect it. The guide lowered his eyes and turned away. Message received. Even so, I would be glad to see the man's back when we arrived in Córdoba.

"We're almost there, Rebecca," my father said, pulling up his horse next to mine. "I just hope your uncle has received my missive and knows we are coming."

Our guide barked out a warning, and I looked up. A column of men on horseback was galloping toward us. Their horses kicked up a flurry of dust from the caked mud on the road, but as they neared, I could see they were a column of Saracen soldiers, dressed in dark gray tunics, white neck gear and turbans, long straight swords sheathed by their sides. I froze, my heart thundering in my chest. Black spots obscured my vision. Were they coming to arrest us or worse? My father grabbed my bridle and pulled my horse to the side of the road. As the Saracens galloped past, the memory of Brian de Bois-Guilbert throwing me on his steed and galloping down the drawbridge came rushing back. Bois-Guilbert had told me the castle where we were being held was on fire and he was taking me to safety. He said the other captives, including my father, were already free and we would meet them in the woods. I only learned later that he was lying, that my father and the other captives were still in the castle, which was being besieged by Ivanhoe and other brave yeomen who had come to rescue us. My father and the others would soon be freed. Only I would remain a hostage, with worse yet to come.

"Rebecca, are you okay?" my father asked in a worried voice.

I came back to myself. I was sitting on a horse on the outskirts of Córdoba and all I saw of the Saracens was a dustbowl settling down the road. My father was staring at me in concern. I drew a shaky breath.

"I'm fine, Father," I said. "Shall we go on?"

Olive groves stretched into the distance as we neared the city; southern Spain was known for its fine olive oil. Closer to the pitted road, small ponds filled with rotting stalks of flax emitted an awful stench, as bad as raw sewage. I pinched my nostrils to keep out the smell and kept riding. We passed tanneries, where foul-smelling hides were being beaten into leather. I withdrew a soiled handkerchief from my bodice and pressed it to my nose. It helped keep out the repellent smell of the hides and smoke belching from the metal-working shops we passed.

As we neared the center of the city, the streets became cleaner and more fragrant. Were those lilacs I smelled, with a hint of wisteria? The streets here were paved, and I stared in wonder at the luxurious villas and water gushing from fountains set back from the street. The falling water sounded faintly like the ocean. My muscles relaxed for the first time in days.

The city of Córdoba seemed laid out like a labyrinth. At its center stood a huge, imposing mosque. I stared at it in wonder as we rode by. It was larger in girth than any of the churches I had seen back in England, and yet, according to my father, it had been built more than two hundred years ago. Several men dressed in garish yellow tunics, hurried through the streets, their faces drawn and eyes averted. Just past the entrance of the mosque, a guard berated a young bearded man dressed in yellow. The man stood slumped, his shoulders rounded, his eyes downcast, accepting the abuse. I could sense that something was wrong but couldn't put my finger on it. All I knew was that I felt acutely uncomfortable and wanted to be far away from this spectacle.

Once we were safely past the mosque, I turned to my father. "Why are some men wearing those ugly yellow tunics? Do you think their garb signifies something?"

My father shrugged. "I have no idea. But don't worry; we're almost there." His lined face gleamed with excitement. "I'm amazed that I remember the way after all this time. We're entering the Jewish quarter now."

The streets here were narrower but immaculately clean. Tall whitewashed walls hid the dwellings from view, and wooden doors latticed with iron barred entrance from the street. Finally, my father stopped in front of a door, which was slightly ajar. He got off his horse and pushed it open. The guide and I also dismounted, and we walked into a small courtyard flanked by tall walls. It was late afternoon but the sun was still high in the western sky.

"I think this is Benjamin's house; it used to be my father's," my father said, his voice husky with joy. He knocked on the front door and after an interval a young woman clad in a simple dark blue tunic opened it. My father bowed to her. "Shalom. Is Benjamin home? I am Isaac, his brother."

The young woman gaped as she took in the three of us, dusty with travel. She uttered something in a language that I didn't recognize and disappeared back inside the house.

After what seemed like an interminable time, a stooped man wearing a long yellow tunic with a matching turban appeared in the door. He squinted at us and his mouth dropped open.

"Isaac, is that you?" he said in a dialect that I could barely understand.

I already knew some French and a little Latin, and on the ship from England, my father had taught me the rudiments of Ladino, the Judeo-Spanish language that Jews in southern Spain spoke. It was the language my father had grown up with, but I couldn't recall him ever speaking it in England, to me or my mother. As my father and his brother conversed, I was able to catch some of their words here and there.

"What in Yahweh's name are you doing here?" Benjamin repeated.

"Did you not get my scroll?" My father stepped up to enfold his brother in his arms. "It is good to see you, Benjamin."

"What scroll? I received nothing," Benjamin said. He embraced my father and then stepped back and looked at me. "And this must be Rebecca—I haven't seen you since you were a baby. You've grown into a beautiful woman."

I felt my checks warm. "Thank you, Uncle." I bowed my head as decorum required.

"Come in, come in, you must be weary and parched after your long journey." Benjamin gestured to us, stepped back into the house, and barked some orders.

My father turned to the guide, dug some gold coins out of his purse, and pressed them into his hand. He thanked and dismissed him. I was relieved to see him go.

My father and I were ushered into the cool shade of the house and stripped of our dusty cloaks. As we were escorted down a hallway, I noticed a plethora of leather satchels, some empty, others crammed with household items, sitting in the hallway. Was the family getting ready to travel somewhere? Had we come at a bad time? Benjamin escorted us into an anteroom adorned with rich tapestries and thick oriental rugs. Plush cushions lay strewn around the room.

"Please make yourself comfortable. Jemila will bring you some refreshments and then, ahem . . . perchance you'd like to clean up from your long journey." Benjamin looked away but I saw his nose wrinkling in distaste. "As you can see, our house is in disarray. We ourselves will be on the move soon. But all of that can wait until you have replenished yourselves."

Three hours later, feeling blissfully clean after a hot bath, I sat down with my father, Benjamin, his wife, Hania, and their daughter, Estraya, for the evening repast. Hania had given me a light silken tunic to wear, which felt much cooler and more comfortable than the woolen tunics I had brought from England. It was early fall and the temperatures in southern Spain were much warmer than they had been in England. Hania's table was laden with delectable dishes: rice-stuffed peppers, lamb kebabs, pickled lemons, a cucumber and tomato concoction, and fried chickpeas. I was famished, despite the refreshments we had been given earlier. Once all the food was served, Benjamin dismissed the servants and muttered the blessing over the wine, followed by the Hamotzi, the blessing over bread.

"We have to be very careful about who sees us practicing our faith," he said in a low voice. "Ever since the Almohads conquered Andalusia, they have arrested and tortured any Jew who openly observes. And they have forced many to convert to Islam. Those of us who have not converted are forced to wear this hideous color." He plucked at his yellow tunic with distaste.

I exchanged a perturbed look with my father; so that was why those harried-looking men had been wearing yellow. They had been Jews, singled out because of their faith.

"And we get spit on when we go out," Benjamin continued. "Sometimes worse. One of our neighbors was beaten to death a few weeks ago because he went out without wearing a yellow tunic."

I gasped. This sounded as bad or worse than the situation in England. Had we made a mistake in coming here?

"What are you saying, brother?" my father asked, as if reading my mind. "I thought the Saracens gave the Jews greater freedom to practice our religion than the Christians who persecute us relentlessly."

Benjamin sighed. "It used to be that way. But the Almohads practice a more militant version of Islam and they consider nonbelievers to be blasphemers. They have made life very difficult for us. That is why we are leaving Córdoba. My older daughter and her family have already left for Toledo, which is not under the Almohads' rule. King Alfonso of Castile has seen to that. He is bent on throwing the Almohads out of Spain."

I felt sick to my stomach. We had just arrived in Córdoba after an exhausting trip and now we would have to pick up and move again. And what guarantee was there that our lives would be any better in Toledo, which sounded like a Christian stronghold.

"Isn't King Alfonso Christian?" I asked. "How do you know we will be any better off under his rule?"

Benjamin smiled sadly. "There are no guarantees, of course. But up till now Alfonso has allowed Jews to live in Toledo with some degree of safety. Most of our people are confined to the Jewish quarter at the edge of town but I am told we can practice our faith and go about our business. It helps that the Jews of Toledo have given generously to King Alfonso's war chest."

I nodded, still feeling queasy. I had almost died because of my faith back in England and had been hoping for an easier life in Spain. But it sounded as though members of our tribe were persecuted here as well.

Even so, our relatives had been so happy to see us and so welcoming that I tried to hide my unease.

"That's good to hear, Uncle," I said. "I pray it stays that way."

"As do we all, my dear," Benjamin said and turned to my father. "And now tell me, brother, what brings you here?"

Our relatives listened in awed silence as my father told the tale of my capture by the Templars and my deliverance at the hands of Ivanhoe.

Estraya, the Manasses' fifteen-year-old daughter, leaned toward me, her eyes wide, and asked, "What is this Ivanhoe like? How could you help but fall in love with him?"

Hania's lips tightened. "Estraya, that is not an appropriate thing to ask."

I laughed and waved a hand. "I don't mind." I smiled ruefully. "To be truthful, I think I was a little in love with Ivanhoe. He is so handsome and kind and he doesn't seem infected by the hatred that so many of his countrymen feels toward our people. But Sir Ivanhoe is in love with the Lady Rowena and she with him. Her own parents, who were Saxon nobility, perished when she was a little girl and Ivanhoe's father, Lord Cedric, raised her as if she was his own. As a result, she and Ivanhoe grew up together. But then Wilfred—that is Ivanhoe's given name—went off to fight with King Richard in the Crusades against his father's express wishes and he was disinherited. Even so, Ivanhoe and Rowena never stopped loving each other. They just had to keep their love a secret—in the beginning."

Estraya's eyes glistened. "What a romantic tale."

I felt a familiar ache in my breast and fought to keep my voice even. "Even if Ivanhoe wasn't in love with Lady Rowena, it could never be. Ivanhoe is a Christian knight and I am a heretic in the eyes of the Church. Even so, Ivanhoe has been nothing but kind to me."

"Unlike that dastardly Bois-Guilbert, a so-called Knight of the Templar," my father said. "He took a vow of chastity to the Church and yet he thought nothing of kidnapping Rebecca and trying to force her to submit to his will. And when she resisted, he left her in the clutches of the Templars to be tried as a witch."

I laid a supplicating hand on my father's arm. "This is true. But at least he tried to help me in the end."

My father snorted. "Well, bully for him. Don't forget, he is the reason you were almost burned at the stake. I hope he is rotting in hell or wherever Christians believe evil men go after they die."

Benjamin looked around fearfully. "Please, brother, lower your voice. Not all of our servants are Jewish and they might take offense."

My father looked abashed. "I'm sorry, brother. I forgot myself."

I patted my father's arm. "Thank you for defending me, Papa. I wouldn't be here if it weren't for you."

CHAPTER TWO

LESS THAN A fortnight later, we all left Córdoba, my relatives' worldly goods piled into two carts led by donkeys. Being unused to horseback, Hania and Estraya nestled on one of the carts alongside the driver, while I rode a steed, as did my father and uncle. Benjamin had retained only two male servants to drive the carts, but he had also hired two armed guards to protect us on the road from Córdoba to Toledo. Since the Almohads' grip on power had loosened in recent years, bandits roamed the roads. Even when we reached Alarcos, the southernmost outpost in Christian Spain, a four-day journey on horseback, we wouldn't be entirely safe.

"These are dangerous times," Benjamin told us during supper the night before we left. "King Alfonso has pledged to take Andalusia back from the Saracens and everyone is on edge."

I tried to hide my concern and twisted a fold of my skirt under the table. I wished, not for the first time, that my father and I had taken King Richard's assurances to heart and not left England. At least there we were known and supported by the Jewish community and I myself had a champion in Ivanhoe. Here, we were completely dependent on two armed strangers and my uncle's understanding of what lay ahead. Would we even live to see Toledo?

To prepare for our trip from England, my father and I had sold or given away most of our household belongings and converted our money into precious stones and gems, which we sewed into our garments. Our relatives now did the same with much of their furniture and household goods and we wore long, shabby cloaks to hide the silken garments holding our jewelry.

We were fortunate not to encounter brigands during our first three days and were able to find inns at night that could accommodate our party. I had to share a filthy cot with Estraya, but at least we didn't have to sleep on the floor, wrapped in flimsy blankets the way the servants and guards did.

On the fourth day, as we slowly made our way to Alarcos, the guard leading the party spied a dustbowl on the road ahead of us. He galloped back to Benjamin and spoke rapidly to him. Benjamin turned around and waved an arm at us.

"Quick, everyone, we must hide in the woods," he yelled, pointing to a small path that wound into the forest just ahead of us. "There, see that path, follow it."

I spurred my horse onto the path, my father close behind, followed by Benjamin. The servant driving the cart carrying Hania and her daughter, plowed onto the path behind us. A few feet in, we saw that the cart was too big for the narrow path. Behind me, Benjamin and one of the guards helped Hania and Estraya onto their steeds. Then we all trotted deeper into the forest, leaving the cart partially obscured by foliage. But the driver of the second cart, who had been lagging in the rear, couldn't get off the road in time. The bandits galloped into view around the bend, and he jumped off the cart and ran into the woods in the opposite direction.

As we cowered behind bushes, stroking our horses in an effort to keep them quiet, a terrified scream pierced the air and was suddenly cut off.

Terror coursed through me, and I was plunged back to that horrid day in Templestowe when the Knight Templars had prepared to burn me at the stake. Ivanhoe still had not come, and that afternoon, I had been taken out of my cell and brought to the field where two knights, one standing in for the Templars and the other for me, were supposed to battle over my fate. But my champion wasn't there. A throne for the Templar Grand Master had been erected at one end of the lists, surrounded by seats for the Preceptors and Knights of the Order. My custodians dragged me to the other end, where two men standing guard could not obscure the pile of wood cluttered around a stake fixed in the ground. I felt dizzy with disbelief and horror; this was where I would meet my end if Ivanhoe didn't arrive soon. I repressed an urge to wail out loud and tried to calm myself by repeating the Shema, the cornerstone of my faith. *Hear O Israel, the Lord is our God, the Lord is one.*

Hania, cowering next to me in the brush, was repeating the same mantra. The brambles in the bushes pricked me through my cloak, and sweat glistened on Hania's face. I gently put a hand on her forearm and squeezed it. She stopped chanting and looked at me with gratitude in her eyes.

"It will be okay," I mouthed, and she nodded slightly. The thieves were yelling at each other as they plundered the cart left on the road.

An eternity later, one of the guards who had crept closer to the road gave the all-clear. We emerged, blinking into the sunlight. The cart we had abandoned in the woods was where we had left it. But the second cart was overturned and almost empty, and the donkey tied to it was gone. My relatives' fine linens and sheets were also gone, along with several vases they had brought with them and other household items. Only a few pots and pans and broken dishes remained scattered in the dust. Benjamin asked a guard to search for the missing driver. While we waited, Hania and I picked up the few remaining belongings and packed them into the first cart. A few minutes later, the guard came back shaking his head. The second driver's throat had been slit and he was dead. Estraya let out a yelp of pain. Hania put an arm around Estraya and hugged her close.

"He gave up his life for ours," Hania said. "He died a hero."

Estraya snuffled, pressing her body against Hania's dusty cloak.

"I wish we had stayed in Córdoba," she moaned.

I too was heartily sick of being thrust in harm's way. I went to Estraya and pulled her into a hug. "We're almost to Alarcos and safety. Would you like to ride with me?"

By this time, Benjamin had conferred with the guards and turned to his family. "We don't have time to bury Ferrando, the banditos might come back. We must be on our way if we want to get to Alarcos by nightfall."

We set off with one cart carrying Hania and the driver and the rest of our worldly goods. With Estraya riding behind me on my mount and only one cart, we were able to proceed at a slightly faster clip and reached the town of Alarcos without further incident. A half-built fortress loomed over the town, and we spent the night in its partial shelter. After eating a cold meal of dried chickpeas and stale bread, I huddled with Estraya under a thin blanket in an effort to stay warm. Although I was exhausted, I couldn't fall asleep. Had coming to Spain been a mistake? Was any place in the world safe for me and my family?

Like Benjamin, my father had been raised in southern Spain, but he traveled widely as an emissary of his own father's business: trading spices, olive oil, and other goods from the Middle East and the Orient. My father had met my mother, the daughter of a wealthy banker in York, during one of his trips to England. He had fallen in love and decided to stay in England. But when I was only four, my mother, Sarah, had died giving birth to a son and a few days later, the infant died too. I had only hazy memories of my mother, a soothing voice, soft hands, the faint smell of lavender.

After my mother's death, my father was lost in grief and could deny me, his only remaining child, nothing. As a motherless child, I had been given freedoms that other girls in my social milieu did not have, allowed to ride my horse in the countryside, accompanied only by my father or the family groom. From a relatively young age, I had been permitted to pursue my interest in healing, and I acted as the mistress in my father's house, entertaining his guests and seeing to the household. As a moneylender, my father made a comfortable living, more than enough to sustain us, and we had two houses, one in York and the other near Ashby. It was only after I was kidnapped and almost killed that my father decided England was no longer safe for us. I shivered as the memories once again engulfed me, and looked up at the night sky, hoping to distract myself. Just then, a shooting star streaked across the heavens amid the thousands of winking points of light. I gasped; this was a good omen. Perchance the worst was past us and we would make it safely to Toledo. I turned on my side and snuggled up against Estraya, who was snoring lightly, and sleep finally took me.

Two days later, we arrived at the outskirts of Toledo. High cliffs surrounded the city on two sides and a river snaked its way through a deep gulley that separated the city from the surrounding countryside. When I asked Benjamin who had built the tall stone walls that encircled the city, he explained that they had been erected first by the Romans, then enhanced by the Visigoths and the Moors, and most recently by the Castilian kings who had reconquered the city in 1085. The walls surrounded Toledo from the west and north, he said; the Tagus River and tall cliffs kept the city safe to the east and south.

Weary and saddle-sore, we rode over an old stone bridge and were stopped at the gate. But we were allowed through after my uncle answered a few questions and dropped some coins in the guard's hand. Benjamin had been to Toledo before, and he led us to the Jewish quarter, a labyrinth of one and two-story wooden houses crowded together on the southwestern edge of the city overlooking the river and steep cliffs. Dirt paths just large enough to accommodate a small cart wound through the quarter, bustling with people trying to finish their errands and get home in time for the Sabbath. Benjamin asked every person he saw if they knew where the Mendes family lived. Finally, a man said he knew a Mordecai Mendes. He pointed down a narrow alleyway.

"I think it's the fifth house on the right," he said.

A young woman, who bore a remarkable resemblance to Hania, opened the door to the house he had pointed out. Her hands were covered in flour and a simple linen coif kept her abundant hair out of her face.

"Isadora, my darling, we're here," Hania cried out.

A joyous smile wreathed Isadora's face. "Mama! Papa! Estraya! Just in time for Shabbat." She saw my father and me and put her hand to her throat. "Who are these people with you?"

Benjamin stepped up and embraced Isadora. "We will tell you everything, but we've had a long hard trip and we're very tired. Where can we stable our horses?"

TWO HOURS LATER, my father and I joined our extended family around a table in the kitchen, which had a stone hearth and was the largest room in the house. The Mendes lived on the first floor of a narrow two-story house they had been able to purchase with Benjamin's money. The first floor had four rooms and an outhouse in the backyard, which was shared by all the tenants of the building. The Mendes rented out the second floor to another Jewish family. Isadora's young children, four-year-old Amada and one-year-old Daniel, had already been fed and put to bed in another room. Benjamin had paid the armed guides and his one remaining servant for their services. The servant had family in Toledo and was planning to seek them out.

Hania, Estraya, and I washed ourselves as well as we could in the basin in the backyard and donned silken tunics for the Shabbat meal. While we finished dressing in Isadora and Mordecai's bedroom, Isadora joined us.

"I'm so glad you're here," Isadora said to Hania as she pinned her hair back up under a fresh lace coif. "But if we'd known you were coming, we wouldn't have rented the second floor. Why did you not send word?"

Hania frowned. "But we did. Benjamin sent a message two fortnights ago with a rider who was bearing a dispatch from another family in our neighborhood. After the Saracen mob beat Salman to death on our very street, we decided it was time to go."

"I remember Don Salman; how horrible," Isadora said. "But we received no message from you."

Hania looked crestfallen.

Isadora rushed to her and hugged her. "Don't worry, Mama, we'll make do. Mordecai and I will talk to our upstairs tenants to see if they can spare a room. They are a nice family, recently from Valencia."

Before the evening meal commenced, Mordecai intoned the blessing over the wine and then the Hamotzi. He tore off chunks of the homemade flatbread and handed it around the table. I marveled at how comfortable he felt in observing the Sabbath. Back in England, my father and I lit the candles every Friday night in the privacy of our home and he never worked on the Sabbath. But ever since the massacre of a hundred and fifty Jews in York four years prior, we had been afraid to openly observe the Sabbath or any Jewish holidays for that matter.

My father and I had been traveling to our other house near Ashby at the time but we knew many of the murdered Jews. My uncle, a banker, and his wife and children had managed to make it to Clifford's Tower, a royal castle, along with many other Jewish families in York. They had thought they would be safe—they were, after all, supposed to be under the protection of the king. But the mob burned the keep down and slaughtered any Jew who survived the fire. King Richard had already left for the crusades and none of the instigators were apprehended and punished for their foul deeds.

For weeks afterward, I felt physically ill with anger, sorrow, and guilt that my father and I, by sheer providence, had managed to survive the butchery. But how could God, a compassionate just God, allow such evil to occur? I came close to losing my faith after that calamity. I had truly never believed in a God-like entity who existed in any corporeal form and regularly intervened in earthly affairs. And the tragedy in York only cemented my skepticism.

After York, I understood that no Jews, no matter how wealthy or high in the king's favor, were truly safe in England. My father and I talked of leaving, but where would we go? The only family we had left in the world was in Spain. But the idea of starting anew in a strange land didn't appeal to me, and my father wasn't eager to give up his business interests and throw himself on his brother's mercy. Even so, we were careful not to observe any Jewish rituals outside the confines of our home.

Yet here in Toledo, my relatives seemed to feel confident that they could safely practice their faith. My father must have been thinking the same, because after the meal was served, he ventured to ask, "So it is safe to openly practice here as a Jew?"

Mordecai, a slender man with a closely cropped beard and long hands, considered his answer as he took a tip of sweet wine from his goblet. "To a point, yes. We can observe in the privacy of our homes and Rabbi Yoachav Abenir reads the Torah every Saturday morning in the courtyard of the Perez house. He always gets a *minyan* for that. I hear there are even plans to build a synagogue in the Jewish quarter."

"A *minyan*?" I asked.

Mordecai smiled. "It means having at least ten men in attendance. According to the Talmud, you can't properly hold a service and read the Torah unless at least ten men are there."

He placed both palms carefully on the table. "But we have to be mindful of not rubbing our way of life in our Christian neighbors' faces. Already, I hear there is some resentment building about King Alfonso's appointment of several Jews to his cabinet."

I stared at him in surprise. "He must be a very liberal monarch—to have Jews in his inner circle."

Mordecai's face reddened, and he exchanged a glance with his wife. Isadora gave him a slight nod.

"As you probably know, King Alfonso is married to Queen Eleanor, a sister of Richard the Lionheart," Mordecai said in a lowered voice. "But she lives in a castle in Burgos, and they rarely see each other. The king spends much of his time in Toledo. He has fallen in love with a Jewess, Rachel Esra, and she wields enormous influence over him."

My mouth dropped open. A Christian king coupling with a Jew. This could never have happened in England.

Isadora leaned forward. "She even convinced the king to appoint three Jews to the royal court, where they advise the king on all matters. I hear tell she is quite attractive. They call her *La Fermosa*, The Beautiful One."

Estraya clapped her hands. "How wonderful. Will she be our Spanish Esther?"

She was referring to the Biblical story of Esther who had saved the Jewish people from certain death in ancient Persia. I quite agreed with her sentiment. I would love to meet this brave beauty who had the King of Castile and Leon wrapped around her little finger. But I doubted that would ever happen.

"Wouldn't it be grand to meet *La Fermosa*?" Estraya said. "Where does she live?"

Hania frowned at Estraya's impulsive question, but the men merely laughed.

"I would like to see her myself," Mordecai said. "Although I'm sure my wife's beauty is quite comparable to hers. Rachel lives in a grand house closer to the king's residence in the Alcatraz. That's across town from the Jewish quarter. But I hear she occasionally comes to the *barrio* with her servants to shop in the market."

I smiled at Estraya. "Well then, we'll have to make sure we make frequent forays to the market."

Everyone laughed.

CHAPTER THREE

AFTER SLEEPING ON the Mendes' living room floor the first night, my father and I were given a room for ourselves upstairs. The Jewish couple who lived there had one toddler, and Benazir, the wife, was pregnant again. Her condition reminded me of when my mother had been pregnant. We had been living in York, and my parents were clearly delighted that I would soon have a little brother or sister to play with. I often wondered what might have happened if Miriam, one of my mother's oldest friends and a renowned healer, had been home when my mother's time came. Miriam was known for getting women through difficult pregnancies. Would she have been able to save Sarah? Perchance. But instead, Miriam had been traveling on the continent with her father, a prominent Rabbi, as he tended to his far-flung flock of devout followers. She had been wild with grief upon returning to find that her beloved friend was dead and the baby with her. I suspected that the guilt Miriam felt for not being on hand to help Sarah had a lot to do with why, from then on, she devoted herself to me. Even though Miriam was often away, traveling with her elderly father, she became a surrogate mother of sorts to me and I loved her with fierce devotion. Even as a child, I often plied her with questions about her healing practice; I was drawn to her steadfast commitment to helping others.

One day when I was almost fifteen, Miriam roused me early and asked me to come and observe the miracle of birth. It was a raw April morning and heavy with mist. The stable hand had already saddled my favorite mare, Bessy. I shivered as I came outside and drew my cloak tightly around me. But I was eager to assist Miriam, and so I mounted Bessy and followed my mentor as she trotted down a rutted road to a small village outside of York. As we neared the village, men were already stooped over in the fields, furrowing the ground for crops that belonged to Philip de Malvoisin, the Norman lord who owned all the land in and around this village. I had heard that Malvoisin was a ruthless knight and nakedly ambitious. He was also known as a womanizer, and my father had warned me to stay clear of him.

After asking directions from a villager, Miriam reined in her horse before a small wooden hovel with a thatched roof. She turned to me. "This is not going to be pleasant. I understand the woman has been in labor for some time and she's having difficulties. Don't hesitate to go outside for some fresh air if you need to."

Miriam dismounted and entered the hovel, with me following behind. As my eyes adjusted to the dim smoky light inside, I could see a woman writhing in pain on a dirty mattress on the floor, attended by a stout woman whose wrinkled face bore the mark of many years.

"The baby won't come," the stout woman said, worry thickening her voice. "I don't know what's wrong. Estrid has been in labor for two days."

"Let's see what the problem is," Miriam said. "Do you have any clean water? I'd like to wash my hands first."

The older woman, who introduced herself as Gwinith, dragged over a bucket of cloudy, clearly dirty water.

"Tis all I have," Gwinith said somewhat belligerently.

Miriam sighed at the bucket, pulled some soap from her bag, and lathered her hands before rinsing them in the pail. She squatted by the bed, and gently massaged Estrid's huge belly, feeling for how the baby was positioned. Finally, she frowned and sat back on her heels.

"It's as I thought—the baby's face is facing front," Miriam said. "We need to encourage it to turn around."

She leaned over Estrid. "I know you're exhausted, but we need to get you in a better position to give birth. Gwinith and I will help, but you need to turn over and get on your hands and knees, like a dog. Okay?"

Estrid groaned. "I can't."

"You must," Miriam said calmly and turned to Gwinith. "Your daughter and the baby may die if she does not do as I ask."

Gwinith whispered to Estrid in a language that I recognized as Anglo-Saxon, a version of old English that I didn't understand. Estrid groaned and tried to sit up. Miriam and Gwinith helped her reposition herself.

"Good," Miriam said. "Now I want you to stick your bottom in the air; that might help tip the baby back up so it can turn around more easily. And if you can sway your hips back and forth, that would help too."

Estrid did what Miriam asked, although it was clear she was close to collapse.

"Now, Gwinith, while we attempt to turn the baby, can you please heat up water and bring some fresh cloths?" Miriam asked.

Gwinith grumbled under her breath, but she got up and went into the other room.

Miriam asked me to take her place and rub Estrid's lower back. As I rubbed, I marveled at how calm Miriam was, how well she handled Estrid and her mother. She showed no hesitation, or the kind of fawning I had observed when my father dealt with Christians, particularly landed gentry. I wondered if Gwinith knew that Miriam and I were Jewish, which meant we were loathed by the vast majority of English peasantry and their lords. She must know; after all, it would have been her mother or Estrid's husband who had sent someone from the village to seek out Miriam.

With Estrid doing her best imitation of a dog, Miriam gently palpated her belly. "Ah, I can feel the baby turning now. Keep swaying."

After some minutes, Estrid started screaming in pain. Her pains were coming fast and furious. Miriam positioned herself behind Estrid. "Okay, now I need you to push as if your life depends on it. The baby is coming."

Miriam felt around underneath. "It's crowning. Keep pushing."

"I can't," Estrid moaned. "It hurts too much. I hate you."

"Yes, you can, you can do this," Miriam murmured. "Just a few more big pushes."

By now Gwinith had returned with hot water and clothes. She squatted by Estrid's side and wiped the hair out of her eyes. "You can do this *min meregrot*. You're almost there."

Estrid howled and gave one final push and the baby slid out into Miriam's waiting hands.

"Well done," Miriam said. "A little boy and he's perfect."

She cut the cord with a knife she had ready, cleaned the mucus from the baby's face and body, and expertly bundled it into swaddling cloth. The afterbirth was expelled a short time later. By this time, Gwinith and I had wiped down Estrid, propped her up against a pillow, and covered her with a thin wool blanket.

I stared in awe as Miriam lay the baby on Estrid's chest. All the sweat, the yelling, the blood and tears had led to this, the miracle of a healthy newborn. I realized then and there that this was a miracle I wanted to participate in, again and again. If this was what it meant to be a healer, I was all in. I watched, tears in my eyes, as Estrid smiled wanly at her son and then fell asleep. I vowed I would do whatever I could to follow in my mentor's footsteps.

Miriam and I stayed until Estrid had revived and begun nursing the baby. Gwinith tried to press a plucked chicken on Miriam but she waved her off.

"Seeing your daughter and grandchild healthy and safe is my reward," Miriam said.

When we returned to York, I told Miriam I wanted to be a healer, just like her. To my surprise, she frowned.

"Are you sure, child? This isn't an easy life, especially for a Jewess." Miriam gently tucked a wayward curl back under my coif. "With your looks you will have no trouble finding a good husband among our people. Getting married would be the much easier route."

I frowned. She sounded just like my father, who had already started asking me if I was ready to entertain suitors. I was not. I could see how constrained life was for married women in York's close-knit Jewish community. My father had given me freedoms not permitted to most girls of my faith. He had taught me to read and write, and I could go riding in the countryside on my favorite mare whenever I wished, as long as I was accompanied by him or the groom. While I certainly wanted to experience romantic love—who wouldn't—I had no desire to have my freedoms curtailed by a husband, or a passel of children. Not yet anyway.

"I want to learn how to be healer," I insisted. "Please."

Miriam merely nodded.

She must have had a word with my father because shortly after that, she began tutoring me in how to heal common ailments, set broken bones, cure a child's jaundice, even deliver a baby. With patience and exactitude, she shared her secrets about which herbs and plants could help with what ailments and how to mix the most effective potions possible. Whenever I could, I would sit in when she treated patients and go on house calls with her.

IN THE YEARS since I attended Estrid's labor, I often wondered why my mother had had so much trouble birthing her second child. Had the baby been turned the wrong way too? Could anything have been done to save her and the infant? Now that I was in Spain, living in the same house with another expectant woman, I prayed that Benazir's second pregnancy would not end the way my mother's had. Mois, Benazir's husband, was often away on business, and I tried to help my pregnant housemate, entertaining her toddler, Bendie, and taking him out to play with Isadora and Mordecai's children, so his mother could rest. At one point, Benazir complained of back pain, so I suggested a soothing ointment that her husband could rub on her back. But while Benazir was happy to have me take Bendie off her hands for a time, she wanted nothing to do with my healing advice.

Shortly after we had arrived in Toledo, my father joined Benjamin in the family business. Just as their father had done, Benjamin imported spices and tea from Persia and India as well as flax from Egypt and then exported the goods, along with olive oil from southern Spain to countries in northern Europe and England, using a network of traders to carry the goods overland and by sea. Mordecai and Mois were two of those traders, and they often traveled abroad, leading caravans with the goods Mordecai's father-in-law procured.

While my father was thus engaged, time felt heavy in my hands. I yearned to put my own skills to work, but I couldn't do that until I had a better command of Judeo Spanish. I enlisted Estraya to teach me the dialect, and we spent hours conversing in that language as we walked around the Jewish quarter, shopped at the market, and helped Isadora and Hania with the household chores.

The first time I visited the market, I was assaulted by a pungent mix of animal entrails and rotting fish, freshly baked bread, sweet-smelling herbs and flowers, and smoke from wood fires. The vendors did their best to keep their own stalls clean but there was always foul-smelling garbage lying around, particularly near the end of the market day. I found the stench overpowering at first, but soon I barely noticed it.

One day when Estraya and I were shopping in the market, I watched in horror as an older woman was stepped on by a horse whose rider was pushing his way through the crowd. The woman screamed and collapsed. I rushed over to her. The woman had hit her head when she fell and was unconscious and bleeding. I asked Estraya to quickly find some alcohol and then extracted a clean cloth from the bag I always carried with me. I used the cloth to put pressure on the gash on the woman's forehead, and when Estraya returned with a flask of wine, I cleaned the wound with the alcohol and bound it with another cloth. By this time, the woman had regained consciousness a curious crowd had gathered around.

"Stand back please. Give this lady some air," I said, trying to speak with authority, the way Miriam would have.

A few people smiled at my mangled Ladino, but everyone obediently fell back, allowing me to prop the woman up against a stall. Squatting next to her, I took a closer look at her injured foot, which was encased in a dented boot.

"You're going to be all right," I reassured the woman, who was still in a daze. She was probably in her fifties, petite and slightly plump, with a round pleasant face and wrinkled, age-spotted hands. "My name is Rebecca and I am a healer."

She grimaced in pain and pointed at her foot. I considered whether I should remove her boot right there in the market and realized that it would only cause her more pain, and she would black out again. It would be better if we could get her out of the crowded marketplace and into her own home. I asked if any of the onlookers could help me get the injured woman home. Two workmen stepped forward and offered to help.

"Can you direct us to your home?" I asked the injured woman.

The woman nodded faintly.

The two men picked up the woman, who yelped in pain, and carried her through the crowd; Estraya and I followed close behind. Fortunately, she did not live too far away. When we got to her one-story house, the men laid her down gently on a bed and went on their way. I offered the woman the flask of wine that Estraya had procured earlier.

"Drink this; it will help with the pain," I said. "I need to take your boot off to look at your foot."

I instructed Estraya to hold onto the woman while I tried to remove the boot. "She may black out again. Make sure she doesn't hit her head."

As I untied the boot and tried to ease it off the woman's foot, she screamed, trying to wiggle out of Estraya's grasp. Finally, I tugged off the boot and the dirty sock underneath. It was as I thought. Several of the bones in the swollen foot looked broken and needed to be splinted and bound. While I was considering my options, a young woman rushed into the house, her eyes wide with alarm.

"I heard my mother was hurt," she said breathlessly. "We got separated in the market." She carefully sat down on the edge of the bed and took her mother's hand. "I'm here, Mama." The older woman smiled through her tears.

"I think she's broken several bones in her foot," I said. "I'm going to splint them, but she won't be able to walk for a while. Do you live with her?"

"Yes, my husband and I live here with her; I'm Rita and my mother's name is Perla," the younger woman said. "And you are?"

I introduced myself and explained that I was a healer. "Do you have any small strips of wood, some clean clothes and mayhaps a wire wrap? And a sharp knife?"

Rita rushed off to fulfill my request, and I used the opportunity to finish examining Perla's foot. Rita returned with the supplies, and I whittled the smooth wood into two small splints and carefully positioned the splints on either side of Perla's swollen foot. I asked Estraya to give Perla another drink from the wine flask and then gently rubbed an ointment I had previously prepared from flaxseed and mallow and carried with me on the swelling around Perla's ankles. I then bound the splints with the strips of cloth and pinned them together with the wire wrap.

"Make sure your mother doesn't put any pressure on that foot for at least two fortnights," I told Rita. "I'll come back to check on the splints in a few days and change the bindings. You might also want to make your mother some wooden crutches."

After I rechecked Perla's head wound and made sure she was comfortable, I stood up.

"Wait," Rita said and went into the other room. She came back and pressed some coins into my hand. "I am so grateful; you are clearly a skilled healer."

Word of that accident got around, and other injured or sick residents of the Jewish quarter turned up at the Mendes' house day and night. I treated these patients as well as I could in the courtyard of our house, but I could tell that Isadora was concerned about Amada and Daniel being exposed to whatever toxic vapors my patients brought with them. I knew this situation could not last. My father and I would eventually have to move but I was loath to leave the comfort of my relatives' household. An incident the following fortnight made the decision for me.

Benazir, whose growing belly made her irritable, was increasingly hostile to me. She had noticed that her husband, a stocky bearded man in his thirties, was wont to cast lingering glances at me when I used the backyard basin to bathe in the morning or came upstairs at night. I had never thought much about my looks, having grown up motherless. But once I reached puberty, many men, Christian and Jew alike, considered me a beauty, with my violet eyes and jet-black tresses, which fell in a cascade of curls down my neck. I found the attention that most men paid me to be burdensome; after all, it was my outward appearance that had gotten me kidnapped and almost killed back in England.

Now living in close quarters with a resentful pregnant woman, I did my best to avoid her husband whenever I could. But it wasn't enough. One morning, Benazir accosted me as I came back upstairs after cleansing myself to change into my day wear.

Benazir leaned heavily against the wall, her large stomach protruding ahead of her. "You have bewitched my husband, you sorceress. Perchance they should have burned you at the stake after all." Isadora must have told her about my misadventures at the hands of the Templars.

I gasped. How could Benazir be so cruel? I had done nothing to encourage Mois, nothing at all.

"You shouldn't say such horrid things," I said, as I brushed past Benazir. "Don't worry; we will be out of your hair soon."

I told my father about Benazir's outlandish accusations, and he was outraged. He wanted to confront Mois and Benazir, but I convinced him that would only make matters worse.

"The best thing we can do is move," I said. "Women in the advanced stages of pregnancy are not always the most rational."

My father agreed to find another place for us to live and within the week, we moved into a small house several streets away from the Mendes. Our new abode came with a private latrine and bathing area, a welcome respite from prying eyes. The house had three rooms downstairs, including a small kitchen, and two bedrooms upstairs. My father and I could still dine with our extended family most evenings, but at least we now had our own space.

A few days after we had moved, we were awakened by a loud knock on the door just after dawn. My father opened the door to find Isadora on the doorstep, breathing heavily, as if she had run the entire way.

"Amada has fallen ill," she said. "Please, can you fetch Rebecca. Perchance she can help?"

I hastily donned a cloak, grabbed the bag with my herbs, and followed Isadora through the still quiet streets. I found four-year-old Amada moaning and restless with fever in the bed she shared with her younger brother. I dropped my cloak on the floor and sat next to her, murmuring words of comfort and resting a hand on her hot forehead. Tell-tale red blotches marred the child's face and neck. I stood up and picked up my bag.

"She has the child pox," I said. "You must move Daniel into your room, although he has probably already been exposed. We need to keep Amada warm and hydrated. I have some herbs that I think will help."

Isadora clutched my arm. "Will she die?"

"I don't think so," I said. "If this is what I think it is, it is not fatal. But you need to keep her still and not let her scratch herself. I'm going to prepare some concoctions. Can you heat up some water?"

Hania, who was now up and dressed, stayed with her restless grandchild, while we went to the kitchen.

"I'm going to mix some belladonna, which should bring down the fever," I said, as Isadora started a fire in the hearth and put a kettle on. "And witch hazel should help with the itching."

Later that morning, Daniel also became hot to the touch. I dosed him with belladonna and witch hazel as well and left careful instructions with their mother for treating the children. In the days that followed, I was called upon by other families in the crowded Jewish quarter to treat their children who had also come down with the pox. Benazir had even sent Mois with an entreaty that I come and treat Bendie, who was showing the telltale signs as well. I agreed and after I had dosed the little boy with herbs and made him comfortable, I made a request of my own.

"I'm running out of my supplies of belladonna and witch hazel," I told Benazir. "Can you please ask Mois, the next time he leaves Toledo, to find more of the plants? I understand they grow just north of here. I will ask the same of Mordecai and draw pictures of the plants so they know what to look for. But tell Mois to be careful. The belladonna plant is toxic; it is known by some as the deadly nightshade, so he must not ingest it or get it anywhere near his lips."

Benazir, her eyes wide, nodded. "I will do that. We need to protect the baby." She patted her huge stomach. She looked down at her feet. "I'm sorry about what I said. I know you're not interested in my husband. Please forgive me."

I felt sorry for Benazir, red-faced and clearly exhausted. "Of course. Now you need to rest; I will stay with Bendie for a while and then maybe Hania or Estraya can spell me. You have to look after yourself for the baby; it is coming soon."

Benazir nodded miserably. "I know. I would be most grateful if you can help when the baby comes."

I nodded. I didn't really want to be anywhere near Benazir and Mois but I couldn't ignore a woman in her time of need. Miriam had once told me that a healer can't pick and choose who to help; she must try to heal all those who seek her help, whatever their life circumstances. She told me she had only drawn the line once, refusing to treat an English nobleman whom she knew had tortured Jews to extort money from them. When this odious individual lay mortally wounded from a swordfight and his henchmen came calling on her, she had her maid turn them away, saying she was not there. Fortunately, they didn't hang around long enough to find out the truth.

"I have to admit it was as much self-preservation as anything," Miriam had said. "If I had gone to him and he had died, which I knew he would, they would probably have killed me in retribution. Being a healer does not always protect one from being a Jew."

How sadly prescient Miriam's words would turn out to be.

AFTER I HAD nursed at least a dozen children through the pox outbreak, people knocked on my door quite often, seeking help with any number of ailments, from an impacted tooth to a listless baby. My father had helped me set up an apothecary of sorts in our spare front room to help those who didn't need house calls. Even so, we were often roused at night by frantic knocks on our door, particularly from men whose wives who were in the throes of childbirth. My father had plowed much of our remaining valuables into the family business and had yet to reap the return, so my services provided us with welcome additional income, as well as bread, eggs, and other food stuff that patients gave me when they didn't have coins.

Every once in a while, someone who sought my help would stare at me in surprise or consternation.

"You can't be Rebecca the healer," one beefy middle-aged man said, looking around. "You're too young and pretty."

I pursed my lips, having heard this too many times. "I'm afraid I am. What can I do for you?"

His pockmarked face turned scarlet, and he looked down at his shoes. Seeing no help there, he finally admitted that he was having trouble urinating.

"I just stand over the pot and sometimes nothing comes out, sometimes a little dribble," he said. "It's very annoying; I don't have time for this."

I tapped my finger on my cheek, a habit I had when thinking. I had never treated this problem myself, but I remembered Miriam talking about it. Although she wasn't sure what caused such urination difficulties in older men, Miriam said she had found some success in crushing the leaves of the garden-tree mallow, a common plant found in England and Spain, boiling them in water or wine, and serving the concoction as a drink. Because the mallow was such a useful herb—it also soothed toothaches and other inflammations—I had been delighted to find the herb on sale at the market in Toledo's Jewish quarter and bought a quantity for my apothecary.

"I think I have some medicine that might help," I said. "Please wait here and I will ready it for you."

I SOON BECAME so busy that I needed a helper. I turned to my family, and whenever they could spare the time from their household duties, Hania and Estraya would assist me. Estraya, in particular, enjoyed the work, listening closely as I explained the secrets of my art. One afternoon after we had finished with our last patient, Estraya sidled up to me as we were putting away the supplies.

"I notice that you often intone Hebrew prayers when you're preparing salves and treatments for the patients," she said. "Why do you do that?"

Her question stumped me for a minute. Miriam had taught me these healing prayers. She said they not only soothed her while she worked, she believed they helped the patients as well. I couldn't tell if they made a big difference in the actual treatments, but I found they calmed my hands and helped me prepare my salves and ointments with quiet efficiency.

I didn't really believe in some heavenly being that interfered in our paltry lives here on earth. But I found that the prayers I said over my work and on the eve of Sabbath every Friday gave me a measure of comfort and peace.

"Do you believe in God?" I asked instead of answering.

Estraya stared at me with a startled expression. "Of course, although I often wonder why he allows other religions to persecute our people so."

"I wonder the same," I said. "But I don't think God, at least how I imagine him, interferes much in earthly matters. I think whatever heavenly body created us has pretty much left us on our own to follow our own inclinations. Why else would there be so much strife and hatred?"

"So, what's the point of religion then?" Estraya asked.

I smiled. Estraya knew just how to get to the point.

"Good question. I think religion, or at least Judaism, gives us the tools to try to help others, to be as compassionate and moral as we can be. It doesn't absolve us of our sins every time we go to confession, as the Christians believe. But as a result, I think we Jews have to work harder at being good and doing the right thing. After all, we only get to ask God to forgive us for our sins once a year."

"At Yom Kippur?"

"Yes, and there's no guarantee he will forgive us and write us into the Book of Life for the next year," I said. "There's no priest in a confession box saying I absolve you of your sins if you do thus and such."

Estraya rubbed a cheek thoughtfully. "You're right—it's not easy being a Jew. But maybe there's a reason for that. Maybe it explains why we as a group tend to be resourceful—we have to be to survive."

I beamed at Estraya, feeling as if I were a teacher and she my star student. My cousin was very keen.

"Precisely," I said. "There's a saying in the Bible that God never gives you more than you can handle. I'm not sure that's completely true, but I think we as Jews have learned to handle a great deal and still remain standing. And now we really must get going or we're going to be late for supper at your mother's house."

CHAPTER FOUR

February 1195 AD

ONE DAY A few months after my arrival in Toledo, I opened my door to a loud knock and a splendidly attired man bowed to me.

"*La Fermosa* needs your help with a pressing . . . ahem . . . medical problem," the man said, leading me to believe he was a servant of hers, perhaps her mayordomo. "Can you come now?"

Rachel, the king's mistress, needed my help? Surely, she had her own healers, no doubt more experienced than me. How did she even know I existed?

"So can you come?" the mayordomo repeated. He made it sound as though I didn't have much of a choice. So much for my plans for the day. But I couldn't deny that I was curious to meet the vaunted *La Fermosa*.

"I'm coming," I said. "Is she ill? What are her symptoms?"

The mayordomo's face reddened. "I don't know, *señorita*. You will find out soon enough. *Por favor*."

I grabbed my bag and cloak and followed as best I could. The mayordomo strode through the narrow dirt-packed streets toward Toledo's Christian quarter. I hadn't been out of the Jewish Quarter since we arrived in Toledo, and was intensely curious to see what lay beyond its crowded borders, where wooden houses were stacked right on top of each other. I was surprised to find that as we climbed up toward the center of town, the streets were even more cluttered with garbage. Did the Christians not have a system of removing their waste, as we did in the Jewish Quarter? I resolved to ask Mordecai about this curious fact.

Halfway up the steep hill, we had to stand aside for a religious procession. Two white-robed priests with tall triangular hats walked in front, swinging a smoky chalice of incense. Behind them trudged a motley group of worshippers, mostly women and children and a few men, chanting a religious dirge. I had been told such holy processions were common in Toledo, but this was the first one I had seen close-up. One of the priests gave the mayordomo a look so filled with venom, I stumbled back in fright. The mayordomo just stood with his eyes rooted downward. As soon as the procession passed, he rushed up the path with me half-walking, half-running behind him. Why would a priest display such open hatred for a servant? Had he recognized him as Rachel's mayordomo? What could it mean? I didn't dare ask.

Finally, we arrived at a handsome two-story house; this must be where *La Fermosa* lived. I followed a maid up the stairs to a sitting room in the back. Colorful tapestries covered the walls and rich oriental rugs muffled the sound of our feet.

"I will tell *la señora* you are here," the maid said and left.

I walked to a window at the back wall and looked out onto a small but beautifully manicured garden. A few daffodils were already in bloom along with a cluster of white flowers that I didn't recognize.

"Those are bridal brooms, I had them brought here from Morocco."

Startled, I spun around to find an exquisitely attired woman with striking auburn hair held neatly in a lace coif, smiling at me with amusement. *La Fermosa* was perhaps a few years older than me and about the same height. And she was every bit as beautiful as the gossipmongers said, with luminous hazel eyes, aquiline nose, and full red lips.

"Come, sit with me," she said, pointing to one of the plush cushions that littered the room. "I am Rachel and you are Rebecca the healer. Yes?"

"I am." I sank onto one of the cushions.

"I have heard only good things about you as a healer," Rachel said as she arranged herself on another cushion. "Where did you learn your art?"

I explained that I had learned everything I knew from a wise healer back in England, a Jewish woman like myself, who had taken me under her wing. I said nothing about what happened to Miriam; it wouldn't be seemly to share such a tragic tale with a stranger I had just met. Rachel nodded, and before she could ask any more questions, I added, "And what can I do for you?"

Rachel pursed her lips and looked around. "What I tell you must not leave this room. Is that understood?"

I drew myself up. "Of course, I never betray my patients' confidences."

"Good." Rachel leaned forward and whispered, "I need your help in getting pregnant."

I rocked back in surprise.

Rachel laughed. "Is it so surprising that I want a child with the king? We have been together for almost seven years, and I want to give him the gift of a baby."

Rachel's eyes clouded over and she looked away. There was something this beautiful woman was not saying. I knew that King Alfonso had a number of children with his wife, the sister of Richard the Lionheart. So, he was undoubtedly virile. Thus, the problem probably didn't lie with him.

"This is no easy feat," I said, rubbing my chin. "Is your monthly bleeding regular? Have you and the king used any form of birth control?"

Rachel raised a jeweled hand. "One question at a time please. My menses are regular and when we first . . . ah . . . became lovers, I did use some oil. But I haven't in a long time."

I couldn't help but wonder why, after seven years of being his mistress, Rachel desired to get pregnant now. Surely, she understood that the king would never divorce his wife and marry her to legitimize any children they might have. Her offspring would be considered Jewish and thus a threat to the Church and the established order. Didn't she understand that?

Rachel narrowed her eyes. "You do know what I mean by inserting oil?"

"Of course. I am a woman after all." As an experienced midwife and healer, I knew as much as anyone about the vagaries of birth control, how unreliable it could be, and how carefully women, particularly those who were having carnal relations out of wedlock, had to tread with the subject.

Rachel considered me. "You are *bella*. I'm surprised you haven't been married off yet. I'm sure you've had many suitors."

My, this woman was a busybody. Yet I felt warmed by her attention. I had no one to confide in; I didn't want to burden my father, and Hania and Isadora were too preoccupied with their own family to pay me much mind. Although it was true that Isadora had raised the subject of suitors with me a month ago. Her husband, Isadora said, had heard about a widow, a man in his early forties whose wife had died recently. He was looking for another bride.

"He has two young children, and he can't really look after them himself," Isadora had told me. "He makes a good living as a butcher, and I understand he's not bad-looking."

"I'm too busy taking care of my patients to think about looking for a husband," I said.

I had been attracted to one of my patients, a muscular young man about my age who had come in with an infected toenail. He worked for his father, a builder, he said; they were hoping to bid on the contract for the synagogue when it was finally drawn up. But as I tended to him and we talked, it became clear he could not read or write. I had been taught to do both, and my father and Miriam had shared their devotional literature and precious handwritten books with me. Ivanhoe had not only been brave, handsome, and compassionate, but he too was literate, a man of the world. I doubted I would find someone of my faith who could measure up to him. But how could I explain any of this to the elegant woman sitting next to me?

"You will find someone who is worthy of you, I am sure of it," Rachel said, as if knowing my thoughts. She straightened. "Now, can you help me?"

I explained that women were at their most fertile in the middle of their monthly cycle. "So that is when you should try to make love," I said, failing to maintain a straight face.

Rachel giggled. "Anything else?"

"Well, there are herbs, like cinnamon, and the berries from the chaste tree shrub, that are said to help boost a woman's fertility," I said. "But I do not have these herbs myself and cannot vouch for their safety or effectiveness."

Rachel nodded. "I already have cinnamon. I will procure these chaste berries you speak of and you can mix them for me in the right doses."

I sighed. It was clear that *La Fermosa* would not take no for an answer. "I will try, but there are no guarantees. And I would hope you won't hold me accountable if the potions don't work."

Rachel's maid rushed into the room and whispered something in her mistress' ear. Rachel frowned and stood up. "One of my advisors has arrived and needs to speak to me. He has important news." She bit her lip. "Thank you for helping me. I will be in touch as soon as I have procured the items you mentioned. And now I must go. Taresa will see you out."

As I made my way back to the Jewish quarter, escorted by the mayordomo, I wondered what "important news" Rachel's advisor was bringing her. No doubt something to do with all the intrigue that must be rampant at court. I recalled something Mordecai had said, that Rachel, as a Jewess with unusual influence over the king, had enemies in the Church. Maybe being the king's mistress was not as glamorous as it seemed. Her position, her very survival, depended on retaining the love of one man and a married man at that. My heart softened toward the beautiful woman I had just met, and I was very glad I was not walking in her shoes.

LESS THAN A fortnight later, I found myself ushered into the same sitting room. I had to wait again and occupied my mind with all that I needed to do now that spring was here. I considered planting some garlic bulbs and basil plants in a tub in my small backyard. I had hoped to ride out into the country outside Toledo and search for wild garlic bulbs, garden-tree mallow and maybe even some healing mushrooms, but Mordecai had warned me that I shouldn't leave the city walls without an armed escort. Talk of war with the Saracens was in the air, he said, and it would be too dangerous for me to ride out alone or even with my father. But the idea of hiring an armed stranger bothered me. The market in the Jewish quarter did occasionally sell ginger and mallow but the herbs were very expensive and supplies were limited. And there was no ginseng or valerian root to be found anywhere in Toledo.

Finally, Rachel walked in and held up two packages. "I have procured the berries you spoke of and the cinnamon as well. Can you ready the potions? My lord is visiting tonight."

I had already pored over Miriam's old leather journal to find something, anything, about how to prepare the right dosage of chaste tree berries, which I knew could be toxic if taken in too large an amount. But Miriam's journal was silent on that subject or on any topic related to fertility, as if she had decided not to interfere with the natural process of conceiving a baby. Miriam had had no children of her own and perhaps she felt this was an activity best left to nature. If that was the case, I could well understand. Women too often died in childbirth, as my own mother had, so why interfere to boost the odds of something so dangerous?

I felt as though I was being pushed into a corner. Rachel's highhanded refusal to throw caution to the wind annoyed me, but another part of me admired her determination to do what she could to retain the king's good will.

"I'll do my best," I said. "But I have to warn you—I've never dealt with chaste tree berries before."

Rachel waved a hand. "I'll take that chance. I trust you."

I took the packages and followed Rachel's maid down to the kitchen, where I asked the cook to heat up some water. I crushed the berries with a knife, sprinkled some into the hot water along with a pinch of the cinnamon, and whispered a Hebrew prayer for healing as I stirred the mixture. I carried the tea concoction back upstairs, where I found Rachel reclining on the cushions as if she didn't have a care in the world.

"Drink this slowly," I said as I gave the tea to her. "I'll stay for a few minutes to see how you do. Does that suit you?"

Rachel smiled. "I would welcome the company." She patted the cushion next to her. As she drank the tea slowly, she asked me about my family back in England. I told her about my mother's death when I was only four.

"My mother also died when I was very young," Rachel said, a faraway look in her eyes. "I can't help but wonder how my life would have turned out if she had lived." She shook her head as if to dispel the gloom. "Tell me more about your life. Did your father remarry?"

I felt warmed by her genuine interest. I explained that although my father had never remarried, the healer who mentored me, Miriam, had become something of a surrogate mother to me. I left unsaid the fact that my father had been a wealthy man in England, a moneylender who, along with even wealthier and more powerful Jews, had lent money to the king and other knights for their crusades. In my native land, I hadn't needed to make a living healing; like my mentor, Miriam, I had done it as a vocation.

"This Miriam sounds fascinating," she said. "I'm surprised she didn't marry your father."

I had often wondered the same. Perhaps it was because Miriam's first allegiance was to her elderly father or perhaps there had simply been no sparks between my father and Sarah's oldest friend. It was just as well, given Miriam's cruel and untimely demise. During the same wave of hatred against the Jews that had prompted the York massacre, Miriam, England's most noted Jewish healer, had been arrested by the Knights of the Templar and tried for witchcraft. I knew that my father and other members of the Jewish community had tried to save her. They had even gone to the royal court, but King Richard had just left for the Crusades and his brother, John, had no interest in saving a Jewish healer he had never met. So, Miriam had been burned at the stake. I blinked away tears as I remembered that horrible time.

Rachel patted my hand. "You don't need to continue if you don't want to. This tea tastes awful by the way."

I couldn't help but smile through my tears. "Miriam's death was a great blow to me; she was murdered simply for being a Jewish woman and healer. The same thing would have happened to me if not for the knight called Ivanhoe. He rescued me from being burned alive as well."

Rachel's eyes widened. "Please, tell me the story, all of it, leave nothing out. Start with how you came to this knight's attention."

I smiled to myself. While the land of my birth had been cruel to my family and me, I had only good memories of Ivanhoe.

"I knew of Ivanhoe because he came to my father requesting the loan of a good steed so he could enter the tournament at Ashby. He had just returned from the Crusades and had no money to his name. You see, his father, Cedric the Saxon, had disinherited him for going against his wishes and fighting in the crusades alongside the Norman King, Richard the Lionheart. If you can believe it, well-born Saxons like Cedric still smart from being defeated two centuries ago by William the Conqueror and they hate the Norman kings who have ruled them ever since. So, Ivanhoe disguised himself and was entered as the Disinherited Knight when he fought in the lists."

"What an amazing story," Rachel breathed. "His own father didn't recognize him?"

"No, he kept his visor down at all times," I said. "He wouldn't even identify himself to Prince John after he had vanquished all his opponents and won the day. But I could tell he was wounded by the way he was walking. When he fainted at the foot of Lady Rowena, after naming her Queen of the Day and depositing the coronet at her feet, I instructed my attendants to place him in a litter and carry him to our house near Ashby."

Once there, I had treated his wounds. He had been lanced in the side and lost considerable blood. I had fallen in love with the fair-headed knight while tending to him. As he convalesced, he would recite epic poems by heart, and we had long talks about the legend of Arthur and the Song of Roland. Those recitations, which he delivered in a fine sweet baritone, melted my heart, although I was careful not to let him see how I felt.

"Ivanhoe, you see, is not only gallant and well-spoken but he is an unusual man for his times—a knight who doesn't harbor the deep-rooted prejudice and hatred that so many of his countrymen have toward us," I said.

"It is the same here," Rachel said. "The Church prelates preach hatred toward our people every chance they get."

I nodded; everyone in the Jewish quarter knew about the Toledo priests' venomous sermons. "It seems to be the same everywhere." I sighed.

"I don't understand why the Church hates us so. Perchance they need scapegoats to blame the ills of the world on."

Rachel waved a hand in dismissal. "They are evil men. But now, I must hear more about Ivanhoe. Did he feel the same way about you?"

"Oh no," I said. "He was most kind to me, but I knew my feelings could not be requited. A good Christian knight could never wed a Jewess, and besides, he has always loved another woman, the Lady Rowena—they grew up together."

Rachel's mouth trembled, her expression pained. "It is hard to fall in love with someone you cannot truly have. Such is my lot too."

"So, why don't you end the affair with the king and look for love within your own faith?" I ventured to ask.

"It is too late for that. If I were to end our relationship now, my life would be forfeit. There are many factions who hunger for my death and without the king's protection . . ." Rachel's face paled, and she stared at the far wall.

Her candor stunned me. Surely Rachel's situation wasn't that dire. Even so, I was curious to know more.

"How did you even come to the attention of the king?" I asked, after a few minutes.

Rachel twisted a lock of her auburn hair and studied it for a long moment. "I was young and naïve and without a mother's guidance when I first attracted my lord's notice. As you know, my mother also died in childbirth when I was very young and I'm afraid my father was too ambitious for his own good. You see, he had loaned money to Alfonso's grandfather, Alfonso VII, and when his grandson assumed the throne after the death of his father, Sancho III, my father continued that mutually beneficial financial relationship with the regent, Alfonso's mother, Queen Soria, who reigned in his stead. Alfonso was only three when he became king and he and his mother were much in need of money and advice. As Alfonso matured, he grew to trust my father and it was only natural that when he visited Toledo as a young king, I was introduced to him."

She sighed. "I was only thirteen at the time, but I must have made an impression because some years later when Alfonso decided to set up a royal court in Toledo, my father made sure I was invited to dine with the king's retinue." She shrugged. "By that time, I was a woman and Alfonso was thirty-three and handsome. The rest is history."

Rachel's story made me angry; her father sounded like a conniving glutton who cared more about his own interests than his daughter's. "Your father has much to answer for. Is he still alive?"

Tears glittered in Rachel's eyes, and she wiped them angrily away. "No, he died of the sweating sickness four years ago. I felt so alone. I still feel alone."

A wave of sympathy engulfed me. I at least had my beloved father and my relatives whom I'd grown very fond of.

"Is there no one left in your family that you feel close to?" I asked.

Rachel frowned. "My uncle, my father's younger brother, is alive, as is his wife. But I'm afraid Ricardo is a weak man, and he is ruled by his wife's ambitions. She has tried to thrust her own daughters at the king but they are not very pretty and my lord finds them annoying." She giggled, but then sighed. "My uncle is a member of Alfonso's inner circle—I have seen to that. But I don't trust him or his wife to have my interests at heart."

I felt a kinship with Rachel. She seemed caught in a web not of her own making, and at the same time, determined to make the best of it.

I patted Rachel's hand. "You haven't had an easy time of it. I think you're very brave."

Rachel smiled. "Thank you. I am grateful you have come into my life." She pressed my hand in return.

Her gesture warmed me. I realized I would do whatever I could to help this brave and gracious woman. Growing up, I had not been close to any of the girls who lived in York's tightknit Jewish community. Most were uneducated and not allowed to roam as freely as I was, and they seemed fixated on boys and fancy new garments. Perchance Rachel could be the friend I never had.

"I too feel blessed," I said. "Now you need to drink a second infusion of this tea in a few days, just to make sure it takes. Shall I show your maid how to prepare it?"

Rachel shook her head. "I'd rather you do it, if you don't mind terribly much. I know I'm asking a lot of you, but I would be most grateful . . ."

"Of course," I interjected quickly. "I will come back in a few days."

Rachel beamed and stood up.

I too rose to my feet, and she hugged me.

"Thank you. Taresa will see you out."

As I passed the mayordomo at the front door, he pressed a small leather bag in my hand. It was filled with silver coins.

CHAPTER FIVE

WHEN I ARRIVED at Rachel's abode a few days later, I was told that Rachel was closeted with her advisors.

"She asks if you can wait a few minutes," Taresa said. "I have put out some nuncheons for you."

I felt a prick of annoyance. I had moved some of my patients around to attend to Rachel and now I had to wait. I followed the maid up the stairs and into Rachel's private sitting room. On a low table was a dish of spiced chickpea paste and some flattened bread. A pitcher of wine stood nearby, with two glasses at the ready.

As I settled myself on the cushions, I could hear voices coming from a room nearby. I helped myself to some chickpeas and bread as my irritation grew. I had better things to do with my time than wait on the king's mistress. Finally, I stood, brushing some crumbs from my gown, and walked to the hallway, unsure of whether I should go or stay. The voices were coming from a room down the hall. Seeing no one about, I edged closer and could discern Rachel's voice, shrill with anger, or was it fear? I crept closer still to a slightly ajar door.

"We must find a way to counter de Pisguera's influence with the king," Rachel was saying. "He is determined to drive a wedge between me and my Lord."

"We must be very careful," a deeper voice interjected. "The archbishop is very powerful and if we force the king to choose between you and his faith, I'm not sure . . ."

"I'm not suggesting we ask the king to choose, God forbid," Rachel said, frustration in her voice. "Perchance there is a way of suggesting that the archbishop is too powerful, that he is usurping the king's authority. We need to come up with a plan to convince the king to rein in de Pisguera, stop his rants about me, about our people. That's why I appointed the two of you to his cabinet. It's your job to come up with a strategy. And now I must go; I . . . ah . . . am late for an appointment."

I turned and strode back to the sitting room. I settled myself back on the cushions just as Rachel burst into the room, apologizing profusely for her tardiness.

"I am so sorry to have kept you waiting," she said. "I'm afraid it couldn't be helped. These are difficult times. Have you prepared the tea?"

I rose. "No, it needs to be fresh. I will go now and make the infusion."

When I returned, Rachel was sitting on the cushions, deep in thought. She hadn't touched the food laid out for us.

"It's best to have something in your stomach before you drink this," I said. "That chickpea paste is delicious."

Rachel obligingly dipped some bread into the paste and chewed slowly. "Please sit down and join me while I sip this potion. You must continue your story—I'm dying to hear about how Ivanhoe rescued you from being burned as a witch."

My father and I had been traveling back to York from the tournament at Ashby with the entourage of Cedric the Saxon and his ward, Lady Rowena. By then, Ivanhoe had healed enough to rejoin Richard the Lionheart's entourage as the newly returned king rallied England's powerful noblemen back to his side. Our trip was uneventful until we entered a deep wood and suddenly a band of men came hurtling out of the trees, screaming and brandishing swords. The outlaws, whom I later learned were actually Norman knights disguised as yeomen, herded our group on a forced march to a nearby castle belonging to Reginald Front de Boeuf, one of the disguised knights. As I eventually discovered, de Boeuf had concocted the idea of kidnapping Lady Rowena in a futile attempt to convince her to marry him. And as I was soon to learn, another knight had designs on me.

"Once we arrived at the castle, I was torn away from my father and imprisoned by myself in a small room high above the castle ramparts," I told Rachel. "It wasn't long before the Templar knight Brian de Bois-Guilbert came to my cell. Bois-Guilbert was lean and dark-haired with a hawk-like nose. He had a reputation as a fearless warrior and fought in the Crusades alongside King Richard. I remember he swept off his green yeoman's hat and came close to where I was seated on a bench by the open window.

"'You are beauty incarnate and I must have you,' he said without preamble.

"I gasped. Surely, he was jesting. As the Knight of a Catholic order, he was sworn to chastity. He would be the last person I expected to be importuning me.

"'You can't be serious,' I said. 'You are a Knight of the Templar.'

"Bois-Guilbert laughed mirthlessly. 'That hasn't stopped me before. I will have you, my lovely lady, just as I had myriad other women as we fought our way down the Syrian coast. Whether they wanted me or not.'

"I put a hand to my mouth to keep from crying out. I had to think of something to keep this predator at bay.

"'But are you not a sworn Christian and thus forbidden to consort with a Jewess?' I asked, trying to stall for time.

"'Hah, as if that stopped me before,' Bois-Guilbert said, drawing closer. 'I have had my share of Jewish and Saracen women. In fact, the more foreign they are, the more I like them.' He smiled wolfishly at me. 'I will take you by force if I have to. You are the captive of my bow and spear.'"

"I felt as though I was a helpless mouse cornered by a large menacing cat. I had no intention of submitting to such a beast; he would no doubt kill me after using me and even if he didn't, my reputation would be forever stained. I looked around wildly and then jumped up on the bench by the window. Without hesitating, I climbed out onto the parapet.

"Taken by surprise, Bois-Guilbert stopped short. And then he moved stealthily toward the window. My stomach lurched and a cold sweat formed at the base of my spine. But somehow, I managed to speak with calm determination.

"'If you come any closer, I will jump to my death rather than become the victim of your brutality,' I told him.

"As I stood perched precariously high above the earth, I tried hard not to look down, knowing it would just make me dizzy. I held onto an edge of the rough stone wall, and took deep gulps of air, trying to steady my breathing. Would I really jump to my death? I didn't know, I just knew I had to get away from this horrid man.

"I heard Bois-Guilbert speaking, and, taking another deep breath to quiet my pounding heart, leaned closer to the window to look at him. He was gazing at me with an expression of awe-struck admiration.

"'Please, my fair lady come back inside; do not jump,' he entreated. 'I swear on the ancient crest of my fathers that I will do you no harm.'

"I hesitated. Could I trust this despicable man? If I came back inside, he might still try to force himself on me. What in God's name should I do?

"Sensing my indecision, Bois-Guilbert added, 'Not only will I not harm you but I can help your father. You must know that he is even now being tortured by Reginald Front de Boeuf who thinks the old Jew will give him money to avoid being maimed. I will put in a good word for your father.'

"I gasped; how could men who called themselves Christian knights do this to my father, to any other human being? My poor father, I thought. I must do something to help him, but could I really trust this lecherous knight?

"Bois Guilbert said, 'Rebecca, believe me. I may have broken many laws, but I have never broken my word. Please come back inside.'

"At that assurance, I let go of a breath I didn't realize I was holding. I climbed back inside but stood on the bench near the window ready to jump out again should he go back on his word.

"But the knight kept his promise and soon left. I dropped onto the bench and waited for my heart to return to its normal rhythm."

I heard a woman speaking to me as if from a great distance. I came back to myself, surprised to find I was still sitting on cushions in Rachel's luxurious sitting room. Rachel was regarding me with a mixture of awe and admiration.

"I'm sorry," I said. "What did you say?"

"I said you are so brave," she said. "I only hope to have such fortitude should something like that happen to me."

I felt my cheeks warm. "Yes, well, it's all in the past now, thank God."

Rachel gazed at me with avid eyes. "Is that when Ivanhoe rescued you?"

I sighed. My newfound friend would not be satisfied until she had heard the whole terrifying tale. I was gratified by Rachel's interest but reliving what had happened to me at the hands of the Templars wasn't easy. As I recalled those horrible moments on the castle parapet, my heart was galloping so hard I thought it would burst out of my chest.

I poured myself a glass of wine to give me time to calm myself. "Later the same day, Ivanhoe and Richard the Lionheart with the help of Robin of Locksley—better known as Robin Hood—and his men stormed Torquilstone castle in an attempt to rescue Lady Rowena, Cedric, and the rest of us being held there. Our captors mounted a defense but when it looked as though the besiegers would win, Brian de Bois-Guilbert forced me to escape the castle with him. He concocted a story about how my father and the other captives had already escaped and were waiting for us in the woods. I tried to resist but he literally threw me onto his horse and galloped down the ramparts during an interlude in the fighting.

"Bois-Guilbert took me to Templestowe, where the Knights of the Templar had massed for a Preceptory gathering. Once there, the bastard tried several more times to convince me to submit to his desires. I refused his overtures. It was only later I discovered that in a cruel twist of timing, the head of the Knights of the Templar known to all as the Grand Master had unexpectedly turned up in Templestowe, determined to rout out venal corruption in the order's ranks. When the Grand Master learned that I was being kept in the castle by one of his own men who was bent on seducing me, he was furious. He wanted to punish both of us, but the head of the Preceptory, a Norman knight who was a friend of Bois-Guilbert's, convinced the Grand Master that I had somehow bewitched his friend, that the knight's willingness to break his vows was all my fault. Then and there, the Grand Master decided to try me as a sorceress and burn me at the stake. At first Bois-Guilbert refused to turn me over to them, but after the head of the preceptory made it crystal clear that the Grand Master would have no qualms about expelling him from the order if he didn't give me up, he relented. In short order, two Templar guards appeared at my cell and told me to come with them.

"At first, I thought I was finally being released. But then I was brought into this Great Hall and all these men, dressed in the garb of Templar knights, were seated on a dais, looking down on me. And this one old man, the Grand Master, said I had bewitched the very Knight who had kidnapped me and tried to force me to his will. It was unbelievable."

Someone cleared their throat. I looked up, surprised once again to find myself in Rachel's richly appointed parlor. Rachel's servant stood at the door, trying to get her mistress's attention.

"It's growing late, my lady," she said. "And the king will be here soon."

Rachel sighed. "Thank you, Teresa; I quite forgot the time. What an incredible tale. You will have to finish it for me some other time."

We both stood, and Rachel started to walk to the door but turned around.

"Listen, I am having a private party next week," she said. "My lord will be away traveling and I'm inviting some of my closest advisors and friends over. I want you to come."

I shook my head. "I couldn't possibly attend. I'm an unmarried woman; it wouldn't be proper."

Rachel laughed gaily. "What's proper? I will send the invitation to you and your father. He might be able to strike up some important business contacts at my party. And what could be more proper than being accompanied by your own father?"

Rachel, I could see, was determined for me to attend. As long as it was all right with my father, I would come. I wanted to spend more time in the company of this smart, enchanting woman.

CHAPTER SIX

A FEW DAYS later, a messenger delivered a scroll to my home, stamped with the royal seal. My father took receipt of the scroll, but waited until I had finished with my morning patients to show it to me.

"What is this?" he demanded as soon as I hung up my apron.

I read the scroll. "We have been invited to a party being given by *La Fermosa*. Many of Toledo's most influential Jews will be there; it might be a good place for you to make some contacts for your business."

My father raised an eyebrow. "Since when have you become so friendly with the king's mistress? I hear she has enemies in the Church; do you think this is wise?"

I stared at my father, dismayed at his judgmental tone.

"She is a good woman, and she is trying to do right by our people," I said. "As long as the king loves her, she is safe. And so, by extension, are we."

My father frowned and rubbed his chin. I knew that he had always encouraged me to stand up and think for myself, but sometimes my outspokenness bothered him. At the same time, I knew he loved me and hated confrontation of any sort.

"You may be right," he said finally. "Let me talk to my brother about all of this. If he thinks it's a good idea, I will be happy to accompany you to this event."

Benjamin agreed that it would make sense for my father to accompany me to the party and try to strike up some useful acquaintances for their business. Five days later, we dressed in the finest clothes we owned and set off for Rachel's home. Twilight would not come for another hour, and I was feeling joyful. This outing reminded me of all the times my father and I had stepped out to visit relatives and friends in York. As we strolled past the stone church in the center of the city, my father stopped to look at it. It was a smaller version of the mosque I had seen in Cordoba, but with a large cross carved into one wall.

"Benjamin tells me this used to be a mosque," my father said. "When the Castilian kings conquered Toledo, they simply appropriated this space for Christian worship."

My father always had his head full of interesting facts, one of the many things I admired about him.

"Is that so?" I asked. "I'm surprised they haven't torn it down and built a proper Christian church."

My father laughed. "Just wait—I hear there are plans in the works to do just that. According to Mordecai, the archbishop wants to build a magnificent cathedral on this spot, he just doesn't have the money for that yet." He frowned. "That may be why he is pressuring the king to conquer the rest of Andalusia—to grab all that revenue from Spain's olive oil trade for Christianity."

I hated hearing talk of war. It reminded me of what a precarious existence we led.

"They talk of religion but wars are really all about money and power, aren't they?" I sighed and continued down the road, my father beside me.

WHEN WE ARRIVED at Rachel's house, the mayordomo who had sought my help that first time stood guard outside the house. He recognized me and waved us both inside. The high-ceilinged chamber was lit up with candles in every possible nook and a table set up in the large room was filled with delicacies, stuffed partridges, almonds, figs, and pomegranates. Two dozen or so richly attired grandees, mostly men, were already mingling. I was glad my father was with me, because I felt uncomfortable amidst such largesse. Due to my father's business prowess, we had been relatively well-off in England, yet we had always lived modestly. As my father often explained, it wasn't smart for us, as Jews, to live lavishly. But at Rachel's party, I could see no such restrictions.

We stood under the front archway, unbuttoning our cloaks so a servant could take them. I noticed a stir at the other end of the chamber and arched my neck to see over the crowd. Rachel, dressed in a stunning teal gown, was standing just inside a doorway. Her long auburn hair was swept up into a twist at the back of her head, with a few curls left dangling, and she looked ravishing, laughing and kissing guests as she greeted them. I used the opportunity to observe the people milling around her as she made her way across the room. I couldn't tell who was Christian and who was Jewish, who was of noble birth versus who were traders and merchants. Most of the men wore expensive fur-lined tunics and leggings; some had heavy gold chains around their necks. A few elegantly gowned women—

wives or mistresses, I presumed—were scattered among the men. I was glad my father had come with me; I would have felt very uncomfortable walking in by myself, especially since I knew no one here except Rachel.

La Fermosa finally approached us and kissed me on both my cheeks, then curtseyed to my father. He bowed back.

"It's my pleasure to meet you, *señor*," Rachel said, her blue-green eyes dancing. "I'm so glad you could come. As I'm sure you already know, you have a very special daughter."

"The pleasure is all mine," my father said, smiling. "And yes, I know how special my daughter is. But she didn't do justice when describing your beauty."

Rachel smiled and pressed his hand. Then she looked around. "Don Enriquez, if you please, I'd like you to meet some friends of mine," she called out to a gray-bearded man standing a few feet away.

Don Enriquiz, wearing a fur-trimmed burgundy tunic and dark leggings encased in boots, strolled to us and bowed low over Rachel's hand.

"Since both of you are successful businessmen and members of our own tribe, you must have much to talk about," she said, after introducing us. "In the meantime, I'm going to show Rebecca around."

She winked at both men, took me by the arm, and led me away. "I am so glad you came," she whispered. "Most of these men are married but their wives, even the Jewish ones whose husbands are getting rich because of my association with the king, don't approve of me. Such hypocrites."

"Yes, they are," I agreed. "I wondered why there were so many more men here. Now tell me, who is Don Enriquiz? Is he a trader?"

Rachel laughed. "Yes, and Enriquiz Perez is also a banker. He has his fingers in many pies. The king recently appointed him to his cabinet, at my suggestion of course."

I looked around. "Are your uncle and aunt here?"

Rachel's mouth twitched. "No, my uncle and aunt are in Valencia, thankfully." She took a glass of ruby wine off the tray held by a servant. "Here, I think you'll like this wine—it comes from the king's own vineyards."

Rachel smiled as another grandee bowed low over her hand. "Ah my dear Don Paulo. May I introduce Rebecca, a good friend of mine?"

Don Paulo, whose fur-lined tunic could not hide his noticeable paunch and stick-thin legs, stared at as me if he was mentally undressing me. How vulgar.

Don Paulo grabbed my hand and bowed low over it. "My pleasure, *señorita*."

I could feel his hot breath on my hand and pulled it away.

Unabashed, Don Paulo turned to Rachel. "*La Fermosa*, I didn't realize you had friends who are almost as beautiful as you are."

Rachel laughed. "Please, Don Paulo, enough with the flattery. Now if you'll excuse us . . ."

Rachel introduced me to several other men and one woman whose names I promptly forgot. She seemed to be keeping one eye on the entrance as she squired me around the room.

"Ah there he is. Come, Rebecca, I have someone else I want you to meet." Rachel led me toward the entrance and whispered, "This is my best friend from childhood. We grew up together. If I wasn't with Alfonso, I might have . . . Bernardo!"

A tall, broad-shouldered man with his brown hair tied neatly into a short ponytail, turned around. Bernardo grinned at Rachel and then stared at me with a glint in his eyes. I felt a buzzing sensation in my stomach. Bernardo was handsome, with an aquiline nose, full lips, and a square chin. The intensity of his gaze made me tingle.

"Hola, Bernardo, better late than never," Rachel greeted him. "May I introduce a friend of mine, Rebecca Manasses of England. Rebecca, this is my good childhood friend, Bernardo Nabaro. He is one of us."

Bernardo bowed low over my hand. "My pleasure, *señorita*." He straightened. "How are you finding our fair city?"

Was there a sardonic note in his voice?

"It's very different from what I'm used to," I said. "But most people—in the Jewish quarter at least—have been quite welcoming. Have you always lived here?"

Bernardo's mouth twitched in amusement. Perhaps he was not used to being questioned by a woman.

"I have lived here all my life, although my family also has a house in Valencia," he said.

"Bernardo's father, Don Esteban, is another of the king's advisors," Rachel interjected. "His family, like mine, have long been bankers to the royal family. Bernardo here has gone his own way, however."

I raised an eyebrow. "And what way is that?"

Bernardo's eyes gleamed at my interest. "I import and export goods, including dry goods and wool from England. As a result, I have been to your country several times. It is a beautiful island but I wouldn't want to live there. Too much antipathy toward our people."

"My friend here would agree. She can tell you quite a hair-raising tale of her own, if she's so inclined." Rachel looked about. "And now I really must circulate." She squeezed my arm and whispered, "Have fun."

Bernardo and I were left to watch Rachel sashay off to greet another guest.

"I certainly would like to hear your story, perchance over some food," he suggested. "Hungry?"

"I am," I said. "In the rush to get to this party, I didn't have time to sup."

After we had loaded up our plates with food, Bernardo guided me through a door at the other end of the house into the beautiful garden I had seen from the upstairs window on my previous visits. A few people were wandering around the garden, talking, drinks in hand, but Bernardo steered me to a bench at the other end, where we could have some privacy. As we ate, I gave him a shortened version of my ordeal in England, my rescue by a knight called Ivanhoe and our escape to Spain. The heat of his body next to mine made me lightheaded.

"So, this Ivanhoe, why did he go to all that effort to rescue you?" Bernardo asked. "Was he in love with you?"

I wasn't sure I was ready to discuss my feelings about Ivanhoe with this stranger, as handsome as he was.

"I understand if you'd rather not discuss this," he said, capturing my eyes. "We can talk about something else."

His concern released a knot in my chest. Suddenly, I wanted to share everything with him. "No, Ivanhoe is in love with Lady Rowena, always has been. They grew up together. They're married now."

"So why did he come to your assistance?" Bernardo asked. "From what I have gathered in my travels, most English knights wouldn't bother to help a Jewess."

"You're right, but Ivanhoe is different," I said, somewhat miffed by Bernardo's skepticism. "We got to know each other when I nursed him back to health after he was wounded in a tournament. Is it so hard to believe that a Christian knight would come to the aid of the woman who helped heal him?"

Bernardo smiled, seemingly unperturbed by my tone. "Actually, yes. You know what I think?"

I didn't really want to hear what he thought but reminded myself to be courteous. I bowed my head slightly.

"I think this Ivanhoe, as much as he was committed to this Lady Rowena, was a little in love with you too," Bernardo said. "You are very beautiful and it is possible, you know, to be in love with two people at the same time." His face reddened.

What did he mean? Oh. Bernardo must have loved someone he couldn't have. And perchance still did. Rachel? I decided not to probe. After all, I wasn't about to confess to my own feelings for Ivanhoe.

"What you say is no doubt true. Human emotions are very complex, are they not?" I waved a hand. "But please I'd rather hear about you. Why did you decide not to go into banking with your father?"

Bernardo uttered a sardonic laugh. "Didn't Rachel tell you? I'm the black sheep in my family. I know that in England it's very difficult for Jews to be anything other than money lenders. As I'm sure you well know, they are not allowed to be in the trade guilds and can only own land by special disposition from the king. But here we are allowed to import and export goods and it's the route I've taken. I didn't want to have Christian kings and noblemen beholden to me for money. At some point, they may decide to rid themselves of their debt by killing their debtors. It has happened before and no doubt will happen again."

I had overheard my father and his friends discuss their own concerns about being preyed upon by the very noblemen they lent large sums to. And hadn't that happened to my own father when we were imprisoned in Torquilstone castle? He might have been killed had it not been for Brian Bois-Guilbert's intercession.

I nodded. "That is certainly a possibility. In England, Jewish moneylenders are dependent on the king's mercy. I assume it is the same here."

"Yes, but the difference between England and Spain is that the Church is more powerful here. And sometimes Church zealots who have it in for us hold sway and then all hell breaks loose." Bernardo looked into the distance, then returned his attention to me. "Has anyone told you about the massacre of Toledo's Jews eight-seven years ago?"

My mouth dropped open. "No."

"There was this big battle in 1108 and the Moors defeated the Christian forces and killed the Infante and thirty thousand of his men," Bernardo said. "The priests in Toledo stirred everyone up and a mob descended on the Jewish quarter. Dozens of men, women, and children were slain and their houses burned. It was an awful night."

I placed my hand on my chest. "Did anyone in your family die?"

Bernardo shook his head. "My father's parents and their family had left for their summer home in Valencia a few days before the riots. They were lucky to survive."

"But surely that is all in the past now?" I asked. "I understand that King Alfonso is favorably disposed toward us. After all, his own mistress is Jewish."

"The Archbishop of Toledo hates Rachel's hold on the king's affections, and he is working tirelessly to break that hold. What's more, he and other Church prelates have been pressing the king to mount another assault on southern Spain, and now that the Yaqub al-Mansur—he's the ruler of the Moors—is in Morocco occupied with other matters, the king has finally agreed the time is right to strike. But if things should go wrong . . ."

I stared at him. What was he trying to say?

"But enough of this. I shouldn't be talking so gloomily at such a festive occasion." Bernardo stood and offered me his arm. "Would you join me in a stroll through the garden? The early spring flowers are blooming."

After a pleasant stroll through the garden, which we spent conversing about flowers and plants native to Spain, I reluctantly announced that I really should check up on my father. He was probably tired and ready to retire. Bernardo escorted me back into the house, where I saw Rachel off to one side, deep in conversation with two men. Rachel's expression was somber, and I wondered what they were talking about so intently. No doubt some palace intrigue. I didn't envy Rachel her position as mistress to the king; I knew from overhearing some of her conversations, it was a precarious existence.

I finally found my father near the entrance to the hall, conversing with another man.

I turned to introduce him to Bernardo, who bowed low over my hand and whispered, "I must leave. I will be traveling abroad for the next two fortnights. But rest assured I will be in touch on my return."

He strode to the door, leaving me feeling stranded and very much alone in the noisy chamber.

CHAPTER SEVEN

IN THE WEEKS after the party, I threw myself into caring for those in the Jewish quarter who sought out my assistance. I tried to put Bernardo out of my mind, yet I couldn't help thinking about the way he made me feel. I sensed that he still had feelings for Rachel, which was probably why he remained single. Rachel had told me that Bernardo was twenty-nine, a year younger than Rachel herself and eight years older than me. And according to Isadora, whom I had confided in, Bernardo was considered quite an eligible bachelor among Toledo's Jewish families.

Fortunately, I didn't have much time to dwell on Bernardo. I was busy every day in my practice, with patients waiting to see me. My reputation as a midwife had grown to such an extent that even some Christian families called upon me for help. I tried not to intercede, however, when another midwife was involved and the birth was not going well. In York, a Jewish midwife had tried to save a Christian woman whose labor had been botched. Her baby had been in a breech position and the original midwife had made no effort to turn it or get help in time. By the time the Jewish midwife was brought in, it was too late. The woman and her baby died—in large part because of the incompetence of the previous midwife. Yet it was the Jewish midwife who was killed by a mob who blamed her, rather than the real culprit. The story behind that unfortunate woman's murder was seared into my memory and my father's as well, which is why he always answered those late-night knocks on our door and asked a few questions before acknowledging that I was home. My father understood as well as I did the risks involved in taking care of gentiles.

One night, I awakened to the sound of loud knocking. The noise also aroused my father, whom I heard clamber down the stairs to answer the door. I got up, wrapped a robe around my nightgown, and stood at the top of the stairs where I could just see the entrance. My father opened the door to two soldiers who were holding up a third man, a civilian whose head was bleeding badly. He looked like he was barely conscious.

"We were told to bring him here," said one of the soldiers, who bore the royal insignia on his uniform. "He has been badly beaten."

My father stood aside and gestured for them to bring the bleeding man into our house. He then turned to call for me, only to find that I had rushed down the stairs to help. I instructed the soldiers to lay the injured man on an examining bed. I asked the soldiers what had happened.

"We were heading back to the Alcazar when we came across four men who were the beating the piss out of this poor soul," one of the soldiers said. "It looked like they were going to kill him. He's a Jew, see, and the priests have gotten everyone all stirred up, with tales of Christian children being murdered and all that. We just couldn't stand there and do nothing."

The soldier sounded disgusted, and I remembered hearing Isadora talk about how every year around Easter time, Toledo priests would deliver sermons ranting about Jews killing Christian children and using their blood in religious rituals. I had heard the same canards spread about shortly before the massacre in the English city of York. I shook myself; I didn't have time to dwell on such horrific falsehoods. I had to tend to this poor man.

While my father saw the soldiers out, I leaned over the man, gently palpating his abdomen and chest. It looked like he was struggling to breathe, a sure sign of broken ribs and possibly a collapsed lung. I put a pillow under the man's head and asked my father to heat up some water and wine and bring them to me. I remembered Miriam showing me a way to decompress the lungs with a slender reed or tube, but it was a delicate operation and I wasn't sure I knew how to do it correctly.

While I was waiting for my father to do as I asked, I gently tried to wipe off the blood on the man's head to see what kind of wound he had suffered there. He had obviously been kicked in the head, but while he might be suffering from a concussion, his skull seemed intact. I breathed a sigh of relief and bandaged his head. I then found the reed Miriam had given me and laid out my instruments. When my father returned, I made an infusion of warm wine and oil and asked him to gently hold the man down by the shoulders should he recoil from the pain.

I took a deep breath to steady myself. I then cut a small hole in the man's upper chest with a sharp scalpel. The man jerked and appeared to lose consciousness. I carefully inserted the reed with the wine and oil mixture into the hole and sucked out the pus that had gathered in the man's collapsed lung. I spit the pus out into the bucket near the table and then plugged the wound with a tent of wine-soaked linen. It was done.

I stepped back. I washed my hands in the basin of warm water, dried them with a clean towel and wiped the sweat off my face with the back of my hand. My patient had not regained consciousness but at least he was still breathing. His injuries might also have caused internal bleeding, but there was nothing I could do about that. I could only pray that the bleeding would stop on its own. I had done all I could for now; the rest was up to fate.

I MUST HAVE fallen asleep in a chair by the man's bed. The weak rays of early morning light awakened me and at first, I was disoriented and didn't know where I was. Why was I sleeping in a chair? And then I remembered and jumped up. My patient was still asleep but he seemed to be breathing easier, thank the Lord.

When I came back downstairs, after dressing and washing up, the man was awake. When he saw me, he gasped, "Where am I? Are you an angel? Am I in heaven?"

I laughed softly. "No, I'm Rebecca Manasses and you are in my home in the Jewish quarter. You have sustained some very serious injuries. Do you remember what happened?"

The man groaned and tried to sit up. I gently pushed him back down. "Please don't exert yourself. Are you thirsty? Here's some water." I put another pillow under his head so he could more comfortably drink the water. He sipped it gratefully.

"I have an awful headache," he said. "I feel like I've been clocked with a hammer."

I patted his arm. "That's to be expected. You were kicked in the head."

The man rubbed his eyes. "Oh my God, it's coming back to me. I was coming back from visiting some customers. I'm a tailor, you see, and, I was doing some fittings. My customers took forever to decide what they wanted. It was after dark when I left, and a bunch of thugs jumped me. I thought they were going to kill me."

"They very nearly did," I said.

My patient shuddered and fingered the bandage on his head. "Am I going to die?"

"Let's hope not. Lucky for you, two of the king's men came to your rescue and brought you here," I said. "Now rest. I will prepare some chicken broth in a little while but first I want to take a look at your wounds."

Leon Torres' brutal beating was all anyone could talk about in the Jewish quarter for days. While everyone had heard of the nasty sermonizing against the Jews, this was the first time in years that a Jew had been set upon in Toledo while tending to his own business. There was mention of enacting a curfew—to protect Jewish residents when they went outside the *barrio*—but in the end the elders decided it would be too restrictive and unfair to their own citizenry. Rabbi Abenir and two of the elders sought an audience with the king to ask him to rein in the clerical rabble-rousers, but Alfonso was said to be traveling and unable to see them. They were left to relay their message to one of the king's advisors.

I kept a careful watch on Torres but he continued to improve. After a few days I was able to remove the reed and close the wound in his chest. Less than a fortnight later, his family carried him home on a litter but not before expressing their profound gratitude to me for saving his life. Torres' wife insisted on giving me a shimmering bolt of silk fabric.

"You must come in for a fitting when you have time; I will make you a beautiful gown," she said. I tried to give the fabric back, saying it was too much, but Aldonza Torres insisted. "No, it is the least we can do. You saved my husband's life."

A FEW DAYS later, I was summoned back to *La Fermosa's* home. Rachel waited for me in her upstairs sitting room and her eyes looked red and puffy. "I am still not pregnant. Is there anything more you can do?"

"I'm so sorry," I said. "We just don't understand why it is so easy for some women to get pregnant but not others."

"I have endeavored to make our trysts as spontaneous as possible and to time them when my monthly cycle is most receptive, as you suggested. But to no avail." Rachel stood up and paced around the room. "My lord doesn't visit me as often these days. He has been increasingly distracted by his plans to recover Andalusia from the Moors. Martín López, blast his evil heart, has been pushing Alfonso to attack, telling him that God is on his side and he cannot lose."

I gave her a questioning look.

"Lopez de Pisuerga is the Archbishop of Toledo; he has his own army and is a very powerful man. But he is pure evil. I think he is trying to turn Alfonso against me, making me out to be some kind of sorceress blinding the king to the true faith. I feel so trapped, like a fly trussed up in a spider's web."

I walked over to Rachel and patted her arm. "Your lord loves you, try not to worry. I'm sure he would never allow anyone to harm you. Let me do some more research and see if I can come up with any other remedies. Fertility is a tricky business."

Rachel sighed. "Thank you. And now tell me, have you heard from Bernardo?"

I felt my cheeks warm. "Ah no, but he told me he would traveling for much of the month. I don't expect to hear from him."

"Oh, that's right," Rachel said. "I forgot he said he would be away for a while. I've been so preoccupied. If you'd like, I can ask his father if he's heard from Bernardo. I'm in fairly regular contact with Don Esteban."

I felt uncomfortable at the idea of Rachel interceding for me. I could manage my own affairs, thank you very much. If Bernardo wasn't interested in seeing me again, that was no concern of Rachel's.

"Please, I don't want you to go to any trouble," I replied. "If Bernardo wants to get in touch with me again, he knows where to find me."

Rachel's mouth quirked upward. "Of course, my dear. And please let me know if you find any other treatments that might work for me."

A FEW DAYS later, I opened the door of my house to a familiar-looking woman. It was Perla, the woman who had been stepped on by the horse five months ago. I had gone to her house several times after the accident to change her bindings and then to remove the splints around Perla's foot. The foot looked like it was healing well. Still, I had cautioned Perla to use the wooden crutches her son-in-law had made for her and not to put too much pressure on the foot. I gestured to her to come inside.

"How's your foot?" I asked.

Perla waved a hand. "Oh, it's much better. I just came by to thank you . . ." Just then my father walked into the hall; he had something in his hand. "I'm sorry, I didn't mean to intrude . . ."

"You didn't." I laughed. "Perla, this is my father, Don Isaac. And Papa, this is Señora Perla, the widow who was stepped on by that horse in the marketplace."

My father smiled broadly and bowed over Perla's head. "Yes, I remember but you didn't tell me how beautiful your patient was."

Perla blushed and smiled up at him. I looked at my father and Perla with astonishment; what was going on here?

"I just came by to thank your daughter for taking such good care of me," Perla said. "You must be so proud of her; she's such a gifted healer."

"Thank you, *señora*; I was just doing my job," I said. "Do you want me to take another look at your foot?"

Perla shook her head. "No, I'm fine." She took a bunch of pink flowers out of her satchel. "The last time you visited me and I asked if I could do anything for you, you mentioned that you needed some herbs. Valerian root you called it. Anyway, my daughter found some of this in the market the other day; the seller told her these were valerian root and that they were useful as a sleep aid. Is this what you were looking for?"

I took the bundle of flowers. "You're a godsend—thank you. I'm completely out of it. Did you know that valerian root also helps with digestive problems and anxiety?"

"No, but I'm glad to be of help," Perla said. "I must get back and start preparing our evening meal. Thanks again."

My father, who had been watching us with interest, stepped forward. "I will see the *señora* outside if that suits."

"Of course," Perla and I said in unison.

We both laughed. I watched them leave with bemusement. Perla looked so petite beside my tall but slight father. This was the first time I'd seen him interested in a woman other than my mother. He must have had liaisons back in England but if so, he'd never introduced me to any of those women. And whenever I had asked if he wanted to get married again, he had always fobbed me off by saying, "I remain devoted to the memory of your dear mother." But now I was seeing a new side of him, a side I welcomed. My father deserved to be happy.

CHAPTER EIGHT
April 1195 AD

ESTRAYA AND I had just finished treating a patient and were washing up when there was a knock at my door. She went to answer the door and returned with a scroll for me. It was from Bernardo, saying that he had returned a few nights ago and would like to see me. Was I interested in going for a ride through the countryside with him the following day? My heart leapt.

"By my troth, you're blushing," Estraya said. "Who is this scroll from?"

"Oh, just a nice gentleman I met at Rachel's party," I said. "He wants to take me for a ride in the countryside. I've been wanting to search for some herbs I can't find in the marketplace."

Estraya grinned, her eyes searching my face. "Hmm, why do I think there is more here than just a desire to find some medicinal herbs?"

I laughed. "Well, this fellow—he's a friend of Rachel's; they grew up together—he's Jewish and he's not bad-looking. I suppose it won't hurt to get to know him better, and replenish my herbs in the meantime."

"Aha, just as I thought," Estraya said. "But don't you need a chaperone?"

"I do," I said. "I don't suppose you'd be interested in joining us?"

"Prithee, yes," Estraya said. "I'd love to get some fresh air myself."

Tomorrow was Sunday, the Christian Sabbath, and we wouldn't be seeing patients anyway. "It's settled then. Just be sure to get your parents' consent." I was sure my father would give his.

The next morning, Bernardo arrived at our house, leading two horses.

I opened the door and he bowed, his hat in his hand. "You are as beautiful as I remember, Rebecca. We picked a lovely day for a ride." He tied the reins of his horse to the post next to my door.

I looked up at the cloudless sky and smiled. "I'm looking forward to some fresh air. Please come in. My cousin, who will serve as our chaperone, hasn't arrived yet."

Bernardo gestured at the saddle bags on his horse. "Then you're both in for a treat. My cook has prepared some nuncheons for us to eat outdoors."

Bernardo stepped into the entryway, where my father waited; he appraised Bernardo with narrowed eyes.

"Welcome to our humble abode," Isaac said. "Come in, come in and tell me all about yourself. I hear we are in the same business."

They talked amiably while I finished my preparations. Estraya arrived soon after and we bid my father goodbye.

Bernardo suggested that Estraya and I mount one horse and he the other. The sun was still in the eastern sky and the air felt refreshingly cool against my skin. We rode out through the eastern gate and the sentries paid no attention to us.

My heart lifted with excitement. I couldn't believe this was actually happening; I had not been outside the city since I arrived eight months earlier. I had wanted to go in search of wild herbs a few months ago, but Mordecai had warned me not to venture out without armed protection. I felt safe today with Bernardo— an imposing figure on horseback with his sheathed sword.

I drank in the sights and smells. Decades ago, the Muslim leaders who ruled Toledo had built sewers beneath the streets of the city, and waste from the latrines spilled into those sewers and was carried to large underground canals, which flushed the waste into the Tagus River. The river that snaked halfway around Toledo was badly polluted, and on days when the winds blew a certain way, we could smell the stink of waste that ended up in its rushing waters. But in the countryside, the air smelled fresh and clean. Bright red poppies covered the hillside, pink and white bougainvillea climbed stone walls. Here and there I could see wild orchids poking their brilliant lavender blossoms out of the grass. I pointed them out to Estraya, who rode behind me.

After riding for an hour or so, we came to a clearing at the top of one of the hills that ringed Toledo. We dismounted, and I told Bernardo I would like to look for herbs at the edge of the meadow where some trees cast their welcome shade.

"Do you think it would be safe to venture into the woods just a bit?" I asked. "That's often where I find basil and medicinal mushrooms growing."

"I will accompany the two of you and play scout." Bernardo's eyebrows drew together. "I've heard of mushrooms that are safe to eat and quite tasty. But healing ones?"

As we walked toward the woods, I explained that I was looking for several types of mushrooms, one of which looked like the tail of a turkey.

"It grows on dead and fallen trees, branches and stumps and is very pretty. Another mushroom I'm looking for resembles an oyster and it tastes delicious."

"But what are they good for, besides eating?" Bernardo asked.

"Well, my teacher Miriam taught me to use the turkey tail mushroom to fight infections, like the ague or the sweating sickness," I said. "And the oyster mushroom is good for problems of the heart and spleen."

"Really?"

I shrugged off the doubt in his voice; I was used to skepticism. At least he seemed willing to hear me out.

"Yes, really. Miriam and I used these mushrooms to good effect in England. But I haven't been able to replenish my store here." I smiled at Bernardo and Estraya. "Maybe we'll get lucky today."

"Maybe we will," Bernardo said. "I want you to know—I'm impressed with how much you know about these natural remedies," he added in a more serious tone.

Once we entered the woods, Estraya and I walked slowly, peering under dead limbs and foliage. Bernardo had attached the horses' leads to the long limb of a tree and they happily munched on grass a short distance away from where he stood watch.

"Ah, here's one," I said, plucking a white fan-shaped mushroom from the underside of downed tree. "This is an oyster mushroom." I carefully dropped it in a small leather bag I carried in my other hand.

Within an hour, we had harvested three different varieties of mushroom and collected a cluster of basil and some wild garlic. I had also unearthed a leafy plant with a small yellow flower. It was *Tribulus terrestris,* a plant that Miriam had once mentioned as being a possible remedy for a number of ills including infertility. Finally, I straightened up and wiped the sweat off my brow.

"It's getting hot," I said. "And I'm hungry."

Bernardo laughed. "I thought you'd never say that. Let's have lunch."

We walked back to the horses and spread a woolen blanket out under a large oak tree. Bernardo's cook had packed a loaf of bread, cheese, olives and grapes along with two flasks of wine.

"What a feast. We must dine with you more often." I put a hand to my mouth, afraid I was being too forward.

Bernardo chuckled. "I would like that very much."

As we ate, Bernardo told us more about his family. His mother was from Segovia but his parents had met as children when their families spent a holiday in Valencia. He had two older sisters, both married. One lived in Valencia with her family and the other had recently moved to Egypt with her husband and his parents.

"Is that where you went on your last trip, to Egypt?" I asked.

"Yes, and I also went to Morocco," Bernardo said. "Won't go back there if I can avoid it."

"Why not?" Estraya asked, leaning forward from her place a few feet away to give Bernardo and I some privacy.

"When I was there, the sultan's younger brother was fomenting rebellion—he wants the throne—and as part of his campaign, he was stirring up anti-Jewish sentiments. No doubt trying to out-zealot his brother. While I was in Marrakesh, a prominent rabbi was hanged and a mob burned down a synagogue. I got out of there as soon as I could."

Estraya and I exchanged horrified looks.

I collected myself and smiled reassuringly at Estraya. "Guess we won't be going to Morocco any time soon."

"Good idea," Bernardo said. He took a sip of wine. "Egypt is probably the safest place right now for Jews."

"Why is that?" I remembered Benjamin saying that after the Almohads had begun tightening the screws on Jews in Córdoba, a few of his neighbors had left with their families for Egypt and never returned.

"Well, from what I gather, Jews are free to practice their own faith there and are not harassed like they are in Andalusia or Morocco," Bernardo said. "Cairo has a flourishing Jewish community and I felt very comfortable there. In fact, one of the sultan's favorite physicians, Maimonides, is a Jew and he apparently comes from Córdoba. He has quite a reputation as a Jewish scholar as well."

What I would give to learn from such a distinguished doctor. "I would love to meet this Maimonides. Have you ever met him on your travels?"

Bernardo snorted. "No. I'm afraid I don't travel in his circles."

Estraya stood and dusted herself off. "I'm going to pick some flowers for my parents' table." She wandered off into the meadow.

Bernardo watched her go and moved a little closer to me. "Your cousin is the perfect chaperone, isn't she?"

I laughed, but I could feel my heart speeding up.

Bernardo leaned over and placed a lingering kiss on my hand. My entire body tingled. Bernardo looked up at me with a question in his eyes. My eyes must have given him the answer he sought because he moved closer and kissed me softly on the lips.

Estraya was slowly making her way back across the meadow, trying to avoid looking in our direction. I sighed.

Bernardo nodded. "We should be headed back."

Estraya approached us while carefully putting her flowers into a pouch. We packed up the remnants of our meal and mounted our horses for the trek back to Toledo.

We finally arrived back at my house just as the sun sat on the distant hills. Bernardo dismounted and held our horse as Estraya slipped off, gave me an encouraging look, and went inside.

Bernardo helped me off the horse and kissed my hand.

I didn't want the day to end. "Would you like to stay for dinner?"

He shook his head. "I have to attend to some business, but perchance we can get together the day after tomorrow."

"I'd like that," I said.

"I'll see you soon." He mounted his horse, nodded his farewell, and trotted down the narrow lane.

I watched until he turned the corner, giddy at the thought of seeing him again. I took a steadying breath, and ignoring the ache in my thighs from riding, walked inside the house.

Estraya rushed up to me. "I think he is quite gallant and it's clear he dotes on you."

My cheeks warmed. "You think so?"

"I do indeed," Estraya said. "But I won't tell a soul, unless you want me to."

"I appreciate your discretion," I said, laughing. "It's really too soon to tell what will come of this but I do enjoy his company."

"It looks like he enjoys yours too," Estraya said, unable to contain her excitement.

I smiled at her enthusiasm. "And now you really should get home and help your mother with supper. Thanks for coming today."

I COULD BARELY concentrate on my patients as two days passed without a word from Bernardo. Finally, a messenger arrived with a sealed scroll from Bernardo. I broke the seal, my heart soaring.

Bernardo had written that his mother, who was at their summer house in Valencia, had taken ill, and he and his father were leaving to be with her. He was very sorry that he wouldn't be able to see me today. But soon, he wrote, soon we would see each other again.

I sank to my stool and stared at the words, trying not to be disappointed. I sighed and pocketed the scroll. Perhaps Bernardo would summon me to take care of his mother. I'd heard Valencia was a beautiful port town on the Mediterranean and I would dearly love to visit it one day. I wouldn't want to be away too long—I had too many patients and expecting mothers depending on me. But surely, I could fit in a short visit to Valencia.

CHAPTER NINE

THE DAYS PASSED with no word from Bernardo. I did receive another summons from Rachel. I prepared a concoction consisting of chaste tree berries and cinnamon and for good measure, I chopped up and threw in the small leafy plant I had found in the woods during that wonderful outing with Bernardo. I knew this latest mixture would probably not work, but Rachel's message had a desperate tone.

"I have no idea if this will help and I'm not sure of the correct dosage," I told Rachel as I handed her the concoction. "It might give you a stomachache. I understand if you'd rather not take it."

Rachel had deep circles under her eyes and it looked as though she had lost weight since I last saw her. "Ha. As if I have any choice. I have to try. I have to do anything I can to get pregnant. I'm running out of time."

"What do you mean?" I asked.

"I hardly see my lord anymore and he is preoccupied when he does visit me." Rachel sighed. "He has been squirreled away with his generals and bishops planning the assault on the Moors. I'm told the archbishop's army is going to march any day now."

"But why the rush? When the king returns victorious, won't that be time enough to renew intimacies?" I still felt I was missing parts of the puzzle.

"Of course." Rachel waved her hand. "But what happens if the king and his allies are not victorious? I love my lord, but he tends to be overly confident. And Yaqub al-Mansur, the Sultan, is a formidable foe. If my lord is killed on the battlefield, I'm afraid the Church will exact its revenge on me."

What a dreadful thought. No wonder Rachel was scared. I knew what it was like to live in fear. I leaned over and enclosed Rachel's hand in mine. "In that case, you must prepare an escape plan. Bernardo has traveled to many places; perchance he and his father can advise you on how to get out of the city safely in the unlikely event that the king is killed in battle."

Rachel ran a hand through her hair. "Mayhaps. When Bernardo returns from Valencia, I will consult him." She rose and straightened her gown. "In the meantime, my lord has sent word that he is visiting me this evening and I must prepare for him. When should I take this concoction?"

"Why don't you take it now while I'm here, just to be on the safe side?" I suggested. "And drink some water with it."

Rachel took the cup with the potion I had prepared and frowned. "I wish I had time to hear the rest of your tale about how Ivanhoe rescued you, but my Lord will be here soon. Perchance there is a shorter story you can tell me about the merry knights of England."

I thought for a moment. I knew just what would fit the bill: the story of how Richard the Lionheart had helped Ivanhoe win the Ashby tournament. King Richard had been shipwrecked on his return from the Holy Lands and forced to march with his dwindling retinue across central Europe. Along the way, he was captured by Leopold of Austria, who turned him over to the Holy Roman Emperor Henry IV. As Ivanhoe told me during his convalescence in Ashby, Henry had demanded an enormous ransom—150,000 marks—comparable to 100,000 pounds of silver—for the beleaguered king. Richard's mother, the redoubtable Eleanor of Aquitaine, had managed to raise the money for his ransom by confiscating the gold and silver of the churches and raising taxes on both clergy and laymen. But no one knew that the king was back in England.

"On the second day of the tournament, everyone else in Ivanhoe's group was vanquished by the opposition," I told Rachel. "Ivanhoe was the only knight remaining in the field and he was set upon by two knights from the other party. It looked as if he would at last be overpowered, when an entrant who called himself the Black Knight rode into the fray. Up to this point, this particular knight, whom no one knew, had shown no interest in helping anyone else in his party, although he had easily beaten off any opponent who challenged him. As a result, he had earned the name of the Black Sluggard from the spectators. But when it looked as if Ivanhoe might finally be overcome, the Black Knight rode to his rescue and helped Ivanhoe defeat his remaining opponents. Yet when the two knights came forward to accept their prizes, neither Ivanhoe nor the Black Knight would disclose their identities."

"Who was the Black Knight? The king?" Rachel asked, her eyes dancing with curiosity.

I smiled. "Good guess."

"But why didn't he want anyone to know who he was?" Rachel asked. "I understand that Ivanhoe did not want his father to know he was back from the Holy Lands because his father had disinherited him for fighting in the crusades. But why was the king so hell bent on remaining anonymous?"

"Because he knew that his younger brother John was trying to usurp his throne," I explained. "Richard was just returned from the crusades himself and he needed to shore up support among the noblemen before he reclaimed the kingdom. He didn't trust John and rightly so. If Prince John, who was presiding over the tournament, had known Richard was in the lists that day, he probably would have had him dispatched then and there. He's a bad seed, that one."

"My lord has to deal with upstarts too," Rachel said, and took a sip of the concoction. "While the kings of Leon and Navarre are loyal allies to him, there is a Castilian nobleman, Pedro Fernández de Castro, who feels he should be the rightful King of Castile just because his mother was the illegitimate daughter of Alfonso's grandfather, King Alfonso VII. From what my lord has told me, this Pedro is so greedy for power that he has allied himself with the Almohads. He thinks that if Alfonso is defeated by the Moors, they will let him rule Castile and Leon. As if. But he has his own army and he's a real thorn in my lord's side."

Powerful men were the same everywhere. The more power they had, the more they wanted. "I don't understand this lust for power. So many people suffer as a result of a few men's obsession with power. And that includes Church prelates," I added, looking around to make sure no one was listening. "I don't understand why they have to impose their religion on others. When I think of all the people killed in the name of religion. The crusades alone have led to the slaughter of thousands of innocents."

"I completely agree," Rachel said, also in a hushed voice. "But be careful whom you say such things to. You are safe with me, but if the archbishop or his minions ever got word of our conversation . . . I am very grateful to you for preparing this concoction for me and for being such good company." She stood. "And now I must prepare for my lord's visit."

A few days later, I heard that the Archbishop of Toledo had marched south to begin the reconquest of southern Spain. According to rumors sweeping the Jewish quarter, his army, which included one of the country's papal-ordained military orders, was ransacking towns in the province of Seville, plundering mosques, killing any men who resisted and even raping women. I was horrified by what I heard; the Christians sounded no better than savages.

Everyone was on edge as my family gathered for our usual Shabbat meal that Friday. Isadora was frantic because Mordecai was traveling on business. As I helped Isadora and Estraya prepare the table for the evening meal, Isadora told me that Mordecai had sailed out of Valencia a few days before for France with goods to trade and was not due back for at least two fortnights.

"What happens if Toledo is under siege by then?" she cried. "How will he get back home? Why, oh, why does this have to happen now?"

I patted Isadora's arm. "I'm sure he will be fine. If it isn't safe for him to travel to Toledo, he can always shelter in Valencia. Bernardo and his family are there now."

During the Shabbat meal, all we could talk about was the impending war between the Christians and the Moors.

Benjamin said that the leader of the Moors, Yaqub al-Mansur, was a crafty and formidable warrior and that King Alfonso should not underestimate him. "The sultan came off of his sickbed to put down a rebellion by his younger brother, Abu Yahya, in Morocco." He forked chicken and chickpea stew onto his plate. "And I've just heard that he's now back in Spain and marching north to meet the Christian army. As much as I dislike the man—he's a fanatic just like his predecessors—he knows how to build alliances and wage war. It would be a disaster if he defeats the king."

My father stopped chewing and looked at Benjamin. "What would happen to us if he takes Toledo? I don't relish the thought of going back to England."

"I doubt very much he will be able to breach Toledo's walls," Benjamin said. "But if he does, he would probably ransack the city and we would need to flee for our lives. And even if we survived, we'd be in the same position we were in Córdoba—unable to practice our faith and under intense pressure to convert to Islam. Not a good scenario any way you look at it."

Hania narrowed her eyes at Benjamin and tilted her head down the table, where Estraya sat in horrified silence.

Benjamin caught her look. "But I'm sure it won't come to that. King Alfonso has been assured by his allies in Navarre and Leon that they will come to his aid on the battlefield. The numbers are on his side."

I remembered what Rachel had said about the king's impulsiveness, but said nothing. Why worry my family needlessly? Besides, I had sworn not to betray Rachel's confidence. Even so, I no longer felt hungry. Hania and Isadora had likewise lost their appetites.

CHAPTER 10

ONE AFTERNOON A fortnight later, I said goodbye to my last patient and walked Estraya to the door. The heat from the late June sun was hotter than anything I had felt back in England. I was glad I was wearing a light sleeveless tunic gathered at the waist with a cord. I closed the door behind me to an empty house. Father was at the Manasses' home, no doubt conferring about business with Benjamin.

Enjoying the quiet, I returned to my healing room to tidy it for the next patient. The silence was broken by a knock on the door. I sighed. Most likely someone who needed a healer. I went to the door and opened it. Bernardo stood there, grinning down at me.

"You're back. Please, come in," I said, returning his grin.

An unmarried woman should not be alone with a man in her own house, but I didn't care.

"Thank you," Bernardo said, as he stepped inside. "I don't have a lot of time."

"Do you have time for some wine and biscuits?" I asked. "Oh yes, how's your mother?"

Bernardo looked away, but I could see the pain in his eyes. He took a deep breath. "The only reason I came back to Toledo is because of Rachel. She summoned my father and he sent me in his stead. He refuses to leave my mother's side."

Tears welled in my eyes. "I'm so sorry. Is there anything I can do?"

"She has the cancer and the doctors fear she may be gone within days." He sighed. "I hope to get back to Valencia before she goes." Tears glistened in his eyes.

I stepped forward and took his hands. "I'm so very sorry."

Bernardo's shoulders shook as he struggled to contain his emotions. He looked up after a few moments. "There is another reason I came back to Toledo. I'm told the sultan has reached Córdoba with his army and will be marching north soon to meet King Alfonso in battle. Things are going to get ugly very soon and I wanted to make sure you are safe."

His words warmed me. I wanted to throw myself into his arms. My eyes must have communicated my wishes because Bernardo stepped forward and folded his arms around me. He sought my mouth, and I abandoned all restraint, kissing him back with heartfelt passion.

Bernardo stepped back. "I have longed to do that for some time."

"As have I," I whispered. "Please come and sit down. I will put out some refreshments."

Bernardo shook his head. "Forgive me, but I must attend to Rachel. I'll be back soon, I promise." He smiled crookedly. "Perchance we can go for another ride in the country—before the hostilities begin."

I hated the thought of losing him so soon, but how could I resent his loyalty to Rachel, who must be feeling increasingly isolated as the king prepared for war. As much as I wanted him to stay with me, I understood that I should not hold him back from doing his duty.

"I would love to go for another ride in the country," I said. "Please give my best to Rachel."

The next morning, I heard a knock on my door. Being the Sabbath, I wasn't seeing any patients. My father had already left the house to visit with Perla, so I answered the door myself. A messenger handed me a scroll. I opened it in haste, hoping it was from Bernardo. To my delight, it was. He wrote that he would be able to break away from his duties at court for a few hours this afternoon. But since it wasn't safe at this point to leave the city, he suggested we could go for a walk in a park overlooking the Tagus.

I smiled to myself and sent the messenger off with a quickly scrawled assent; I knew my father would agree to it, since we would only be going for a walk within city walls.

By the time Bernardo arrived on my doorstep that afternoon, I was already sweaty from the heat despite wearing my lightest, sleeveless shift. I draped a wet scarf over my neck to keep cool. I gave Bernardo a wet cloth covering as well but he declined to wear it. Laughing, I draped it over his tall shoulders.

"It will keep you cool," I insisted. "You can always take it off when we leave the Jewish quarter."

"Yes, *la jefe*," Bernardo replied. "Whatever you say."

I laughed; I was no one's boss, but I didn't mind his good-natured ribbing.

I didn't see many other civilians out and about as we walked through the narrow streets, heat rising from the stone walls of the buildings that crowded us on either side. As we left the Jewish quarter, I noticed a few soldiers standing at guard. They took little notice of us, just another young couple out for a stroll. But even so, they made me nervous.

"Is it safe for us to leave the *barrio*?" I asked as we climbed up the narrow cobblestoned streets that led to the park.

"For the time being, yes . . ." He shrugged and looked down at the cobblestones. I heard the "but" in his voice, but I decided not to ask. Why ruin our outing with dark thoughts?

I had never been to this park before, and as we wandered along the meandering pathways, the flowering plants delighted my senses. A slight breeze came off the river but we were at a high enough point that I couldn't smell any stench from its rushing waters. A shallow pool of water spread out between the Alcazar and the cliffs, and I wished I could splash in it. I had vague memories of splashing in a fountain near my house as a child.

Bernardo gestured a a bench under a leafy oak tree. "Would you like to sit? I brought a flask of wine and some bread and cheese with me."

How thoughtful of him. "Sounds lovely. Yes, let's sit for a spell."

We sat down and Bernard took the food out of his leather shoulder bag and laid it on the bench next to him. He unscrewed the flask, put it down next to him, and reached back into his bag, He bumped the flask with his elbow, spilling a little wine.

"Mierda. I'm very sorry," Bernardo said, as he frowned and righted the flask.

"It's only wine and you didn't spill any on me," I said, laughing. But I could tell something was bothering him. "Are you upset about your mother? Is there anything I can do to help?"

Bernard brushed a hand over his eyes, as if to wipe away his sorrow. "Thank you but no. It's not just that. This is a very dangerous time. Rachel is very worried—about the king's safety and her own. This war is a gamble, no telling who will win and how many people will die. Rachel is concerned that the king may be killed on the battlefield. No surprise that she's been having bad dreams of late."

I felt terrible for Rachel; she was so brave and true. "I've heard that some of Toledo's priests have been sermonizing against her, calling her a Jezebel who is turning the king away from the true faith. Is there anything that can be done?"

Bernardo looked off at the shimmering hills surrounding the city. "Yesterday, Rachel and I discussed a possible escape plan for her should the king fall in battle. I can't go into the details—the less you know the better. Enriquez Perez and my father are helping with the arrangements."

Bernard tore off a chunk of bread and handed it to me. Then he cut me a piece of cheese. "I think you'll like this; my cook baked it fresh this morning." He tore off another piece of bread for himself.

"Thank you." I took a bite. "It's delicious." I put the rest of the bread on my lap. Bernardo's news and the sun's heat had left me with little appetite.

"And what about us? Will the Jews of Toledo be safe if the king dies?" I asked.

"If Alfonso is killed, it will be very bad for all of us," Bernardo said, frowning. "If history teaches anything, it's that the Church would like nothing better than to wipe us out. The Jews survive only at the whim of rulers like Alfonso who tolerate us for our money lending skills."

Despite the heat, I shivered. "Are you saying that we should be prepared to flee Toledo if the King dies?"

"It could come to that," Bernardo said. "Listen, I know of a hiding place that leads to secret route out of the city. I want to show it to you on our way back."

I didn't really want to think about an escape route, but Bernardo obviously thought it was important. I sighed. "Might as well show me now; it's very hot here even in the shade."

I crumbled up the rest of my bread and scattered it on the grass for the birds. As we left the park, I asked the question uppermost in my mind. "How long will you be in Toledo?"

"As you know, my mother doesn't have long to live," Bernardo said, frowning. "I must leave tomorrow and head back to Valencia to sit vigil."

"But isn't it too dangerous for you to leave Toledo right now, with both armies on the march?" I asked, my voice cracking.

Bernardo drew closer and turned my face toward him with a gentle hand. "Don't worry, my sweet. The roads between here and Valencia are quite safe and I will be back again before you know it."

Bernardo led the way through the narrow streets of the Jewish quarter until we came to an area where several of Toledo's wealthiest Jews lived in large, stand-alone houses built on the southern edge of a cliff that overlooked the Tagus River. He stopped in front of one imposing mansion surrounded by high stone walls.

"Don Paulo lives here, but I happen to know that he and his family are in Valencia at their summer home. He won't mind if we look around."

Even so, Bernardo put a finger to his lips as he opened a wooden gate in the wall. I followed him onto a grassy path, feeling uncomfortable. Wouldn't Don Paulo have left at least one servant to guard the house? What if we were caught trespassing?

Bernardo stopped in front of an unobtrusive wooden door set into the thick stone wall lining one side of the property. The door was painted the same gray color as the wall, and I doubted anyone would have noticed it if we weren't looking for it. Bernardo opened the door, gestured for me to follow him, and stepped inside a small enclosure built into the wall. I walked into a dark and damp place and shrank back from the scratching of tiny feet, no doubt rats scurrying away.

"Ah, here it is," Bernardo said, grasping an unlit torch from against the wall. Bernardo pulled a tinder box from his pouch and lit the torch. Bernardo stomped around the dirt and hay packed floor until his boot struck what sounded like wood. He bent down and lifted a round wooden board to reveal a hole in the floor.

"Here we are," he said. "These steps lead down to a hidden tunnel. Follow me and be careful. The stairs are very old and some of them are uneven."

"Must I?"

"Yes, you must," Bernard said. "I want to show you where you and your family can hide if God forbid, King Alfonso loses the war and Toledo's Christians decide to take it out on us. Don Paulo showed my father and me this hiding place a few years ago."

Bernardo climbed down the worn stone steps. I sighed and followed him, placing a hand on the damp wall to keep my balance. The stairs finally came to an end and I stepped onto packed mud. Bernardo stood a short distance away, his torch illuminating a long narrow tunnel held up by old wooden beams. I shivered; would the wood give way on us?

"If you follow this tunnel a short way, you will come to a slightly larger chamber, where there are built-in benches and a few more unlit torches," Bernardo said, gesturing into the distance. "During the riots in 1108, several Jewish families hid out here and survived the mayhem, Don Paulo's grandparents, among them."

"Oh god, I hope it never comes to that. I don't think I could survive being stuck down here for more than a few hours." I could feel the walls of the tunnel pressing in on me.

"It's better than being burned alive in your homes," Bernardo said.

I shuddered, remembering how close I had come to such a gruesome fate.

Bernardo stepped closer to me. "I'm sorry, that was the wrong thing to say."

I waved a hand. "Do you know where this tunnel leads?"

"I've never had the time or opportunity to explore it, but Don Paulo says it leads out of the city," Bernard said. "A secret passage of sorts."

I peered into the darkness and shivered. Pray God, my family and I would never have to find out where this foul-smelling tunnel led.

Bernardo turned around and pointed the torch back up the crumbling stairs. "And now I'd better get you back home before your father sends out a posse."

Bernardo ended up staying for an early dinner with my father and I, a meal that I prepared with the fresh fish my father had bought in the market that afternoon. After dinner, my father took himself off to visit Perla. I was grateful for his thoughtfulness; he must have sensed that I desperately wanted more time alone with Bernardo. Who knew when I'd see him again?

After Bernardo helped me clean up, we went to our tiny living room with a flask of wine. Bernardo sat close to me on the cushions and took my hand in his. His intense gaze made my entire body tingle.

"I love you, Rebecca, and I want you to know that I haven't felt this way for a long time. "When this"—he waved a hand—"is over, I'd like to ask your father for your hand. If you'll have me, that is."

My eyes misted with gratitude and joy. But would this man accept me for who I was?

"I love you too, Bernardo," I said. "But I could never give up my vocation for healing. Would that be a problem for you?"

"Not at all," Bernardo said. "I know that is an essential part of who you are and I wouldn't want to take that away from you."

A smile cracked open my heart. "Then there is nothing standing in our way."

Bernardo wrapped his arms around me and captured my lips in a long, sweet kiss I never wanted to end.

"My God, I want to keep kissing you. And more." Bernardo sighed. "But you are a woman of virtue and I would do nothing to besmirch your honor."

Bernardo's concern for my well-being touched me, so unlike that dastardly Templar Knight back in England. Even so, I just wanted to keep kissing him and feel his body pressing against mine.

"I really must get going," Bernardo said as he stood up. "I have to consult with Rachel one more time and then leave for Valencia first thing tomorrow." His eyes grew sad.

I looked away to keep the disappointment out of my eyes. I knew his duty to Rachel and to his mother must come first. But I couldn't wait for us to be together again.

CHAPTER 11
July 1195 AD

A FEW DAYS after Bernardo left for Valencia, King Alfonso marched south with his army. The sultan was heading north through the plains of Salvatierra, but no one knew how big a force he had. Most of the wealthiest families in the Jewish quarter had already left for their summer homes in Valencia, and everyone still in the city was on edge. Mordecai had not yet returned from his travels and Isadora was beside herself with worry. Estraya still came every day to help me with my patients, and she reported that no one in the family was sleeping well.

"I came downstairs to heat up some chamomile tea late one night because I couldn't sleep, and my mother and sister were already there. They had already made tea and it was spiked with wine." Estraya giggled. "We all slept in a little the next day."

A few days later, Elazar, Rachel's mayordomo, knocked on my door with a summons from her. I was in the middle of seeing some patients, so I told Elazar I couldn't leave until around noon. Could he come back then?

"My mistress isn't going to like that," Elazar said.

I stifled a rush of annoyance. Rachel might be the king's mistress but I was not at her beck and call. Yet Elazar looked so worried I bit off my response.

I raised my hands. "I can't leave my patients stranded. I promise I will be ready to go at noon."

Elazar frowned and scratched his chin. "I'll be back at noon sharp. Please be ready to come with me then." He took a step and turned. "I don't dare go back without you. Do you need anything from the market?"

How kind of him to ask. "As a matter of fact, I could use some more cilantro and chamomile. I'd be happy to reimburse you."

Elazar returned shortly before noon with the items I had requested. After giving Estraya detailed instructions on how to treat our last patient, who had an infection in his big toe, I took off my apron, grabbed my medicine bag, and followed Elazar out the door.

The streets were quiet without the soldiers, but here and there people went about their business, shopping for food and other essential items. A few clusters of older men were gathered at an outdoor café in the plaza, playing backgammon. Intent on their games, they paid no attention to us.

We arrived at Rachel's house, and I went up to her sitting room. She wasn't there but some light refreshments were laid out on a low table near the cushions. I helped myself to bread and olives. I was famished, having not eaten anything after a quick breakfast that morning. A few minutes later, Taresa came into the room.

She curtseyed. "My mistress is lying abed. Can you come with me?"

I put down my plate and rose. What was the matter with Rachel? I hoped it was nothing serious. I picked up my bag and followed Taresa down a hallway into Rachel's private chambers. *La Fermosa* was sitting up in bed, doing embroidery. She did not look at all sick. In fact, she looked positively radiant.

Rachel looked up. "What took you so long?"

"I had to see to my patients this morning," I replied, trying to hide my irritation. "I came as soon as I could. What's going on? You don't look ill."

"I think I'm pregnant," Rachel said, beaming. "I haven't bled in six weeks and my breasts are tender."

I stifled my surprise. "I am happy for you. Would you like me to examine you to make sure?"

Rachel waved me forward. "Yes please."

I put down my bag. "I have to take a look at your private parts. Are you comfortable with that?"

"Better you than one of the king's doctors," Rachel said, laughing. "I hear they're butchers."

I smiled. Rachel's forthrightness was refreshing.

"First, I need to wash my hands. Can you ask Taresa to bring me some soap and water?" Miriam had taught me the importance of cleanliness in examining patients and delivering babies, but many doctors and even a few midwives ignored this crucial practice. I had heard horror stories of doctors with dirty hands who delivered babies, only to have the mothers die of inflammation afterward.

While we waited for Rachel's maid to return, I sat in a chair by her bed.

"Why are you lying here?" I asked. "It's important for a pregnant woman to be up and about."

Rachel tilted her head. "Really? I don't want to do anything to jeopardize the baby."

"The baby will be fine if you get up and go about your day normally," I said. "I wouldn't go galloping anywhere but otherwise . . ."

Taresa brought back a basin of water and soap, and I washed my hands thoroughly. Then I instructed Rachel to lie at the edge of the bed and bring her knees up. I gently parted the lips of her cunte and looked inside. The cunte had taken on a purple-red hue and I knew from experience that this was an early sign of pregnancy.

"It looks like you may indeed be pregnant." I straightened up.

Rachel giggled and swung her legs out of bed. "I can't wait to see my lord's face when I tell him I'm expecting his child. I didn't want to say anything before he left, since I wasn't sure."

"A wise move," I said. "You have plenty of time to tell him once he returns from the battlefield, victorious."

Rachel frowned. She shook her head and called for Taresa to help her get dressed. "Go ahead and make yourself comfortable in my sitting room. I'll be right there."

We lounged on cushions, enjoying nibbles, grapes, and flat breads. Rachel was almost giddy with happiness. She couldn't stop talking about how the babe growing in her belly, the daughter of a king, would want for nothing. She was sure it would be a girl, and I suspected that her certainty had something to do with the fact that she knew that having a boy child, the illegitimate son of a king, would be too much of a threat to Spain's established order. But a girl, especially a girl as winsome as Rachel herself, could be useful in cementing alliances. Who wouldn't want to be married to the daughter of Alfonso VIII?

Rachel popped a grape into her mouth.

"I find I have quite an appetite now that I'm eating for two," she said gaily. "Oh, I know what I wanted to ask you: can my lord and I continue to, um, bed each other?"

I couldn't help but laugh. "Of course. As long as he's gentle with you."

"My lord is always gentle. He's quite a good lover, you know." Rachel smiled.

My face warmed.

Rachel winked. "You'll see how enjoyable it is once you and Bernardo finally commit to each other." She had an unerring sense of what other people were thinking. "When that time comes, I will give you some pointers."

"Ah, thank you, but let's not get ahead of ourselves here," I said, and we laughed.

I didn't want to spoil Rachel's good mood but I knew my family was desperate for news about the war. There were so many rumors, that the Sultan had taken back some of the towns the Archbishop of Toledo had ransacked the previous month; that Alfonso had already defeated the Moors; that the Moors had killed the king and were on their way to Toledo. No one knew what to believe.

"Have you heard anything about whether the two forces have engaged in battle? Or what's going on?" I asked tentatively.

Rachel frowned and tucked an errant curl back under her coif. "I have heard nothing since my lord left Toledo. But I understand he is going to make a stand around Alarcos. I just wish he had waited for the additional soldiers that Alfonso of Leon and Sancho of Navarre promised to send his way."

"I'm sure the king knows what he's doing," I said. "Perchance he was concerned that the sultan would make inroads into Castilian territory if he didn't stop him."

"Perchance." Rachel looked around to make sure no one else was listening. "My lord tends to be reckless at times. But this is not a time to be reckless—too much is riding on the outcome."

She put a hand on her belly. "I want this baby to have a good future."

Taresa appeared in the doorway with word that one of Rachel's advisors needed to see her.

Rachel stood up. "Mierda. I wanted to hear the rest of your story about how Ivanhoe came to your rescue. It will have to wait. Thanks again for all your assistance."

CHAPTER 12

LESS THAN A week later, a few of the wounded Christian knights who could still ride began dribbling back into Toledo. My father said the news was not good. The battle had been joined on a small hill south of Alarcos, and despite valiant efforts by the king's eight-thousand-strong calvary, the Christian forces had been routed. Diego Lopez de Haro, the Lord of Viscaya who had led the calvary charge, had retreated with a few of his surviving knights into the half-finished fortress of Alarcos, where he was surrounded by enemy forces. The infantry under King Alfonso's command had been decimated, and the king himself had barely managed to elude death or capture by being removed from the battlefield by his bodyguards. I stifled a groan when I heard this; I remembered what Rachel had said about the king's recklessness. Would his defeat put my friend in danger? According to the rumors floating around the city, King Alfonso was either on his way back to the city or had already arrived and locked himself away in the Alcazar.

In the Jewish quarter, almost everyone stayed home behind locked doors, afraid of what might happen next. The market and most shops closed down—no one wanted to be on the streets in case the Christians decided to once again blame the Jews for this humiliating defeat. For the first time since I started my practice, I had no patients to treat. Fortunately, Mordecai had gotten back a few days earlier, putting Isadora's fears to rest. His return was fortuitous in another way. His family now had whatever protection he and Mois could give them. I prayed that Bernardo was safe in Valencia with his family, and that Rachel would be able to comfort the king.

That evening, while my father and I were eating supper, we heard loud knocking on our door. I cast a worried look at my father.

"Should we see who it is?" I asked.

My father rose from his seat as if he was going to his execution. "It might be someone we know. I will check."

I picked up a cudgel and followed my father into the hall. I prayed I would have the strength to slug anyone who tried to force their way into our house.

"Who's there," my father called.

"It's me. Bernardo," he said, muffled by the thick door.

"Let him in," I cried.

My father unbarred the door and opened it. Bernardo, dusty and dressed in riding clothes, stepped inside.

I dropped the cudgel and ran into Bernardo's arms, not caring what my father thought. Bernardo squeezed me tight and then released me. "There's no time to waste. The Archbishop of Toledo is blaming the Jews for the sultan's victory; he says the king lost because he has grown too close to infidels. He's stirring up the Christian rabble. You and your family need to get into hiding before the monsters of hell are loosed."

I couldn't move a muscle, and my father's words sounded garbled.

"Rebecca, please, focus." Bernardo gave my shoulders a shake "I have to get back to Rachel. She is in danger. The archbishop is specifically blaming her for causing the King's defeat. He has called her a sorceress, a witch who has made the king weak."

My head pounded. "If anything, the Church is to blame—"

"I know, we know, that Rachel is not to blame for anything of this," Bernardo said. "But the Church has been looking for an excuse to get rid of her for years and now they think they have it. Her uncle and Don Enriquez are with her and I need to get back as soon as I can."

I grabbed Bernardo's arm. "Has she been able to see the king? He will protect her, won't he?"

"The king has locked himself into his quarters in the Alcazar and refuses to see anyone," Bernard said, shaking his head with disgust. "He is a coward. Now, please, there's no time for this. You and your father need to pack food, water, some wine, blankets, clothes, and whatever else you think you'll need in case you have to stay in hiding for a few days, or worse, leave the city in a hurry. Anything you can carry with you. I'm going to your uncle's house and alert them. Meet me there as soon as you can, in twenty minutes or less."

"Wait." I put a hand on his arm. "How is your mother?"

His face crumbled. "She has passed. We buried her yesterday. I can't dwell on that right now."

"I'm so very sorry." I hugged him tight. "May God comfort you among the other mourners of Zion. Remember that she will live on in your fondest memories of her."

Bernardo shut his eyes. After a long moment, he stepped back, his face a mask of determination. "You have to get moving. I'll see you at the Mendes' on the half hour."

I hurried to tell my father about Bernardo's warning. He went off in search of our valuables and important papers, and I rushed into the kitchen. I tried to keep my hands steady as I filled a few flasks with weak wine and water, but I was trembling with fear and haste and some drops spilled. No time to clean them up now. I packed some food in a leather satchel and rushed upstairs. I threw two woolen blankets and some warm clothing in two more satchels.

My father and I walked quickly to the Mendes' house, where the front door was ajar. Inside, I heard a shrill voice crying upstairs and the rush of feet pounding in haste. Daniel sat on the floor in the entryway, sucking his thumb and crying. I walked into the kitchen, where Hania and Isadora were throwing food into satchels.

Isadora looked up. "Mois and Benazir want to come too; is there room? We can't leave them here."

"We'll make room," I said. "How can I help?"

We finally gathered at the door, overladened with bundles. Bernardo unlatched the door, looked around outside, and pushed the door all the way open. He put his finger to his lips and stepped outside. As we followed Bernardo into the quiet street, no one said anything and I could feel my heart pounding. Benjamin and Isaac, who had attached swords to their belts, brought up the rear. Benazir carried her baby in a sling, and Mois carried two-year-old Bendie, two heavy satchels strung from his shoulders. Mordecai, who was similarly laden, carried Daniel, and Hania and Isadora guided the two older children in front of them. I walked behind Bernardo with Estraya. Twilight darkened the sky and I had to step carefully to avoid stumbling over the cobblestones.

I allowed myself to breathe a little as we entered the lane where the larger mansions stood. Just around the next corner, the high wall of Don Paulo's mansion loomed in front of us. Bernardo approached the gate and looked around. He again put a finger to his lips and unlatched the gate. A dim light from the mansion enabled us to see our way through the gate. My father flashed me a questioning look. I gave him a reassuring nod.

We shuffled through to the grassy patch and waited as Bernardo shut the gate. He beckoned us and stopped in front of the gray unobtrusive wooden door. He pushed the door open, stepped inside, and reappeared a few moments later with a torch.

"Quickly," he whispered.

We shuffled into the darkness. Bernardo walked around us and stomped on the dirt and hay-strewn floor until he hit wood. He lit the torch, handed it to me, and pulled up the trapdoor.

"I've got to leave and get back to Rachel," Bernardo said. "Rebecca knows where to take you from here. Please stay hidden. God willing, I will be back soon."

Desperate, I put a hand on his arm. "Shouldn't you come with us? The streets are not safe."

Bernardo patted my shoulder. "I'll be fine. I'll be back as soon as I can. God speed!" He turned and disappeared into the gloaming.

Estraya gave my arm a squeeze. I gave her a small smile and adjusted the weighty bag on my shoulder. Expectant eyes glistened in the torchlight. Their safety was now in my hands.

"Watch your footing. These steps are treacherous."

I gingerly stepped on the crumbling stone and put my hand on the damp wall as I took one step at a time. The children slid down next, followed by the others.

Hania stumbled and Mordecai, behind her, caught her and helped her keep a hand on the wall.

We took a moment to catch our breath at the bottom of the stairs, as I looked around, getting my bearings.

"This way." I hefted my bag and led the way down the tunnel, the stench from the damp dirt growing stronger as the walls opened up into a chamber.

Rough-hewn wooden and rough stone benches sat next to the walls. I shivered from the cooler air, glad I had packed extra blankets and warm clothes and had told the others to do the same.

Amada pointed to a piece of rusty metal attached to one wall. "What is that?"

Mordecai went to study it. "That, my darling, is a sconce. To hold our torch."

I gave him the torch and he mounted it on the sconce.

"I hope there are more torches down here," Mordecai said, looking around.

"Bernardo said he saw a few torches stored somewhere the last time he was down here." I gazed at the children, who were taking in the chamber with wonder. "First one who finds another torch gets a treat."

Amada and Bendie, Benazir's son scrambled around the chamber and found two torches behind a stone bench. I dug through my bag and pulled out a pouch of sweets.

"I have a sweet for each of you," I said as all the children gathered around.

I then sat onto a wooden bench next to my father and watched as the others took over parts of the chamber to settle in for who knew how long.

After we all found a place to sit, Mordecai straightened and slapped his hands to his knees. "I think I'll go check for rioters in the Jewish quarter."

"I'll go with you," Mois said.

"You can't leave me here all alone with these babies," Benazir cried. "Some husband you are."

Isadora crossed her arms and faced Mordecai.

"We'll be very careful," Mordecai said. "I promise."

Mois put a consoling arm around his Benazir. "We won't go far. We just want to see what's going on. We'll be back soon."

After they left, I spread my cushions on the damp bench and my father and I wrapped ourselves in blankets. Estraya played a game of dice with Amada and Bendie until they wearied and fell asleep, nestled against their mothers. Dim light from the torch cast flickering shadows on the wall, and the faint sounds of rushing water came from somewhere in the distance. I couldn't stop thinking about Bernardo and Rachel; were they safe? Had Rachel told the king that she was pregnant? Surely, he would protect her from the Church zealots. And what would happen to all the Jewish families who had nowhere to hide? Was the sultan even now on his way to Toledo to besiege and ransack the city?

I drank some wine from my flask to tame my thoughts and try to sleep.

Sound penetrated a dream and I opened my eyes and looked about, disoriented. Mordecai and Mois were rushing into the chamber, holding Benardo, with blood splattered on his face, between them.

I stood. "Quick, put him here," I pointed to where I had been resting. "I need some light."

Mordecai grabbed the torch from the sconce and held it above Bernardo as he sat on the bench. I held Bernardo's face to the light. The blood was seeping from an ugly gash on his forehead. I pulled away a long slash on his sleeve to reveal another long bleeding gash on his forearm.

"I was attacked when I tried to . . ." Bernardo began in a hoarse voice.

"Let me take care of your injuries and then you can tell us what happened," I said as I wiped away the blood from his head and arm with a wet cloth.

I glanced around and was relieved to find all the adults awake and anxiously watching us. "Can I borrow someone's wine flask please?"

My father gave me his flask, and I poured some wine on Bernard's gashes. He grunted.

"I'm going to stitch you up. This will hurt, but you need to keep still." I pulled the curved needle and thread from my bag. I looked up to see Estraya hovering nearby. "Estraya, can you find my cloth bandages? Mordecai, please keep the light steady."

I threaded the needle with shaky fingers, pushing down my anger at Bernardo for charging out into danger. I took a breath and concentrated on making neat stitches on the surprisingly deep gash on his forehead and the shallower slash on his forearm. I carefully cleansed the wounds with the wine, and wrapped with the clothes.

I then handed the wine flask to Bernardo. "Take a drink of this. You're going to be fine."

Bernardo drank deeply and leaned back against the wall. "Thank you. I needed that."

Bernardo fingered the cloth wrapped around his head and took a deep breath. He leaned forward with his elbows on his knees, his eyes glistening with tears.

"They killed Rachel, the bastards killed her," he whispered.

"What? No," I cried.

The torchlight wavered as Mordecai straightened. "How do you know? Were you there?"

"I had just arrived at Rachel's house when a woman came bursting out of the alley near the servant's door and ran to me. It was Rachel's maid. She told me not to go inside, that a cadre of assassins wearing insignias of the Calatrava military order had broken into the house. They slaughtered everyone who was with Rachel—her uncle, Don Enriquiz and Rachel's mayordomo. Then they stabbed Rachel to death even as she pled for her life and told them she was carrying the king's baby. The maid saw everything from the second-floor landing. She escaped down the back stairs. She said if I went inside, they would kill me too."

I gasped as I tried to take in a breath. "How did you get hurt?"

"I tried to get into the house anyway." Bernardo rubbed his watery eyes. "I thought perchance there was something I could do. The assassins had posted a guard in front of the house to make sure no one came to Rachel's aid. I charged the man with my sword and we fought. That's how I got this." He pointed to his head. "I had just managed to dispatch him when another man came out of nowhere and rushed at me with his dagger. He slashed me on my arm before I could free my sword. I managed to disable him as well, but with the other thugs still inside, I knew that if I tried to fight all of them . . ." He hung his head.

"You would have been killed," I said. "Thank God you thought better of it."

"You did your best," Benjamin said. "What can one man do against a horde of trained assassins?"

Bernardo's cheek muscle jumped as he impatiently shook his head. I knew him well enough to know that he thought he hadn't done his best, that he had taken the coward's way out.

"Do you think the king authorized Rachel's murder?" Mordecai asked as he returned the torch to the sconce. "I doubt the Church would have done such a heinous deed without his permission."

"I have no idea," Bernardo replied. "From what I understand, the king is not himself."

"If that's the case, he may not protect us from anti-Jewish mobs." Mordecai cast a grim look at Benjamin and turned to Bernardo. "Did you see any rioters on your way here? When Mois and I were walking around the Jewish quarter a little while ago, we didn't see any, but we stayed pretty close to Don Paulo's mansion, just in case."

"No, the city seems quiet," Bernardo said.

"The calm before the storm I'll wager," Mordecai said. "I think we should be prepared to flee Toledo."

Isadora groaned. "But where would we go? The Moors may be encircling the city as we speak. We could be killed once we leave."

"There's no need to make a decision now," my father interjected. "We're safe for now. Let us get some rest and see what the morning brings."

Bernardo quickly dropped into an uneasy sleep, but I lay awake for what seemed like hours. I couldn't believe that my vibrant, beautiful friend was dead. Rachel was only thirty years old and she had been so happy the last time I saw her, so sure that the king would be pleased that she was carrying his child and would protect her from the archbishop's malevolence.

If only the King had waited for the reinforcements from Leon and Navarre before clashing with the Moors. If only he had been victorious, Rachel would be alive now as would her baby. Bernardo had told me that he had offered to spirit Rachel away to Valencia once the king left Toledo with his forces, but she had refused to go, trusting that the king would protect her when the time came.

Her trust had been sorely misplaced; King Alfonso had betrayed her. And if he had failed the woman he loved, then he would probably fail us as well. What a dastardly coward. That man didn't deserve Rachel's love, he didn't deserve to be the monarch of Christian Spain. I half hoped that the Saracen commander would cut the king down in battle, or better yet, capture him and the archbishop and execute them both. Of course, if the sultan besieged and destroyed Toledo, we would probably be caught and killed in the carnage. Unless we fled beforehand. But how? My desperate thoughts ran in ceaseless circles until I finally succumbed to sleep.

CHAPTER 13

THE NEXT MORNING, I awoke to the sound of a baby crying. At first, I didn't know where I was but then it all came back. The flight to the tunnel, Rachel's murder, Bernardo's injuries. Bernardo was still sleeping next to me. I stood up and stretched, my back aching from sitting all night, and looked around. Hania's eyes opened and she sat up and looked around. My father groaned as he tried to stand up.

"I'm afraid this hiding business is not good for old bones like mine," he said, as I hastened over to help him up.

I walked around a bend in the tunnel and squatted in a dark corner to do my business. When I got back, everyone was awake. Benazir was breastfeeding her baby, and Isadora and Hania pulled bread and dried meat from their satchels to give to the children. I gave my father some food as well and we sat back down on the benches to eat.

"I'm going back upstairs to check on my horse and see what's going on," Bernardo said.

I groaned. "But you're wounded. You won't be able to defend yourself if it comes to that."

"I'll go with him," Mordecai said, touching the sword attached to his in its scabbard attached to his belt.

"So will I," Mois said.

Benazir wailed. "You're going to leave me down with these two?" She gestured at Bendie and the baby at her breast. "It's not safe!"

"We have to see what's going on, my dear," Mois said in an imploring tone. "Don't you want to know when it's safe to go home?"

That quieted his wife down. I ran a hand through my tangled hair. I must look a sight but I couldn't worry about that now. I turned to Bernardo, who looked haggard and drawn. "Well, if you insist on going, at least let me examine and clean your wounds."

Bernardo sat back down. "Aye. But please, be quick about it."

As I examined, cleaned and rebandaged his injuries, I thought about how much I wished I could go with him. I was heartily sick of camping out in this damp, depressing tunnel.

The three men soon left. Amada and Bendie were running around the enclosure, making shrill noises and pretending to be hunting vermin.

I turned to Estraya. "Why don't we take the children on a little expedition? I really need to stretch my legs and the others could use some peace and quiet."

"Great idea," Estraya said. She grabbed Amada's hand as she zoomed by, and I did the same with Bendie.

"Let's go for a walk. Maybe we can find some buried treasure further down the tunnel," Estraya said.

Bendie squealed with delight and dashed into the tunnel.

"Come back here," I said. "If you want to go on a treasure hunt, there are two rules: you can't run and you have to hold onto our hands."

I lit two torches and handed one to Estraya. As we walked deep into the tunnel, scurrying sounds greeted us, no doubt from rats or other creatures who lived underground. Amada and Bendie didn't seem to notice. They peered into every dark corner, looking for treasure. As the tunnel wound downhill, we were assaulted by an awful stench.

Amanda covered her nose. "It stinks down here."

"Yes, it most certainly does," I peered down the tunnel at the faint glimmer of light. "I wonder if this is where the waste from our latrines is flushed out into the river."

A fierce desire to find out gripped me. With Rachel murdered and the king in hiding, there was no telling what evil Toledo's archbishop might unleash on us. If this tunnel did indeed lead to the river, it might provide a safe route out of the city for us all.

I turned to Estraya. "Can you take the children back by yourself? I'm going to do a little exploring,"

"Are you sure that's a good idea?" Estraya said in a low but urgent voice. "What if you fall into the canal and get hurt?"

"I'll be fine," I said. "If the canal looks too dangerous, I promise I'll come right back. Please, I have to do this for all our sakes."

"Better you than me; that waste stinks," Estraya said. She turned to the children. "Come Amada and Bendie, let's go back and get something to eat."

She and the children disappeared into the gloom. I walked toward the glimmer of light. Just as I suspected, the tunnel led into a canal with muddy, foul-smelling water flowing toward the light. It didn't look too deep. I took off my slippers and my long tunic; no use befouling them.

I carefully laid the torch against one wall; the light was strong enough here that I could see without it. I took a deep breath and stepped into the rushing water in my undergarments. The cold current took me by surprise and I almost fell. But I was able to steady myself at the last moment by planting a hand onto the damp wall closest to me. Oh God, the water stank!

I planted one foot carefully in front of the next and inched through the filthy water toward the light. It grew stronger, and I soon came upon a large opening. There was a place where I could step out of the muck onto a path alongside one wall. Holding onto the wall for support, I walked a little further and gasped.

I had been right. I was standing in a large hole in the cliff, and I could see the sewage water I had just been walking in flow downhill toward the Tagus River. Off to my right, a narrow path meandered from where I stood down the hill towards the San Martin bridge. This was indeed a way out of the city, one that previous residents of Toledo had no doubt availed themselves of in troubled times.

I feasted my eyes on the countryside across the river. I would give anything to be riding through the grassy fields with Bernardo by my side. But this was no time for daydreaming. I had to get back before my family started worrying about me. I couldn't wait to tell them what I had found.

I walked into the chamber and Hania gave a small shriek of surprise.

My father rushed up to me. "Are you okay my dear? Ooh, I smell something bad."

"Yes, I know," I said, laughing. "I've been wading in raw sewage, but it was worth it. I found a way out of the city if it ever comes to that. There's an opening in the cliff and a path that leads right to the bridge, where we could cross if we had to."

"That's good news, although I don't relish the idea of wading through all that excrement," Benjamin said.

Benazir wrinkled her nose in disgust. "You won't catch me doing that."

Estraya and I exchanged knowing looks.

"I'm sure it won't come to that," Isadora said, unable to hide the worry in her eyes.

Mordecai and Mois trudged into the chamber a short while later.

"Good news, there's no sign of rioters in the Jewish quarter," Mordecai said. "Not a lot of people in the streets."

"Where's Bernardo?" I asked.

"He said he was going to ride up to the Alcazar and see what was going on," Mordecai said.

I stifled a groan. Why did that foolish man have to keep putting himself in harm's way.

"Have they opened the market?" Hania asked. "Did you talk to any of the farmers selling produce?"

Mois nodded. "There were only a few stalls open. People said they'd had no problem getting into the city and thus far there's been no sign of an approaching army. Nor any angry mobs heading our way."

Hania muttered a brief prayer of thanks under her breath.

"So, can we go back home now?" Benazir asked. "It's not healthy for the baby down here. And I need more swaddling bands."

Mordecai ran his fingers through his hair. "You and Mois can do whatever you like. My family and I are going to stay here until Bernardo returns and we hear what he has to say."

Benjamin nodded in agreement, and in the end, everyone decided to stay put until Bernardo returned. Estraya and Isadora took turns telling the children stories while the men muttered among themselves, pacing up and down in the small space. I had already taken off my foul-smelling leggings and washed my legs as best as I could with soap and a little water I had left. I tried to busy myself by sorting through my medicine bag and making a list of supplies I needed replenished, trying not to worry about Bernardo.

I finished rearranging my medicines for the fourth time and thought I heard a sound. Mordecai picked up a torch and planted himself at the opening. He squinted into the darkness.

"It's Bernardo," Mordecai announced.

"Thank you, lord," I said to myself.

Looking haggard, Bernardo dragged himself to a bench and plunked himself down. I handed him a flask. He gave me a grateful look and took a deep drink.

"I think it's safe to go back to your homes," he said. "The king has personally pledged our safety."

"What! Tell us everything," Benjamin demanded.

Bernardo said that when he rode back up to Rachel's house to see what was going on, a soldier guarding the door told him the bodies had been removed. "He suggested I go to the Alcazar, where the king was holding court. So that's where I went next."

Estraya and I both gasped. Bernardo glanced at us.

"I had no trouble getting into the royal chamber. The king was talking with his courtiers, including Don Paulo and my own father who must have just returned from Valencia. The king looked pale and broken with grief."

"As he should be," I interjected. "Did he know that Rachel was carrying his child when she was so cruelly slain?"

Bernardo nodded, his face drawn with pain. "Yes. My father took me aside and told me that this morning the king finally came out of seclusion and summoned the archbishop. He ordered de Pisuerga to stop fomenting anti-Jewish hatred. He said he could do nothing to bring Rachel back but he didn't want any more bloodshed. He said that as long as he was king, the Jews of Toledo would be protected."

I slammed a hand down on the bench.

"How can we trust the king?" Hania cried. "He probably gave the archbishop the go-ahead to assassinate his own mistress."

Bernardo sighed heavily. "I agree. De Pisuerga would not have done this without the king's tacit consent. I suspect the archbishop convinced the king that he needed a scapegoat for his humiliating defeat and Rachel was the perfect goat. In the mind of Toledo's Christians at least."

"How can we believe anything this man says?" I said, sick to my stomach.

"I understand how you feel," Bernardo replied. "But what choice do we have? We have to keep in mind that the sultan is even now consolidating his victory. The king's castles in Malagón, Benavente, Calatrava, and Caracuel have all surrendered to the sultan's army, and there's no telling when he will march north to Toledo. We may have no choice but to support King Alfonso and pray he can hold the city."

Mois stopped pacing around the chamber to quiet his four-month-old son in his arms. "Yes, yes, but is it safe to go back to our home? My wife can't take much more of this."

"Yes, I think it is safe to return to our homes," Bernardo said. "I think the king is serious about preventing further bloodshed."

It struck me that Rachel had been the sacrificial lamb for the archbishop's appetite for vengeance this time around. If she had somehow managed to escape, no telling what retribution would have been unleashed on Toledo's Jewish population.

We packed up our belongings and trudged back up the stairs. The warmth from the sun barely registered on me as I walked, numb with grief, through the mostly empty streets of the Jewish quarter. Like everyone else in the group, I was silent and fearful, expecting to see a swarm of rioters around each bend. But the quarter was eerily quiet. Most residents were still staying indoors behind bolted doors.

My father had only recently begun courting Perla. He said he was going to check on her and her family.

Once we reached Mordecai and Isadora's house, Benjamin turned to Bernardo, thanking him once again for showing us the secret tunnel.

"You must join us for dinner Friday night—for Shabbat," he said to Bernardo. "I'm sure we will have much to discuss."

"I will try to come," Bernardo said. "Can't promise anything though."

Bernardo walked his horse next to me. He looked pale and exhausted.

"You really need to rest so your injuries can heal," I said. "Why don't you come in for a nap? You can have my bed."

Bernardo grinned. "I only want to be in your bed with you in it."

I turned my head away to hide my warming cheeks.

"I'm only jesting." His expression turned grave. "I don't have time to rest. They are burying Rachel and her uncle this afternoon and I promised my father I would be there."

Of course. According to Jewish tradition, the deceased must be put into the ground quickly, within a day or two if possible. This age-old tradition, I knew, came from the concern that the living not be exposed to disease or decay. I could well understand that.

"I'll come with you," I said. "I would like to pay my respects too."

Bernardo walking and turned to me. "No. That is not a good idea."

"Why not?" I asked.

Bernardo looked at me as if I was being deliberately obtuse. "Because you are a healer and you are Jewish. And you are a beautiful woman. The last thing we need is you coming to the attention of the archbishop or, for that matter, the king. Also, don't forget that I killed or seriously injured two members of the Calatrava military order at Rachel's house so if they try to arrest me, I can't risk you're getting hurt."

"What about you?" I asked.

"Now that the archbishop has been called off, I don't think I have to worry," he said. "The king has his own soldiers guarding the city, but I don't want to take any risks with your safety."

At my doorstep, Bernardo stepped back and bowed his head. "I'll be in touch. Stay safe."

He mounted his horse and trotted away, the sound of the hooves echoing after he was gone from sight.

CHAPTER 14

A FEW DAYS later, Bernardo sent word that he and his father would be able to attend our Sabbath meal that evening. Benjamin and my father were excited to meet Don Esteban. They knew who he was of course—who didn't—a wealthy moneylender and one of the king's trusted advisors. Yet as Bernardo had confided to me, his father would no doubt have been killed along with Don Enriquiz and Rachel's uncle had he been with Rachel at the time of her murder. And Bernardo would also have been slain had he not been seeing to the safety of my family. On the other hand, if both men had been at Rachel's side, perhaps they could have fought off the assassins and saved her. How cruel and capricious fate could be.

I forced myself to put these sad thoughts aside as Isadora lit the Sabbath candles and said the blessing. Isadora had already put her children to bed, and she stood next to Mordecai as he recited the blessings over the wine and bread. Then we served the meal.

Don Esteban had good tidings. The sultan, he said, had moved his army back to Seville instead of continuing his march north to Toledo. "From what Lord Lopez tells me, the Moor's forces also sustained heavy losses. I gather that Yaqub al-Mansur wants to rest and restock his troops before any further expeditions."

"Does that mean Toledo is safe for the time being?" Mordecai asked.

"I believe so," Don Esteban said. "But who knows for how long. Our infantry has been destroyed and Lopez had to pay a heavy ransom to win his own freedom and those of his surviving knights. So many men were killed, it was truly a disaster. It will be a while before the king has sufficient arms to retake the battlefield. If the sultan decides to mount a siege against Toledo, the road is wide open. All the defending castles have fallen and there's virtually no one and nothing standing in the Moor's way."

Estraya gasped.

Don Esteban looked abashed. "I'm sorry my dear, I didn't mean to upset you. Perchance this is not an appropriate conversation with . . . ahem . . . women present."

Estraya waved her hand. "No, no, we all need to hear this. Please do continue. I was just surprised is all."

Benjamin cleared his throat. "Not to change the subject, Don Esteban, but do you really think we can trust the king to protect us from the zealots who blame us for his defeat?"

Don Esteban took a sip of sweet wine, put his wineglass down, and turned to Benjamin. "King Alfonso needs us now more than ever—to help replenish the royal treasury and build his army back up. I think the Jewish community is safe for the time being. Of course, I have no crystal ball with which to predict the future."

The men went out into the courtyard to continue their conversation and I helped Hania, Isadora, and Estraya clean up. I wished, not for the first time, that I could join the men so I could hear what they were saying. As I washed the dirty wineglasses from dinner, I wondered if Bernardo and I had a future. I knew he was racked by guilt at not being able to save his childhood sweetheart. Yet he would surely have been killed if he had tried to fight his way into Rachel's house while the assassins were still inside. There was nothing he could have done to alter the outcome.

To my surprise, Don Esteban rode back to his house by himself after dessert and Bernardo insisted on walking me home. My father had already left, pleading exhaustion. We strolled at a leisurely pace through the *barrio's* darkening streets, talking about the conversation over dinner. But I could sense that Bernardo was not at peace, that he was struggling to find the words to tell me something. Was this going to be when he told me it was over between us? I braced myself for what was to come. Finally, Bernardo stopped and ran a restless hand through his hair.

"I've got to go away," he said. "With the war and my mother dying, I've been putting off my trip to the north. But the flax and spices I brought back on my last venture won't be any good in a few months. I should go now while the roads to Valencia are still open and the weather is decent."

"But is it safe to travel?"

"Aye, for the time being at least," Bernardo said. "It will probably be weeks, maybe months, before the sultan resumes his advance."

Bernardo looked away. I could tell there was more he wanted to say but something was stopping him. I bit my lip in frustration. We reached my house, and Bernardo made no move to kiss me.

He bowed low over my hand. "Please forgive me—my mind is in tumult," he muttered. "I will send word when I return." He looked up and tried to smile, a crooked effort that did not reach his eyes. "Stay safe."

In bed that night, tears welled up and dripped down my face. I rubbed my eyes angrily. Why were men so apt to run away or shut down at difficult moments like this? I sighed and pounded a pillow. I would just have to endure and pray that time would heal Bernardo's wounds, inside and out.

CHAPTER 15

IN THE DAYS that followed, the residents of the Jewish quarter ventured out and soon the streets around the market were clogged with shoppers. Those in need once again waited to see me. One of my patients, an older man complaining of shortness of breath, told me that king had just left for Burgos to visit the queen.

"There's some who say he's running away from the memory of his mistress," the man said bitterly. "That was a foul deed, her murder. Did you know she was Jewish?"

I nodded but said nothing. I didn't want to add to the gossip swirling around the Jewish quarter by acknowledging that I had known Rachel. My poor sweet friend, how I missed our time together. I stuffed my feelings of loss back down my throat and listened to my patient's chest.

"You should lose weight or you're a candidate for heart collapse," I said. "You need to cut down on your consumption of wine and sweets. I will send you home with some herbal medicine, which I want your wife to brew into a tea and give you once a day."

My patient nodded obediently.

ONE AFTERNOON, I was just finishing up with a patient when Estraya came rushing into the room and pulled me aside.

"There's a priest at the door," she whispered in a panicked voice. "He says he wants to talk to you."

I pushed down a bubble of anxiety. "I'll be done with this patient in a few minutes. Please ask him to wait."

After I dismissed my patient, I removed my dirty apron, washed my hands, and walked into the entryway. A young man, dressed in a cleric's black tunic, shot up from the chair. He bowed to me.

"It's my sister, she is in distress," he said. "This is her first pregnancy and I think the baby is turned wrong. She has been in labor a long time and I'm afraid they are both going to die. Please, can you help?"

I took in his anxious, imploring eyes. I know he wouldn't have sought me out if he weren't desperate.

"I won't hold you accountable if things go wrong, I promise," the priest said. "Please!"

I studied his open, honest face. His brown eyes locked on mine, and I had to go with my instinct that I could trust him.

"I will come and see what I can do," I said. "There are no guarantees of course."

I told Estraya to tell any patient to wait for my return, grabbed my medicine bag, and followed the lanky priest as he hastened through the streets of the Jewish quarter and into the Christian section of the city. I had to swerve to avoid bumping into other pedestrians on the narrow streets and struggled to keep with the priest's brisk pace. I pinched my nose to keep out the stench from uncollected garbage on the streets.

The priest introduced himself as Father Menendo.

"My sister is the only kin I have left in the world," he said as he strode, his black robes swishing around his legs. "Her husband was killed in the battle of Alarcos and she took his death hard."

He led me to small house down a dirty alley, opened the door, and gestured for me to go inside. A woman was lying on a bed in the back room, groaning in pain.

Another woman, really little more than a girl, crouched over her. Splotches of blood were splattered on the floor, and the room was hot and humid and reeked of sharp bodily odors.

Father Menendo approached the bed. "Sonifrida, I've brought Señorita Manasses to help. She is a respected midwife. Please do what she says. This is Toda, she is my sister's helper."

I put down my bag and turned to Toda. "I need some clean water to wash my hands. And then can you please heat up some water?"

Toda rushed out of the room, and I gazed down at Sonifrida.

"I'm going to reposition you so I can examine you," I said. "Try to take deep breaths through the pain."

Toda came back with a basin of cloudy water, and I washed my hands with the soap I had brought with me. With her brother's help, I moved Sonifrida so that she was propped up at the edge of the bed. I pressed down several times on her belly and she groaned in pain.

I straightened up. "The baby is breech and we don't have a lot of time. Your sister is exhausted, and she may lose consciousness any minute." I turned to Father Menendo. "I need you to support her while I try to turn the baby. And you, Toda, take the other side. You both need to keep Sonifrida still."

Between contractions, each more powerful than the last, I pressed hard on the relaxed belly, trying to push the baby downward. I inserted my other hand into Sonafrida's cunte, and she screamed in pain and tried to wriggle away. But Menendo and Toda kept her in place. I pushed and prodded the baby's head and shoulders downward.

I kept at it until my shoulders ached, as did my hips and knees from kneeling on the floor for so long. Sonifrida's belly and cunte was slick with sweat and hot under my hands, and I could feel beads of sweat running down my own face.

After what seemed like an eternity, I felt the baby turning. To keep its head down, I coaxed Sonifrida onto her hands and knees and kneaded her lower back. Sonifrida was barely conscious and moaning in pain, but her brother and Toda helped support her.

Finally, I could feel the head crowning. I leaned over Sonifrida and said firmly, "You have to push now. Give it everything you've got."

Sonifrida screamed and gave an enormous push. As she lost consciousness, the baby slid out into my palm. The umbilical cord was wrapped around its neck and I quickly cut the cord, turned the baby over and smacked its behind. I prayed that the baby, a girl, would live. She was blue and floppy, and I was afraid she had been deprived of air for too long. I had seen this before and many babies in this state did not survive. I held my breath.

At long last, the infant gasped for breath and turned pink. Thank God! Only then did I take a deep breath myself. I handed the infant over to Toda and instructed her to wrap the child in a soft cloth. But the afterbirth had not yet been expelled. I gently wiped Sonifrida's mouth and nose with a cloth dipped in a vinegar and salt mixture I prepared. She startled awake and moaned again in pain. I urged her to keep pushing and the bloody afterbirth slid out onto the floor.

I asked Toda to put down fresh bedding for Sonifrida and cleaned up the little girl, whom, I was pleased to hear, was now busy exercising her lungs. Then I laid the child in the arms of its tired mother.

"You have a beautiful baby girl," I told Sonifrida. "I'm going to show you how to feed her but first take a draught of this." I pressed a flask of wine to Sonifrida's lips until she gulped a little down.

I then went into the kitchen and prepared a healing tea for Sonifrida. After she had drunk some of it, I checked again to make sure she was not bleeding from the birth. She soon fell asleep, the baby at her breast. As I prepared to leave, Father Menendo pressed some coins into my hand.

"I can't tell you how grateful I am to you for saving my sister's life and the baby with her," Menendo said, his eyes moist. "I am in your debt."

Although my experience with clergy led me to mistrust his flowery words, I wanted to believe that this priest was being sincere. "I'm happy that I was able to help."

A FEW DAYS later, I went over to the Mendes' house to help prepare for the Shabbat dinner. It was mid-August and still hot. An afternoon shower had cooled things off a bit but even so, Mordecai dragged the dining table into the backyard, where a light breeze made eating outdoors slightly more bearable than being inside.

"Mordecai and I are thinking about leaving Spain and starting a life somewhere else," Isadora said, as we were setting the table for dinner. "We no longer feel safe here. Mordecai says the archbishop has started preaching against the Jews again."

I had heard the same disturbing rumor yesterday from one of my patients, a construction worker. I had been too busy stitching up an ugly gash on his hand to pay much heed then. But I trusted Mordecai with the truth, however uncomfortable it was to hear.

"I feel the same way," I said. "Bernardo said he thought Egypt was probably the safest place for Jews right now. He said Jews are free to practice their faith there and the Saracen ruler there even employs a Jew as his private physician."

"How interesting; I'll share that with Mordecai," Isadora said. "The problem is that my parents don't want to leave. They've lived their entire lives in Spain and my father is not eager to start over."

I could understand that. My own father had taken a long time to acclimate to our new life in Spain. Now that he was courting Perla, he was happier than I had seen him in a long time. I doubted he would want to leave Perla and uproot himself once again. And how could I leave Toledo without my father?

At dinner that evening, no one mentioned the archbishop's anti-Jewish sermons or the family discord over leaving Toledo. Instead, we sang traditional Sabbath songs, ending with Adon Olom, a comforting melody about God, the "everlasting sovereign." Adon Olom, Benjamin explained, had been written by a famous Jewish poet and philosopher who lived in Andalusia a century ago.

My uncle seemed determined to keep the conversation cheerful.

"If our business does as well next year as it did until the war, we might be able to buy a house in Valencia," Benjamin said. "It would be good to get away from Toledo for a few months, wouldn't it? The children would love it. Remember the summers we spent in Malaga, Isaac? Those were the days."

My father laughed, his eyes brimming with nostalgia. "Yes, those were the days."

What he and Benjamin left unsaid was it was no longer safe for non-Muslims to travel to Malaga, a town on the Mediterranean southeast of Toledo, with the war going on.

TWO DAYS LATER, I was sorting through my medical supplies—it was early Sunday afternoon, and I was alone—when I heard a knock on the door. I rushed to the door and yanked it open. To my vast disappointment, it wasn't Bernardo standing there, but a man garbed in clerical robes. I recognized him—it was Father Menendo.

"I'm sorry to disturb you on this holy day, *señora*, but I bring bad tidings." The priest glanced around furtively. "May I come in for a moment?"

"Of course." I stepped back to let him in and closed the door. "How is your sister?"

Menendo's face brightened. "She and the baby are doing well—thanks to you." His smile faded. "You must go into hiding at once. The archbishop and his minions preached against the Jews again this morning and called on their congregations to teach your people a lesson. Many are even now massing in the streets. They say they are planning to march on the Jewish quarter and burn it to the ground."

I gasped. Surely, he was wrong; the king had pledged our safety.

"The king is not here to protect the Jews," Menendo added, as if he could read my thoughts. "Do you and your family have a place to hide?"

Not again, I couldn't face going down into that dark, dank tunnel again. And yet what choice did I have? "Thank you for the warning, Father. It is I who am in your debt now."

I SAW HIM to the door and quickly threw some food, wine, water, blankets and clothing into two satchels. I had to find my father, who had said he was going to visit Perla an hour or so ago. I rushed out the door and walked as fast as I could to my relatives' house. Isadora opened the door, gazing at me in confusion.

"The bishops are preaching against us again and I've just been warned by a priest that they may be coming soon to burn down the Jewish quarter," I told her, feeling the sweat pool down my back. "We've got to go back to the tunnel."

Isadora gasped and clutched her throat. "No!"

"Yes, I don't think the priest would lie about something like this. I just delivered his sister's baby." I thrust my satchels at her. "Please get everyone ready to go. I have to go find my father. He's probably at Perla's. Can I leave these here with you?"

My father wasn't at Perla's house; no one was home. Dear God, my father and Perla must have gone for a walk, but I had no idea where. Using a quill and ink I kept in my bag, I scrawled a message on a piece of scroll and tucked it onto Perla's door, instructing my father to come at once to our hiding place. He would know what I was talking about; I had already left a similar message at home. By the time I got back to the Mendes' house, my relatives were packed and ready to go. Mois and Benazir had left for Valencia a fortnight ago; lucky them.

"I'm worried about my father," I told Mordecai. "I can't find him anywhere. What should I do?"

"I will go look for him," Mordecai said. "The rest of you, get to the tunnel."

Isadora clung to him, imploring him to come with them. "Please, our children need a father."

Mordecai hugged her wordlessly and set off in the direction of Perla's house.

As I unlatched the gate at Don Paulo's residence, I could hear angry shouts in the distance and smell smoke.

"Hurry," I said and gestured at my family to come inside. Benjamin relatched the gate when we were all inside, and I hastened toward the door in the wall. I opened it and groped around the small enclosure for the torch. I couldn't find it. With my foot, I tapped around for the wooden trapdoor. There it was. I lifted up the door. A dim light wafted up from down below. Somebody must already be down there, but who? I told the others about the missing torch and the light in the tunnel.

"We have no choice," Benjamin said in a hoarse voice. "If we stay up here, we're doomed."

We tumbled down the steps and at the bottom, regrouped. Benjamin led the way, armed only with his sword, with me following close behind him, my hands gripping the jeweled dagger that my father had given me back in England. I had never had to use it before, but its grip felt oddly comforting.

As we came into the larger enclosure, Benjamin stopped short. Six other people had already laid claim to the benches. I recognized one of them as Don Paulo, the banker whom I had met at Rachel's party five months ago. Had it been that long ago? So much needless tragedy. Benjamin also recognized Don Paulo and gave a gusty sigh of relief. He raised his arm in greeting and strode forward with a hearty hola. Don Paulo returned the greeting.

"Welcome to our hiding place," he said. "I'm glad you found your way here."

Don Paulo's party, which consisted of him, his wife, one of his married daughters and her two young children, made room on the benches. Hania and Isadora spread their blankets and sat down on one bench, with little Daniel nestled in his mother's lap. Don Paulo came over to Benjamin and whispered something to him. Benjamin turned around to the rest of us.

"We're going to take a walk down the tunnel," he said. "We'll back soon."

I was too restless to sit down. "May I come with you? I'm worried about my father."

Benjamin glanced at Don Paulo, and he nodded.

"This is going to be a bad one," Don Paulo said, once we could no longer be heard by the others. "I just pray they don't burn down my house. I left two of my Christian servants guarding the premises. I hope they'll be able to ward off the mob."

He emitted a bitter chuckle. "I instructed them to tell the mob, if necessary, that the house is owned by one of the king's advisors, an absentee Christian grandee. I told them I would pay them well for standing guard."

Don Paulo's deception seemed to me to be one more example of how the wealthy were often able to skirt the disasters visited on those less fortunate. But I said nothing. Benjamin must have been thinking the same thing because he said, in his usual diplomatic way, "You're lucky you have Christian servants. We've locked the door to our house but if the horde is intent on burning down the Jewish quarter, I'm afraid it won't be spared."

Nor, I thought despairingly, will ours. But as long as my father survived, I could deal with the loss of our house. What were material possessions next to the lives of those I loved?

"As soon as I heard about de Pisuerga's vile preaching, I sent word to the king," Don Paulo said. "But even if the king leaves Burgos as soon as he receives my missive, I doubt he will arrive in time to avert this catastrophe. I should never have brought my family back from Valencia." He scowled and slammed his fist into the palm of his other hand.

"How could you know?" I asked. "We all believed the king's assurances."

A little while later, I heard sounds in the tunnel. I heaved a sigh of relief as Mordecai stumbled in, panting heavily; his tunic smelled of smoke. I jumped up in anticipation but neither my father or Perla were with him.

"They are burning down the *barrio* and killing any Jew they can get their hands on," Mordecai croaked. "There is so much smoke everywhere. I wasn't able to find Isaac or his lady friend and I had to turn back, otherwise I would have been killed. I'm so sorry."

I doubled over with a moan, and Hania and Isadora grabbed me and helped me down on a bench.

"Take deep breaths, dear, and try not to despair," Hania said. "Your father is a resourceful man; I'm sure he'll be okay."

Don Paulo gripped Mordecai by the arm. "Is my house still standing?"

Mordecai nodded. "The mob hasn't gotten to this part of town yet." He looked at Isadora. "I didn't have time to check on our house. It was too dangerous."

Isadora folded herself into his arms. "I'm just glad you're safe and here with us. That's all that matters."

I stared in an unseeing fog at my feet. I couldn't believe my father might be lying injured or dead somewhere in the city and I couldn't help him. I prayed he had found a safe place to hide.

Benjamin approached me and awkwardly patted my arm. "Don't worry about your father. From what he has told me of his escapades in England, that man has nine lives."

We all settled down again for the long night. As I leaned against the damp wall of the tunnel wrapped in a blanket to keep out the cold, the faint smell of smoke brought back that hellish day in England when I had sat for hours on the jousting field, awaiting my execution. Three days prior, when I had been brought into the great hall to learn my fate, the Grand Master had given me the chance to find a champion who would fight on my behalf. Of all the bitter ironies, he had designated Brian Bois-Guilbert, the miscreant who kidnapped me, to joust for the Templars. The only knight I could think of who might come to my rescue was Ivanhoe, so I had scrawled a message to my father, pleading with him to find Ivanhoe and bring him to Templestowe within three days. But on the final day when I was brought to the jousting field to await my fate, there had been no sign of Ivanhoe or my father, and I feared my missive had never reached him.

Some spectators had brought food and ale to the field and they milled around eating, drinking and enjoying the mild early summer afternoon. But no one offered anything to me and my throat felt parched and raw. At one point, a Templar official had walked over to me and asked if I wanted to continue waiting for a champion or was ready to yield to my fate. I stood, squaring my shoulders, and requested as long a delay as possible.

Another hour or so passed and still no champion emerged. Just as the sun was beginning to lower in the western sky and the knights of the order began grumbling among themselves that it was time to get this over with, a rider on horseback appeared on the plain advancing toward the lists. Every eye turned toward him as he trotted into the tiltyard, and as one, the spectators yelled, "A champion! A champion!"

I stood up, shielding my eyes from the setting sun. It was Ivanhoe! But at the sight of him, my heart sank. His steed reeled with fatigue, and Ivanhoe himself, whether from exhaustion or his wounds, could barely support himself in the saddle. Even so, he was here, at last. He rode up to me, and bowing in the saddle, asked if I would accept him as her champion.

"I do, I do," I said, overcome by emotion. But then I checked myself; Ivanhoe was in no condition to fight. "On second thought, no, no, your wounds are still not cured; you should not joust with this Templar knight; why should you perish also?"

But by the time I had finished speaking, Ivanhoe was already at his post and had closed his visor and grasped his lance. Brian de Bois-Guilbert did the same. I wanted to close my eyes and put my hands on my ears. Instead, I couldn't help watching in horrified suspense. The Grand Master, who held in his hand the gage of battle, my own glove, threw it into the lists and cried, "*Laissez aller.*" The trumpets sounded and the knights charged each other at full speed.

They clashed, and as expected, Ivanhoe's weary horse went down with its rider before the Templar's well-aimed lance. I gasped in horror and clapped a hand to my mouth to keep from crying out. But even though Ivanhoe's lance had only touched Bois-Guilbert's shield, to everyone's astonishment, he too fell off his horse and lay on the ground motionless. Ivanhoe, having extricated himself from his fallen horse, was soon back on his foot and had drawn his sword. Even then, his opponent did not move. Ivanhoe placed his foot on Bois-Guilbert's breast and with the sword's point on his throat, commanded the other man to yield. There was no response.

I moaned. What did this mean? Was my kidnapper playing dead? Would he spring to his feet at any moment and slay Ivanhoe? I watched, barely daring to breath, as the Grand Master strode over to the two knights. I could see by his gestures that he was asking Ivanhoe not to kill Bois-Guilbert, even though that was his right. The Templar Master commanded two attending guards to un-helm Bois-Guilbert. He knelt by the prone man's side and examined him briefly. He then rose to his feet, sorrow clouding his features.

"He is mort," the Grand Master said. "It is a judgement from God."

The Templar walked over to me. "He was no doubt a victim of his own immoral passions. But Ivanhoe has won this joust and you, Jewess, are free to go."

I collapsed back into my chair, dizzy with relief. I felt overcome with gratitude for Ivanhoe, but I was also angry, no, furious at what I had been put through. Was I really free to go? My heart was hammering in my chest and I didn't think I could stand on my own. As I was trying to collect myself, two more horsemen galloped into the lists, fully dressed for combat. One of them, a tall, broad-shouldered man with a proud bearing, jumped off his horse and strode over to Ivanhoe and the Grand Master. He took off his helmet. I gasped. It was Richard the Lionheart, King of England. He clapped Ivanhoe on the back.

"I see you have vanquished your opponent without my help," Richard boomed. "Quite a feat given the extent of your injuries."

Ivanhoe, his face ashen from the strain of standing upright, bowed slightly. "God was with me."

Richard frowned with concern. "We need to get you to a doctor." He smiled. "Or perchance the beautiful healer you just rescued can help."

To my surprise, Richard bowed to me and turned to the Grand Master. "This fair lady is no more a witch than I am an imposter for the throne of England. I am glad that Ivanhoe arrived in time to save her but I want to hear no more about Templars attempting to burn innocent Jewesses at the stake. Mayhaps it is time you returned to France."

The Grand Master stiffened, but he too bowed to the king. "Mayhaps."

In the distance, I could see a familiar figure on horseback riding toward the lists, accompanied by someone I didn't recognize. It was my dear father, who had no doubt alerted Ivanhoe and saved me once again. A surge of happiness lifted me up from the chair. I stood and waved at him.

Just then, I was distracted by a soft voice speaking nearby. I opened my eyes to the gloom and saw that I was back in the dimly light tunnel underneath Toledo, Hania crouching next to me.

"You need to keep up your strength, so you can find your father when this is all over," Hania said. She pressed a napkin with bread and dried meat into my lap. I reluctantly took a bite and discovered I was indeed hungry. I washed down the food with some wine in a flask that Hania offered me. It felt cool and bracing and I drank some more.

Still later, I dreamed that I was bound to a stake and I could smell smoke all around me. It was clear I was going to die, but suddenly my father appeared on a horse and rode up, vanquishing my enemies with his sword. He leaped off the horse and untied me and told me to jump on the horse and get away. My father smacked the horse's rump and it galloped off with me holding on for dear life. The last glimpse I had of my father, he was surrounded all sides by Knights of the Templar, wielding his sword like an avenging angel.

I woke with a cry and looked around me. The tunnel was dark and bodies lay sprawled on the benches and the dirt-packed floor. What time was it? My mouth felt dry and my back was sore from sleeping propped up against the wall. I walked off down the tunnel to do my business. When I got back, everyone was still sleeping, so I decided to venture upstairs. The fresh air might do me some good. I made my way past the slumbering bodies and up the worn steps. I took a deep breath and opened the door. A weak light greeted me; it must be just past dawn. I stepped out into the yard. It must have rained overnight because the grass was wet and the air felt cleansed and fresh, although I could smell the lingering scent of smoke. Don Paulo's house sat undisturbed a few yards away and I could hear some birds chattering away. I heard no other sounds; the mobs must have gone home to sleep off their rampage.

I breathed deeply; Don Paulo would be happy to hear he still had a home. But did I or my relatives? And most importantly, where was my father? I had to find him.

By the time I returned to the tunnel, a few people were stirring.

Mordecai, sitting on a blanket on the floor next to his wife, looked up at me with glassy eyes. "Where have you been?"

"I went up to get some fresh air," I replied. "Don Paulo's house looks untouched. I'm going to look for my father and see if our house is still standing."

Mordecai stood up and stretched. "I'll come with you. Give me just a minute." He shook Isadora's shoulder and her eyes fluttered open. "I'm going to search for Isaac with Rebecca. The mobs seem to be gone, but I'd like you to stay here with the children until we get back. Oh, and tell Don Paulo when he awakes that his house is still standing."

Isadora rubbed her eyes and nodded. "Be careful."

Mordecai and I made our way through the still-quiet streets, we could see the results of last night's pillaging. Many of the wooden houses in the Jewish quarter were partially burnt and still smoldering, but the rain overnight had kept most buildings from being completely destroyed. Even so, the acrid smoke crept into my lungs, making me cough. Here and there I saw dead bodies splayed on the ground and I had to force myself to look closely at each and every one. My father was not among them. Most of the dead were men, but one was a youngish woman whose skirts were bunched up around her waist. Her mouth was stretched into a grimace of unbearable pain. I almost threw up. The poor woman must have been molested before being killed. I gently pulled the woman's skirts down around her legs. How could God let such evil loose in the world, I asked myself, not for the first time.

I felt like sagging to the ground and sobbing. But I couldn't let myself grieve, not until I had found my father. Mordecai put an arm around me and we staggered on. We rounded the bend onto another street, and he stopped and groaned. His house had not been spared; its roof was partially burnt and caved in in places, but the walls still stood.

"I must go inside and see what the damage is. Can you wait?" Mordecai asked.

"While you do that, I am going to check on my house, and see if my father, God willing, is home," I said. "Can you meet me there in a few minutes?"

Mordecai nodded and strode off.

I turned down my street, and gasped. My house still stood, as did the dwellings on either side. How could that be? As I drew closer, I saw why. Someone had painted a white cross on my door. I hadn't noticed it when I had left in a hurry yesterday afternoon. This must have been Father Menendo's doing.

I opened the door with shaking hands and peered inside. Everything was intact, even though I had left the door unlocked in case my father came home. I called out for him and searched every room. There was no sign of him. I sank into a chair and wept. I was still there when Mordecai rushed into the house a while later.

"You didn't find Isaac?" he said. "How is it your house was left untouched?"

I showed him the cross on my door. "I have no idea who did this."

"It was probably that priest who warned you," Mordecai said. "Luck found you."

I wiped my eyes with my sleeve. "Not if my father is dead. We have to find him. I just remembered that he and Perla enjoyed strolling through that small park at the edge of the *barrio*. Why don't we look there first?"

We passed other residents of the Jewish quarter. Many had soot on their face and clothes from fighting fires and everyone looked stricken and dazed, as if they had just wakened from a nightmare and didn't know where they were or what they should do next. I stopped and peered closely at every dead body lying in the street. I had to push myself to keep moving because all my body wanted to do was fold up and collapse. Mordecai put his arm around me, but he too was trembling from shock. Any minute now I expected to see a mob of armed pillagers surge toward us, eyes filled with murderous rage. We stumbled forward, one step at a time.

As we neared the park, I saw a familiar-looking body crumpled by the side of the path. I felt a scream tear out of my throat. I rushed over to the body. My father. His head lay at an awkward angle to his body as if someone had tried to decapitate him. I fell to my knees, wailing. This couldn't be happening. My invincible father who had protected me at every turn, was dead. When I was kidnapped by the Templars, he had raced to find Ivanhoe and inform the knight about my plight, thus saving me from a similar fate. My father had been my champion in all things. And in his hour of need, I hadn't been there for him. Cradling his broken body in my arms, I sobbed, each sob a wracking reminder of what I had lost.

Mordecai stood by, looking on helplessly. After a time, it could have been minutes, it could have been an hour, I felt him grasp my shoulder.

"I see some men coming," he said. "I think we should leave. I can carry Isaac's body back to your house so we can prepare him for a proper burial."

I numbly rose to my feet. Mordecai lifted Isaac's body into his arms, and we made our way back into the *barrio*.

"My father said he was going walking with Perla, but I didn't see a woman's body anywhere in the park. Did you?"

"No," Mordecai said. "Perchance she got away."

Back to my house, I asked Mordecai to lay Isaac on the examining bed in the front room. I hastened to the well out back and filled a basin with water.

Mordecai washed the dried blood from his hands. "I have to get back to the tunnel. Can you stay here by yourself?"

I nodded and sobbed, acutely aware of how alone I was now. "Yes."

Mordecai hugged me awkwardly.

"I'm not looking forward to telling them about your father or our ruined house," he said mournfully. "This has been the worst day of my life."

"At least your family is alive," I said between sobs.

I sat by my father, tears running down my face. I was now an orphan, my one remaining parent butchered by an enraged mob. If my father and I had stayed in England, he would still be alive. We should never have come to Spain. I wanted out of this villainous country, but where would I go now that my father was dead? I felt destitute, spent, and so alone.

Drained, I forced myself to stand up. How was I going to go on without my father? He had been my north star, my avatar, for as long as I could remember. I couldn't let my relatives see him in this condition. I needed to wash the blood off his face and ready his body for burial. And I had to scrape that cross off my door.

THE NEXT MORNING, I heard a knock on my door. Perhaps Mordecai had come by to drop off more of his family's belongings.

Yesterday my relatives had salvaged what they could from their house and brought most of their belongings, damp and smoky, over to my house. Don Paulo had offered to host our entire family at his house, but while Mordecai and Isadora took him up on the offer, Benjamin and Hania decided to stay with me. Benjamin wanted to stand vigil over his brother and Hania insisted on helping me prepare my father for burial.

I opened my door to find Perla, seemingly unhurt, standing in front of me.

"He's dead, isn't he?" Perla asked, tears in her eyes.

I nodded.

Perla hung her head. "I'm so sorry. He saved my life."

"Would you like to come in and see him?" I said.

"Yes, please. I loved your father."

Perla stood before Isaac's body, sobbing, her head bowed. I went into the kitchen and busied myself making some tea. After a time, I came back into the front room.

"Would you like a cup of tea?" I asked, and she nodded.

I gave her a soft cloth. She wiped her eyes and followed me into the kitchen. Perla, Hania, and I sat around the table. Perla clutched the cup tightly as though it would save her from the reality of what she was about to divulge.

"We were walking in the park when we heard shouts," Perla said. "We hurried away, but before we could get far, a horde of angry men accosted us. They were drunk and they carried torches, axes, pitchforks, it was awful," She paused and hiccupped. "Isaac told me to run and not look back. He said he would . . ." She fought back her sobs. "He said he would find me when he could."

Perla's hands were shaking and she put down her cup. "I ran for my life. I looked back once and saw Isaac standing in front of mob. His arms were raised in supplication as if he was trying to calm the men down. But then . . . then . . . one of them raised an axe."

I gasped in horror. Hania buried her face in her hands.

Perla moaned. "I turned around and ran for my life, up one street, down another. I finally made it home. My daughter was hysterical with worry. We packed a satchel and ran to a friend of mine who lives near the southeast gate. She's not Jewish and she sheltered us for the night."

"And your house? Was it burned down like ours was?" Hania asked.

"They busted in the door and tried to set it on fire, but it failed to take hold," Perla said.

She passed a hand over her eyes and then looked at me. "Isaac stood his ground to give me time to get away. He died so I could live. I am so sorry." She buried her face in her hands.

THE KING RODE into Toledo that afternoon. Soon after, soldiers were posted around the Jewish quarter to protect its residents from further attack. Soldiers were also at the Jewish cemetery so families could begin burying their dead. We heard that as many as thirty Jewish men, women, even children, had been murdered and dozens of homes destroyed or damaged by fire. King Alfonso was reportedly furious at the archbishop for fomenting the mayhem, but by the time he returned to Toledo, de Pisuerga had already left the city, ostensibly to call on the Pope and plead for more money and arms with which to fight the Moors.

My father was buried that evening as the sun slowly descended in the western sky. Mordecai had borrowed a horse and cart from Don Paulo, and we used that to transport my father's body to the cemetery. Isadora had remained at Don Paulo's with Amada and Daniel, reluctant to venture out with the children despite the increased presence of soldiers on the streets.

I barely noticed the men gathered around the graveside, bowed as I was with grief. Other than Mordecai and Benjamin, I didn't recognize any. I assumed they were business associates of Benjamin and my father. Perla and her family had come and were standing in the back. Hania stood next to me, holding my hand, Estraya on my other side.

At the graveside, Benjamin spoke briefly about how happy he was that his brother had come back to Spain and they'd had a chance to be together again. "Isaac was a wise and generous man and had been a wonderful father to Rebecca."

"As you all know, Isaac stayed in England after meeting the love of his life, Sarah. And when she died, he devoted himself to his only child, the lovely and gifted Rebecca," he said. "I remember when I got the letter from Isaac telling me his beloved wife had died and their baby son with her. I wrote back suggesting he and his little girl come to Spain and live with us. And what did Isaac write back? That little Rebecca loved riding in the English countryside and gathering wild flowers and that he could not bear to uproot her, not after all they had both suffered."

Tears coated my cheeks as I heard this story for the first time. My father had made all his major life decisions with me in mind, including not remarrying. Hania, next to me, hugged me.

Benjamin turned to me. "Do you want to say anything?"

I shook my head, barely able to get through the fog of my grief. As if from far away, I heard my uncle recite the mourner's Kaddish, a Jewish prayer that is said when a loved one passes away. I could hear some of the men murmuring the Kaddish along with Benjamin and tried to follow along, the unfamiliar sounds feeling like pebbles in my mouth. After Benjamin intoned one more prayer, the men took turns dropping a handful of dirt on my father's shroud. Mordecai filled in the grave and one by one each of my relatives placed a stone on top of the fresh dirt. When it was my turn, I kissed a smooth rounded stone I had picked up a while back and placed it carefully on top of my father's grave.

"Goodbye, Papa, my best friend and champion," I whispered. "You will always be in my heart. May you rest in peace."

CHAPTER 16

A FEW DAYS later, I heard glass shattering and rushed into the kitchen to find Hania in tears. She was bent over the broken glass, weeping uncontrollably. I put my hand on her arm.

"Are you hurt?" I asked. "Did the glass cut you?"

Hania straightened up. "No, my dear, it's not that. The broken glass just set me off . . ."

I pulled out a chair at the small kitchen table. "Sit and tell me what's going on. The broken glass doesn't matter. I'll sweep it up and make us some tea."

Hania slowly lowered herself into the chair and hugged her arms against her chest. "Did you hear? Mordecai and Isadora are intent on leaving Spain. They don't think it's safe to raise their children here. But Benjamin doesn't want to go, and of course I can't leave without him. But the thought of not seeing my daughter or grandchildren ever again . . . I can't bear it."

I could understand Hania's pain. If I had children, I'd want to live close to them. I sighed and pressed her hand. "I'm sure Benjamin will come around. I think leaving Spain is wise. As long as the Church wields so much power, Spain is not safe for the Jews. I too would like to leave."

LESS THAN TWO weeks later, Benjamin, Hania, and I were just sitting down to a late supper when we heard insistent knocking on the door.

Benjamin started to stand up but I waved him down. "It's probably just the husband of one of my pregnant ladies. I have two who are about to give birth."

I opened the door. Bernardo stood there, his eyebrows furrowed with worry.

"You're safe," Bernardo said. "Thank God. I was so worried."

I threw myself into his arms. Bernardo smelled of hours of hard riding on horseback, but I didn't care.

He gave me a quick hug and kissed the top of my head. We were outside on a public street; perchance that was why he was so restrained.

"I'm sorry—I'm just so happy to see you and it's been such a horrid time," I said. "Won't you come in?"

Bernardo wiped his dusty boots on the steps and followed me inside. Benjamin and Hania had come into the entryway and greeted Bernardo joyously.

"Come and eat with us," Benjamin said. "We have enough to go around, don't we, Rebecca?"

"Of course," I said, leading the way into my small dining area. "I'll just get another plate."

I returned to the table with Bernardo's plate of food.

He stood up and took me in his arms. "I just heard about your father. I'm so very sorry."

My face squashed against Bernardo's chest, I cried for a long time. Finally, I wiped my nose and stood back. "I got your shirt all wet—I'm sorry."

Bernardo smiled down at me. "No bother. My shirt needs a good washing anyway."

I laughed through my tears, and everyone joined in. Benjamin and Hania caught Bernardo up on all that had happened after he left town as I reveled in Bernardo being safe and here with me.

"How is your father?" I asked.

"He was in Valencia during the riots but out house was not touched since it's in the Christian section of Toledo," Bernardo said. "My father was furious at the king for not doing a better job of reining in the archbishop and for abandoning Toledo to the mercy of the mob.

"My father is seriously considering leaving Toledo and moving to Valencia, where one of my sisters live, mayhaps even leaving Spain altogether," Bernardo continued. "With the Moors and the Christians at each other's throats, he doesn't see an end to the scapegoating of our people any time soon. The problem is that the King owes him a great deal of money and if my father leaves the country now, he knows he won't get repaid."

Benjamin stared at Bernardo, a piece of chicken speared on his fork and halfway to his mouth. Finally, he lowered the fork to his plate. "I too am reluctant to leave Spain but it would be easier for me to restart my business in another country than it would be for your father. You need connections to lend money at the level he does. But with trade you can be based almost anywhere."

Hania darted a hopeful look at him. "Are you saying you might consider leaving Spain? I would so love to go with Isadora and Mordecai."

"Well, if such an august personage as Don Esteban is considering leaving, then it might not be a bad idea," Benjamin said. "I have to give it some more thought."

Hania's face lit with joy.

Benjamin rose from the table and Bernardo followed him into the other room. I began clearing the table and went into the kitchen to help Hania.

She shooed me away. "Go, be with your man. I can finish up here."

I found Bernardo in the sitting room, engaged in conversation with my uncle.

"We were just talking about Egypt," Benjamin said and pointed at Bernardo. "Your suitor here thinks that's where we should go. I'm inclined to agree with him." He stood up and yawned. "I think I'm going to retire. It's been a long day."

I felt a rush of gratitude for my uncle. I kissed his paper-thin cheeks and he shuffled out of the room.

I turned to Bernardo. "He's getting old. I hope the journey to Egypt or wherever the family decides to go is not too strenuous. It will be hard on my aunt and uncle."

"Yes, but Mordecai and Isadora will take good care of them," Bernardo said. "And now my dear, would you care to go for a stroll?"

"Yes, I could use some air. But can we walk in the direction of the river or the market? Anywhere but to the park at the edge of the quarter?" My voice quavered. "That was where Papa was killed. I have no desire to ever revisit that spot again."

Bernardo took my hand. "I completely understand. We can talk another time if this is all too much for you . . ."

"No, no, I am so happy to see you, to have you back with us again," I said. "I'll be fine."

Twilight was upon us as we walked in the direction of the river, but I felt safe with Bernardo beside me. The late summer evening was lovely, and others were out and about, enjoying the cooling breezes off the Tagus. As polluted as it was, the river was Toledo's saving grace, the only part of town not enclosed within tall forbidding walls.

We reached a pathway near the cliff.

Bernardo stopped walking and turned to me. "It seems like Benjamin is now willing to entertain the possibility of leaving with Isadora and Mordecai. And I seem to have sold him on Egypt."

"That's great news," I began.

Bernardo held up his hand. "I too would like to leave this damnable place. But until my father and sister are ready to leave, I feel I have a duty to stay here. I'm sorry."

My hands clenched into fists by my side. Bernardo hadn't even asked what I might want to do. "You're right—I do want to leave Toledo," I said. "Even if it was safe to stay, there are too many bad memories for me here. But there are other places in Spain we could move to, Valencia for instance."

Bernardo looked pained. "I . . . I love you Rebecca, but I'm not in a position to ask for your hand. I need some time." He hung his head. "With the war, my business is in arrears and I can't ask my father for help. He loaned a great deal of money to the king for his recent campaign, and with Alfonso's disastrous defeat, he is not going to recoup it any time soon."

"I don't care about the money, you know that," I said, trying to restrain my anger. "I think something else is going on here."

Bernardo jerked his head back in surprise. "What are you talking about?"

"I think you still feel guilty about not being able to rescue Rachel, that you are still a little in love with her," I replied, and saw the truth in his eyes. "That's the real reason you won't commit to me, isn't it?"

Bernardo flinched as if I had hit him.

I walked away from him. Bernardo caught up to me and tried to take my hand. But I swung away from him.

"You may be right," Bernardo said. "I'm sorry—I don't know my own mind. I need time. Please forgive me."

"There is nothing to forgive." I worked to control my anger. "You said you loved me, but it's obvious you love your dead sweetheart more."

Bernardo lowered his eyes as he shuffled next to me.

In that moment, I knew what I had to do. I couldn't very well stay in Spain by myself as an unmarried woman. So, I would go to Egypt and try to begin again there with my family. I would seek an audience with the famed healer Maimonides and try to learn from him. I would devote my life to healing. I had the skills and the fortitude. If Bernardo wanted to be part of that life, he would know where to find me. Then I could decide if I wanted him in my life.

CHAPTER 17

August 1195 AD

IN THE DAYS that followed, the streets of Toledo seemed calm and the residents of the Jewish quarter began to rebuild their lives and homes. During dinner one afternoon, with everyone crowded around the table in my small kitchen, Benjamin argued that we should postpone our departure, to give him and Mordecai time to move their remaining stock of olive oil, flax, and spices and notify their trading partners of their plans.

"What's the rush?" Benjamin asked. "The king has committed himself to our safety."

I could see that Mordecai was frustrated by the delay but reluctant to confront his father-in-law, who was, after all, his employer. I didn't mind waiting. It gave me time to wind down my practice. I told each patient that I would be leaving Toledo soon and referred them to other healers in the Jewish quarter.

Bernardo had sent one message requesting a rendezvous with me to say goodbye, but I ignored it. Seeing him again would only open the wound I was desperately trying to let scab over.

Early one morning, Mordecai hastened in my house. Benjamin, Hania, and I were in the kitchen having breakfast, and we all looked up in surprise. It was Saturday, and Benjamin was adamant about not conducting business on the Jewish day of rest. Mordecai pulled up a chair at the table and sat down heavily.

"Don Paulo tells me that the king is leaving Toledo today with a small force of men," he said. "Now that the Sultan has drawn back to Seville, he wants to shore up a few of the castles between here and Alarcos, so we are not completely defenseless when the Moors march north again. Which they will, eventually."

"So?" Benjamin asked, raising an eyebrow.

"Don Paulo is concerned that with the king away, there might be more attacks on the Jewish quarter," Mordecai said. "He is sending his family to

Valencia today and plans to follow as soon as he finishes some business. I think we should plan on leaving soon too."

"I won't be rushed," Benjamin said, scowling. "We stand to lose too much money in unsold goods if we leave now. Besides, I'm sure the king has left instructions with his soldiers to guard the Jewish quarter, as promised."

Mordecai's face flushed purple. I could see that he was trying to restrain himself from saying something disrespectful to Benjamin.

I laid a hand on his arm and turned to Benjamin. "This is concerning news. As we all know, the king could not be relied upon to protect us before. Surely there is no harm in seeking out more information. Why don't you write to Don Esteban and see what he thinks?"

Benjamin glared at Mordecai and stood up. "The Sabbath is meant to be a day of rest and reflection and I will not break it because of a few scaremongers." He shuffled out of the room.

"My husband is afraid of leaving his country of birth; it is all he has known. I will talk to him." Hania began gathering the dishes from the table.

Mordecai looked at me, a grim set to his mouth. "I cannot risk the lives of my children because of an old man's intransigence. If Isadora and I have to leave without her parents, so be it."

I hated to see this rift in my family. I knew Mordecai was serious about leaving now that the King was no longer here to protect us and I agreed with him. There was no reason to disbelieve Don Paulo. With his connections to the court, his information could surely be trusted. I pursed my lips in thought. I would have to swallow my pride and look past my own private wounds.

"I will write to Bernardo," I said. "He or his father will know what we should do."

Mordecai flashed me a grateful smile. "I will deliver the message myself."

ON HIS WAY back to Don Paulo's, Mordecai stopped by my house and told me that neither Bernardo nor Don Esteban had been at home when he delivered my scroll.

"I left it with one of their servants to give to them," Mordecai said, his face gaunt with concern.

"I'm sure they will read it soon and respond quickly," I said. "Please, try not to worry."

LATE THAT NIGHT, long after I had gone to bed, I was roused by a loud knocking. Groggy from sleep, I raised my head in confusion. Who could it be at this hour? I had already turned most of my pregnant patients over to the care of another midwife and none of them were close to their due date in any event. Perchance whoever it was would go away. But the knocking persisted, so I got out of bed and slipped on my tunic. I was met on the stairs by a bleary-eyed Benjamin, dressed in his smock and gripping a sword, and together we clambered down the stairs.

Before opening the door, I called out, "Who is it?"

"Bernardo," came the swift response.

I quickly unbolted and opened the door.

Bernardo, breathing heavily, slipped through the doorway. He wore a plain woolen tunic, leggings, and riding boots and his hair was disheveled. Even so, I had never seen a more welcome sight.

"What is it, man?" Benjamin demanded. "You look like you've seen a ghost."

"I'm sorry to disturb you at this late hour, but I just received word that with the king gone, the Church is at it again," Bernardo said. "The priests are preparing to sermonize against us in Mass tomorrow and there could be more riots—as soon as tomorrow afternoon. If you are going to leave Toledo, you must leave now."

Benjamin's jaw dropped. "That can't be. The king promised his protection."

"You heard what Bernardo said: the King is not here. You must remember what happened the last time he left the city." I turned to Bernardo. "We will start packing now. Could you possibly ride over to Don Paulo's house and alert Mordecai? If we start now, we can be ready to leave by morning."

Bernardo gazed at me with an intensity that almost frightened me. "Yes, I will ride on to Don Paulo's and then I have to get word to the king about what the clergy are doing." He hung his head. "I wish I could accompany you safely out of the city, but . . ."

I laid a hand on his arm. I might never see this beautiful man again. "You have our undying gratitude. Go with God."

After Bernardo left, I didn't stop to remonstrate with Benjamin, who was still standing there. I woke Hania and explained the situation. I then then went to get dressed and start packing.

Luckily, Mordecai had already sold the Manasses' badly damaged house for a pittance to another Jewish family. Mordecai had also purchased two horses as well as two carts and donkeys, all of which he had stabled at Don Paulo's, waiting for Benjamin to give the go-ahead for their departure.

Hania and I had already packed our essential belongings by the time Mordecai and Isadora arrived in the darkest hours of the morning, driving the carts and donkeys, with two sleepy children nestled beside them, the horses tethered behind them. Benjamin had not stirred from his chair in the living room, and we all bustled around him, careful to leave him alone with his thoughts. I wondered what would he do when it was time to finally depart. If he refused to budge, would Hania stay with him or go with the rest of our family? I fervently hoped it wouldn't come to that.

CHAPTER 18

WE WERE FINALLY ready to go two hours after dawn. Our carts were loaded down with linens, towels, clothing, a few essential pots and plates, and food and water for the two-day journey to Valencia. In the end, all it had taken was a soft word from Hania to rouse Benjamin and get him onto one of the horses. I mounted the other horse and Mordecai and Isadora drove the carts, Hania, Estraya, and the children sitting beside them.

The Jewish quarter was still quiet as we made our way down its well-trodden paths. We had decided to leave by the southwestern gate and make our way around the city, before turning southeast toward Valencia. That way, there was less likelihood of running into armed Christian gangs on their way out of church. Even though I had only gotten a few hours of sleep before Bernardo's arrival, I felt intensely awake, every nerve fiber in my body lit in anticipation of danger. Even if we made it safely to the gate, there was no telling the guards would let us out of the city. I was carrying the dagger my father had given me and both Mordecai and Benjamin had swords. But we would be no match for armed guards or an angry mob. Not for the first time, I wished that Bernardo was with us. He was a skilled swordsman, and since he had standing in the court because of his father's status, the soldiers at the gate might listen to him. I sighed and clenched my fist around the horse's reins; Bernardo had other important duties to attend to, and I had to accept that my family and I were not his first priority.

At the southwestern gate, two soldiers stood at attention. One of them, a stocky young man with a scar running down his face, barked out an order for us to halt. Mordecai explained that we were on our way to Valencia to visit relatives.

The soldier smirked and waved a dismissive hand. "Go home. I have orders from the bishop not to let anyone out of the city today."

I gasped. "Anyone" most certainly meant any Jews.

Mordecai began to rise from the seat of his cart, clearly intending to argue with the soldier. I spurred my horse forward and motioned him down. I trotted up to the other guard who had been staring at me intently. I drew a ruby, for emergencies, out of a pocket in my tunic.

"*Señor*, I beg your forbearance. I am a healer and we are on our way to Valencia to help a very sick relative." I held the ruby my father had given me for my eighteenth birthday out to him. "Please take this gem and share it with your comrade as a token of our appreciation for letting us pass."

"I know you," he said. "You are Rebecca the healer; you helped deliver my son a few months ago."

Estraya gasped in the cart behind me. I didn't remember this man and couldn't recall how his son's birth had gone. A few months ago, a Christian woman gave birth to a stillborn child—I had been brought in as a last-minute consult, breaking my own rules—and although the family never blamed me, the tragedy haunted me still. Pray God that was not this soldier's family

"How is your son doing?" I asked.

"He is well, milady," the soldier said. He took the proffered gem and walked over to his compatriot. They conferred in low voices.

The lanky soldier handed his scar-faced compatriot my ruby. The soldier closed his hand around the ruby, scowled, and grunted something.

He glared at us. "This is your lucky day. You may pass."

Mordecai cracked the reins on the donkey tethered to his cart, and the two carts rumbled forward. I waited until both carts and Benjamin's horse passed and then guided my horse to fall in line behind them. Only when we had passed through the open gate and crossed most of the bridge did I let out a deep sigh of relief.

As we rode past the city to our left, Isadora and Hania stared sadly at the proud walls of the city that had been our home. I myself felt no sense of nostalgia. If anything, I was glad to put Toledo behind me. It had brought me nothing but heartbreak.

The rest of the trip was uneventful. We spent one night in a filthy roadside inn but it was better than sleeping outdoors.

Late on the afternoon of the second day, we arrived at the seaside town of Valencia. I was tired and sore from riding a horse for two days and desperate for a bath. We went to Don Esteban's house. Well before our rushed exodus, Bernardo had told Benjamin that his father would probably offer to put our family up until we sailed for Egypt. Don Esteban was happy to see us and welcomed us in.

As I walked into his spacious abode, I half-hoped to see Bernardo there. He wasn't there, of course, no doubt still riding with the king somewhere, but I couldn't help the leaden feeling of disappointment once I realized he wasn't there. We were shown to our rooms, and Estraya and I gratefully sank into a hot bath that Don Esteban's servants prepared for us.

The next morning, Benjamin and Mordecai went down to the dock to find out when the next seaworthy ship would be leaving for the Holy Land or Egypt. They returned some hours later with good news.

"There's a boat bound from Genoa that will be putting in here in a day or two and then sailing onto the Holy Land and Egypt," Mordecai announced. "We should be able to book passage on that ship."

The Genoese, he explained, were hardy seagoers and had built a robust city-state on the northwestern curve of Italy. They plied a fleet of ships both for trade and raiding enemy vessels. Amada and Daniel were thrilled at the prospect of sailing to Egypt and none of us said anything to dampen their enthusiasm. But after the children were put to bed, we talked of the hazards involved. We had all heard of travelers captured by pirates trolling the Mediterranean and sold into slavery in North Africa. And it wasn't just Muslim pirates who preyed on European travelers.

"Genoese pirates often ransack ships from Byzantium and North Africa," Mordecai told us, his voice thick with disgust. "And they sell the travelers they kidnap in European ports."

I gasped. Wouldn't we be courting attack from Byzantine or Muslim pirates by flying under a Genoese flag?

"Perhaps we shouldn't be traveling on a Genoese ship," Isadora said with a quiver in her voice.

"We have no choice. With the ongoing hostilities between the Muslims and Christians here, we'd be waiting a long time for a Spanish or French ship to take us where we need to go." Mordecai looked sternly around the room. "This is a risk we need to take."

Two days later, Mordecai took the children and Estraya and I to see the ship we were to sail on. The *Santa Rosalia* was a two-masted wooden vessel with triangular sails and steering oars. It had two side rudders and a broad stern, which sat above the deck.

"See those small cabins in the back?" Mordecai pointed toward the stern. "That's where we'll be sleeping. The crew sleeps on or below deck, and cargo and food are stored below deck."

"It's going to be tight quarters," he added. "Benjamin and I will be staying with the captain and you women and the children will be billeted in the other cabin. But at least none of us has to sleep below deck. It stinks down there and except for where the oarsmen sit in the stern, you pretty much have to crawl around on your hands and knees."

"I'll make sure not to go below deck then," I said. "It looks like a seaworthy vessel. That's all that matters, right?"

"Yes," Mordecai replied.

One evening, a few days before our departure, Bernardo's older sister joined us for dinner at Don Esteban's. Her husband was traveling on business and she had left her three young children at home with their nursemaid. Palomba did not share her brother's striking looks but there was a lively kindness in her gray-green eyes that drew me in. Don Esteban had placed Palomba next to me at one end of the table near him. It didn't take long for the conversation to turn to what might have happened in Toledo in the days since we left. None of us had heard anything. It was as if a dome of silence had descended on the city, with no one breaking free to bring word to those who lived outside its walls.

"I fear the worst," Palomba said. "If the archbishop can stoop to killing Rachel and inciting a mob to burn down the Jewish quarter, there is no telling what he is capable of."

Don Esteban cleared his throat. "I'm not sure this is suitable talk for the dinner table, my dear. I don't know that I mentioned it, but Rebecca lost her father in the mayhem a fortnight ago."

Palomba clapped a hand to her mouth. "I'm so sorry, no, I didn't know. Please forgive my reckless tongue." She looked down at her plate, chastened.

"There is no need to apologize." Even so, I hastened to change the subject. "Did you know Rachel growing up?"

Palomba's face brightened. "I did. She was a year younger than me and we were friends. A mischief-maker, that one." She chuckled and turned to Don Esteban. "Do you remember the time she talked Bernardo into helping her steal some ripe pomegranates from our neighbor's tree. She got away, but he got caught red-handed. Oh, was Don Emilio angry."

Don Esteban laughed. "I do remember that. I'm afraid with Rachel's mother gone, she was allowed to run wild." A shadow passed over his face. "Perchance a little too wild . . ."

I wasn't sure I wanted to hear more about Rachel and Bernardo's bond as children, but I had to admit I was curious. Anything to help me understand him better. "And when they got older?"

Palomba glanced at her father.

Don Esteban shrugged.

"Bernardo may already have told you this but when they were teenagers, they pledged themselves to each other," Palomba said, her eyes soft with remembrance. "They had grown up together and they fashioned themselves in love, or at least Bernardo did." She paused and took a sip of wine. Her mouth twisted. "But then the king set up court in Toledo and Rachel's father threw her at him. And Rachel decided he was the man for her."

She gazed at me. "She broke my brother's heart. That's why he took up trading—to get as far away from Toledo as possible. I think it made him wary of ever falling in love again."

Don Esteban smiled at me. "That is, until you came along."

Did Don Esteban not realize that was no longer true? That Rachel's death had thrown Bernardo into a tailspin from which he had yet to recover? I would be leaving Spain in a few days and I might never see Bernardo again. Tears formed in my eyes and I stood up, determined to retain my dignity.

"Excuse me, *señor*, I'm feeling a bit weary. I think I'll go lie down." I walked out of the room as a distraught look flashed across Don Esteban's weathered face.

THE DAY BEFORE the *Santa Rosalia* was set to depart for the Holy Land, Mordecai and two of Don Esteban's servants brought most of our belongings down to the dock, where they were loaded onto the ship. We would board that evening, and our vessel was slated to sail out of Valencia's harbor on the early morning tide.

Late that afternoon, I was taking a stroll with Estraya in the Nabaro's verdant garden when I heard a commotion out front.

"It sounds like someone has arrived—maybe someone with news of Toledo," Estraya said, looking toward the house. "Shall we go and see?"

"You go. I think I'll sit here for a while." I had no energy to care about what might have happened in Toledo. I just wanted to put this episode in my life behind me.

I sat on a bench surrounded by a profusion of flowering jacaranda bushes, my head in my hands. I heard footsteps coming my way. I looked up.

It was Bernardo. He looked tired and dusty, his boots caked with mud, as though he had been riding hard. I stood up quickly and felt dizzy. I swayed, and Bernardo reached out a hand to steady me.

"What are you doing here?" I asked.

"I was afraid I'd miss you," Bernardo said, smiling down at me. "I rode as hard as I could. I am so glad you and your family made it to Valencia safe and sound."

I could not seem to find my voice. Bernardo sat on the bench and beckoned me to sit next to him. My head still felt dull as though I had been sedated by the musky scent of the jacaranda flowers.

"I was so worried you and your family didn't make it out of Toledo in time," Bernardo said. "I'm sorry that I couldn't have been there for you."

The note of sincere apology in his voice wasn't enough. "Yes, we got out," I said, leaving unsaid my thought: No thanks to you.

Bernardo's eyes flashed. "They burned the Jewish quarter down and this time there was no rain. More than fifty people were killed, like calves to the slaughter."

His words shocked me out of my lethargy. "Such evil, how can it be allowed to exist. Were you there, in the city?"

Bernardo shook his head. "When I reached the king and told him what was happening, he turned right around and headed back to Toledo. I was with his entourage. We returned a day too late to stop the carnage."

"He is always too late," I said bitterly.

"Yes, but at least this time he clamped the archbishop's right-hand man, Bishop Engracia, in the dungeon," Bernardo said. "Martin Lopez de Pisguera, blast his demonic soul, is still overseas, but there is no question the bishop was acting on his orders."

What did it matter if the King had imprisoned one clergyman? The bishop would just be released in a matter of days and there would be no justice for all the men, women, and children he had seen fit to have murdered. But at least Bernardo was alive. There was that.

"I'm glad you are safe," I said. "You've arrived just in time to bid us goodbye. We board our ship tonight."

"So, my father tells me," Bernardo said, sadness in his beautiful eyes. He clutched at my hand. "I'm so sorry, Rebecca, that I'm not ready to leave Spain with you. I have things I have to do first, I have to see to . . ."

I stood up. His excuses were breaking my heart all over again. "I feel a chill. I'm glad you're here and safe. And now I must go inside and finish packing."

"But wait," Bernardo said. "I wanted to tell you where my sister and her family live in Cairo, in case you need their assistance."

I turned away from him to hide the pain in my own eyes and waved a hand. "Mordecai and my uncle have already written to family and friends who moved to Egypt. I'm sure they will be able to help us. Goodbye, Bernardo."

Head held high, I strode to the house.

CHAPTER 19

EARLY THE NEXT morning my family and I sailed on the morning tide. A brisk wind pushed us out of the harbor and onto the open seas. I enjoyed feeling the breeze on my face as I walked along the deck with Estraya, her niece and nephew in tow.

On the second day at sea, Amada asked to go below deck just to see what was there.

"Papa says there are pilgrims living below deck," Amada said. "What's a pilgrim?"

I laughed. "A pilgrim is someone who wants to visit the Holy Land so they can atone for their sins."

"Can we go see them?" Daniel piped up.

I looked at Estraya, and she shrugged.

"Aye, but we have to be very careful on the ladder. I don't want any accidents," I said.

Halfway down the rickety rope ladder, I was assaulted by a repellent smell—a disgusting mix of rotting fish and unwashed bodies that made me want to climb back into the fresh air.

"It stinks down here," Amada said. "Can we go back up?"

"Aw, do we have to?" Daniel pleaded. "I want to see the peegrims."

"Pilgrims," Amada corrected. "I'm going back up."

Estraya nodded. "Daniel, I don't think it's safe for us to be down here. Maybe one of the pilgrims will come up on deck and you can see him then."

At first, the weather was fine, mild and sunny with a light breeze, and only Hania got seasick. Estraya and I took the children off Isadora's hands every day so she could tend to her mother. We spent most of our time on the deck, looking for sea creatures and watching the crew work the sails. On the third day we were rewarded when Amada spotted a pod of dolphins off the starboard side.

"Look," she shrieked. "They're racing us."

Sure enough, the dolphins easily kept pace with the ship, their sleek black bodies glinting in the sunlight. Two-year-old Daniel was so entranced by the sight that he climbed up on the railing, using some rigging to haul himself up. As he dangled from the rigging about to fall into the sea, I grabbed his arm and managed to pull him back onto the deck.

"That was a close call," a deep voice with a Scottish brogue said.

I wheeled around. A broad-shouldered man blocked the sunlight. He was one of the two pilgrims who had sailed with us and were quartered below deck. The man, who looked to be in his late thirties or forties, was dressed in a brown homespun tunic and his head and feet were bare. He had a long scar across one side of his face. But his smile seemed kindly.

"I am Walt Rolston," he said in broken Spanish. "I'm doing pilgrimage to the Holy Land to atone for my sins."

"You're Scottish, aren't you?" I replied in English. "I'd recognize that brogue anywhere."

Rolston's smile broadened. "You're English. This is my lucky day. I thought you and your family hailed from Spain."

"I moved to Spain a year or so ago to be with family," I said, feeling a spasm of pain at the thought that my father had been alive then. "What sins do you have to do atone for?"

Rolston's smile faded but he didn't seem put off by my directness. "I fought in the Third Crusade alongside Richard the Lionheart and carried out horrible atrocities. This pilgrimage is an attempt to ease my conscience."

Daniel broke loose from my grip and went running across the deck.

"Sorry to cut our conversation short, but I must see to him." I gathered up my tunic and hastened after the little boy. I would have liked to hear more of Rolston's story, but it would have to wait.

I didn't see the Scottish pilgrim again for several days. But then he turned up at dinner one evening. This time, I noted he had a distinct limp, a war injury, I supposed.

"Your cousin was kind enough to invite me to join you for a meal," Rolston said, smiling at me. "I am grateful for the company."

I smiled in him. "Isn't there another pilgrim traveling with you? Where is he?"

"The other pilgrim isn't much company, I'm afraid," Rolston said. "Henry has been feeling poorly since we sailed."

"That's a shame," I said. "My aunt is also still feeling under the weather, which is why she hasn't joined us tonight." Amada and Daniel had already eaten and were bedded down for the night with their grandmother.

As we ate a paltry meal of dried meat and hard biscuits softened with thin gravy, Mordecai and Benjamin plied Rolston with questions about the crusade. Since his Spanish was limited, I translated for him. Rolston described how he had been part of a massive thrust by England, France, and the Holy Roman Empire to reconquer the Holy Land in 1190, three years after it was taken by the Muslim Sultan, Saladin.

"Isn't that the same Saladin who ruled Egypt?" I asked. Bernardo had mentioned that name when he had told me about his travels to Egypt.

"Yes, the very same," Rolston said. "He was a formidable foe. He also conquered Syria and had himself proclaimed Sultan of Syria and Egypt. But from what I understand he died two years ago, less than twelve months after we left the Holy Land."

"During my recent trip to France, I heard they are considering a fourth crusade—now that Saladin is gone," Mordecai said.

Rolston grimaced. "I hope not. It's an unforgivable waste of men's lives. Why do we need to take Jerusalem when the Muslims who control it allow Christian pilgrims to come in peace?"

Mordecai and I exchanged wry looks; why indeed.

"Rebecca tells us that you are doing this pilgrimage to atone," Mordecai said. "Do you feel comfortable telling us what makes your heart so heavy?"

"My heart has been heavy ever since my Bessie died in childbirth five years ago," Rolston said, looking down at his plate. "The baby died too. That's why I enlisted in the crusades in the first place. After Bessy died, I didn't have much to live for. But I had no idea what I was in for."

I laid a hand on his arm. "I'm sorry to hear this. Losing loved ones is so hard. My father was recently killed by a mob in Toledo, which is one of the reasons we left."

"I am sorry for your loss," Rolston replied. "There is too much evil afoot in this world."

My relatives also extended their condolences.

Rolston waved their concern away. "I know Bessie and the little one are in heaven. I am the one who must seek salvation—after what I've seen and done."

Rolston described how he and hundreds of men had sailed with King Richard the Lionheart to the Holy Land and laid siege to Acre. Armies from France and Armenia soon joined them.

"Acre, where is that?" I asked.

"It's one of the largest cities on the coast of the Holy Land, about thirty-three leagues north of Jerusalem," Rolston explained. "If my recollection is correct, we captured Acre in July 1191. But then Richard and Philip—the King of France—started squabbling over the spoils of victory and who should reign over Jerusalem once it was captured."

"Frustrated with Richard's intransigence, the French king took most of his army and left the Holy Land in August," Rolston said. "He did leave seven thousand French crusaders under the command of the Duke of Burgundy.

"After that debacle, Richard requested a face-to-face meeting with Saladin, but the sultan refused and negotiations over prisoners captured by both sides seemed to be going nowhere.

"That's when Richard ordered the deaths of the Muslim prisoners," Rolston said, his voice cracking. "We had to kill almost three thousand people, men, women, and children, in full view of Saladin's army. It was horrible. I can still hear their screams; it felt like we were drowning in their blood."

Isadora and Estraya gasped in horror. Tears stung my eyes; how could the king I knew as gallant and chivalrous, the same one who had come to my aid at Templestowe, been responsible for such a bestial action? I would never understand these Christian rulers; they were just as bloodthirsty, if not more, than the people they considered infidels.

Mordecai stood up. "We should not talk of this in mixed company."

"I shouldn't have been so graphic," Rolston said, bowing his head. "Forgive me."

The talk turned to Saladin's successors to the sultanate, and none of the men spoke again of the crusade until Isadora and Estraya retired for the night. But I lingered. I was moved by Rolston's obvious anguish and felt as though I needed to hear the rest of his story.

"Uncle, do you mind if I tarry a bit? I would like to hear what happened next, why Richard the Lionheart was unable to take Jerusalem." I dipped my head. "I promise not to be squeamish."

"It wouldn't bother me if you were," Benjamin said. "This sad tale strikes at all our hearts."

After the massacre at Acre, Richard decided to march on Jaffa, an ancient port city just south of Jerusalem. As Rolston explained, the English king knew he would have to hold Jaffa if he intended to recapture Jerusalem since it was the holy city's link to the coast. Saladin tried to ambush

Richard's army at Arsuf, thirty miles north of Jaffa, but to everyone's surprise, Richard's army defeated Saladin's forces and won the battle.

"This was a major victory for us," Rolston said. "It cut into Saladin's aura of invincibility and in short order, we were able to take Jaffa."

After establishing a foothold in that port city, Richard advanced inland toward Jerusalem. Saladin's forces were in tatters and hopes were high that the crusaders could take the holy city.

"But by this time, it was November, and the cold weather, together with heavy rain and hailstorms, forced us to retreat back to the coast," Rolston said. "It haunts me still—how close we were to victory."

Over the winter, the crusaders fought several skirmishes with Saladin's forces from their stronghold in Jaffa. "In one battle, my left leg was slashed up badly and I almost died from loss of blood," Rolston said in a matter-of-fact tone. His leg still wasn't healed by the time the crusaders left to conquer Jerusalem in March so he was forced to remain behind.

"I understand the army came within sight of the holy city only to retreat again," Rolston said, his voice thick with disgust. "This time it was because of an argument between Richard and the Duke of Burgundy, who was leading the French contingent. They disagreed on how best to attack Jerusalem, Richard wanted to force Saladin to relinquish Jerusalem by attacking Egypt and the Duke was adamant about launching a direct attack on the holy city. In the end, Richard refused to lead his army on a direct assault. His men had no choice but to retreat back to Jaffa."

Rolston said his spirits were already low, and when he saw how angry and dispirited his compatriots were when they returned to Jaffa, he decided he had had enough.

"My leg was not healing well in the Mediterranean heat so I couldn't fight anyway," he said. He sailed on the next ship bound for France and then England. He later learned that Richard the Lionheart had also grown weary of fighting and negotiated a treaty with Saladin that allowed unarmed Christian pilgrims and merchants to visit Jerusalem and left Christian forces in control of Cyprus and key cities up and down the Syrian coast. Richard himself left the Holy Land in October 1192, Rolston said. "The Pope and other church officials were furious that Richard left Jerusalem in the hands of the infidels. And then only months later, Saladin himself died of the sweating sickness. So now there is talk of another crusade." Rolston shook his head wearily. "More wasted bloodshed."

I thought it reflected well on Rolston that he was so honest about his part in such a monstrous deed and seemingly committed to doing penance. I looked forward to more conversations with this burly Scot.

A few days later, Mordecai, Estraya, and I were walking with Amada and Daniel on the deck when Mordecai pointed to a slight rise in elevation in the shimmering distance.

"That's the foot of Italy," Mordecai said. "If I recall correctly, we're close to where Odysseus and his men were almost devoured by the Sirens."

Amada's eyes widened. "Who are the Sirens? Will we see any?"

Mordecai chuckled. "No, they are mythical creatures. Have I not told you about the Odyssey? It's an epic story that was written by a Greek named Homer many centuries ago."

"Please, Papa, tell us the story," Amada demanded.

"Yes, Papa, we want to hear about those bad irens," Daniel cried.

I laughed at Mordecai's helpless expression.

"It looks like you don't have any choice," I said. "I'd love to hear it again as well."

Mordecai settled himself in an unoccupied corner of the ship's bow and pulled Amada and Daniel onto his lap. Estraya and I sat a short distance away. "Odysseus was sailing back to Greece after many years away fighting in the Trojan war."

"Who is Odysseus and what is a Trojan war?" Amada demanded.

Mordecai sighed in mock despair. "Odysseus was the king of Ithaca, a Greek island, and a famous warrior. Troy was a city in what we now call Byzantium. Back then it was part of the Greek empire, and the son of Troy's ruler, I think his name was Paris, fell in love with Helen, the beautiful wife of the King of Sparta. He eloped with her and brought her back to Troy. The Spartans were furious, and they mounted an attack on Troy but couldn't breach its walls for ten years. Finally, they got in through a trick—by hiding some soldiers in a large wooden horse that a supposed friend of Troy had gifted to the city. At night the soldiers hiding in the horse opened the gates to the Greek army and they slaughtered the Trojans. Odysseus was among the warriors who helped take Troy."

"Go on, Papa," Amada commanded.

"Well, Odysseus got into all kinds of trouble on his way back to Greece. He had to fight this enormous monster called the Cyclops, and he only prevailed after blinding the Cyclops. But it turned out the Cyclops was the son of Poseidon, the god of the sea, and Poseidon was so furious at

Odysseus that he tried to stop him from getting home. But another Greek goddess—I don't remember who—warned Odysseus that he and his men would have to sail by these bewitching creatures called the Sirens who lure sailors with their singing to sail close to their island and then they capture them. Odysseus gave his men beeswax to put in their ears so they couldn't hear the Siren's songs. But he himself wanted to hear the songs so he had his men tie him to a mast so he couldn't steer the ship closer. And sure enough, when he heard the sirens' songs, Odysseus screamed at his men to untie and let him go. But his men refused and they rowed safely by."

Daniel's mouth had dropped open, and I could almost hear Amada's little mind working furiously.

"What made their songs so bewitching?" she asked.

Mordecai looked at me. "Do you remember? I can't recall."

I smiled. I remembered well this epic tale; Miriam had told it to me. "I think the Sirens in their songs promised to give Odysseus all the knowledge and secrets about the world. Something irresistible like that."

"Caramba," Amada said. "So, what happened after they got by the Sirens?"

Mordecai frowned. "I'm a little fuzzy on the details, but he eventually made it back to Ithaca. There he was finally reunited with his long-suffering wife, Penelope, who had resisted all the suitors who tried to convince her that Odysseus was dead and wanted to marry her and reign in his place. By this time Odysseus had been away for more than thirteen years, but his wife never gave up hope he would return."

"What a great love story," Estraya said. "This Odysseus must have been quite a man."

Mordecai snorted. "That's one way to look at it. I guess I see the Odyssey as a cautionary tale about hubris and the price of pride. Odysseus was a bit too arrogant for my tastes, too sure he could best any opponent. When he tricked the Cyclops and blinded him, he mocked him and shouted his victory for all to hear. That's how Poseidon found out and made the rest of his journey a living hell."

I had first heard the story from Miriam when I was on the cusp of puberty, and Miriam had imparted a very different lesson from the epic: that through the ages there has always been a double standard as far as men and women were concerned. Odysseus could cavort with whatever beautiful nymph or goddess threw herself at him, but if his wife, Penelope, had given in to any of her suitors during the long years of her husband's absence, she would have been roundly condemned and quite possibly killed. It was no different now. Men like Brian de Bois-Guilbert could ravage their way across the Holy Land and get away with it, but if he had besmirched my virtue, who knows what would have become of me. Growing up in England, I had heard stories of unmarried women who had lost their virtue, only to be cast out by their families and left to fend for themselves on the streets. I doubted my father would have been so cruel if Bois-Guilbert had had his way with me, but I was exceedingly grateful that I never had to find out.

I watched Amada and Daniel's innocent faces as they sat in their father's lap. This was not a lesson they needed to hear, not at their age.

CHAPTER 20

SOME DAYS LATER, the weather turned bad. Dark glowering clouds creased the sky and the wind grew stronger. The captain sent us to our cabins to wait out the storm and his crew sprang into action, reefing the sails and preparing the ballast. It soon started to rain and huge waves rocked the boat.

Inside the cabin, Amada and Daniel nestled close to their mother as she attempted to read to them. But she soon turned pale and moaned.

"I can't read any more," she said. "I feel like I'm going to throw up. Lie down, children."

Hania was already on her knees, retching into a small basin by her bunk. When she had nothing left to bring up, she sank onto her bed and started to chant the *Shema*, no doubt sure she was going to meet her maker. The ship tossed and bucked for hours. I too was sure it would sink and we would all be drowned. I swore to myself that if we ever made it to Egypt alive, I would never set foot on a boat again.

At one point, I heard a sharp snap and something crashed to the deck outside our cabin. I heard a shriek of terror, and then nothing. I gasped and caught Estraya's eye, wild with fear. She was no doubt thinking the same as I was; should we venture outside to see if someone needed our help?

The door to our cabin banged open and the first mate stood there, panting heavily. "We have a man overboard. No one must come outside until this tempest is over."

The door banged shut behind him as he left. Miraculously, Amada and Daniel did not wake up; I hoped they would never hear about the drowned sailor.

Isadora sat up in her bunk. "What do you think happened?" she whispered, panic in her voice.

I fought to stay calm. "Perchance a mast had broken and struck a sailor? I don't know. Try not to worry. We'll be fine." But I didn't believe my own words. Surely, we were doomed. How could we possibly sail through this dreadful tempest with just one mast? The ship would sink and all its passengers with it. So, this was how my life was going to end. I would never see Bernardo again, never taste his passionate kisses, never know the pleasure of bringing another baby safely into the world. As I lay back on my narrow bunk, I dug my nails into my palm in an attempt to banish my dark thoughts. After a time, I felt too queasy to even think; I just wanted it to end.

I awoke the next morning, dry-mouthed and depleted to a steady boat and no wind or rain. I no longer felt queasy. In fact, I was hungry. None of us had eaten anything while the squall raged. I got up, smoothed out my wrinkled tunic, and spilled some water from a large skin into my basin to splash water on my face. Everyone else still lay asleep, so I decided to go out and get some fresh air. The sky was metallic gray but clouds were parting to the east. The crew was busy on deck. Some sailors tried to untangle the sail from what was indeed a snapped mast. Another climbed the rigging in an effort to detach the sail at the top and take a bearing.

The ship seemed to be making way on one mast. Ahead of the ship off to the port side, I saw a distant land mass. The captain was talking to the helmsman and I approached cautiously.

The captain stopped talking and strode toward me. "Tough night."

"Yes, but I'm very thankful that we're still afloat," I said, squinting up at him. "What happened to the man who went overboard last night?"

The captain flinched. "We lost him. He was hit by the falling mast. There was nothing we could do."

That poor man. "I'm so sorry," I murmured.

The captain crossed himself and started to turn away.

I cleared my throat. "Excuse me, but what is that land mass?" I pointed to the purplish blur of land off to our port.

"That's the island of Crete. We're going to have to put in there to repair the boat. We can't sail to the Holy Land with a broken mast."

"Crete?" I rolled the strange sound on my tongue. "Who lives there?"

"A better question would be who controls Crete," the captain said. "Unfortunately, it is under the control of the Byzantine Emperor who is not exactly a friend of Genoa."

He pointed up at the bowsprit. "That's why we're flying a Spanish flag. As far the Cretans will be concerned, we are a Spanish vessel bound for the Holy Land. I will alert everyone about our new status before we arrive."

He chuckled at my look of consternation. "Sailing in these waters is a tricky business. I'm sure you understand."

As our ship neared the northern tip of Crete, the captain bade all the passengers assemble on the deck and relayed what he had told me.

"When we anchor in the port, you are welcome to disembark and walk around Chania—it's a nice little town and the food in the tavernas is delicious," he said. "But if anyone asks, we are a Spanish vessel bound for the Holy Land."

He leveled his gaze on Mordecai, whom I had already told. "That won't be a problem for your family, I trust. You are Spanish after all; just speak your natural language and there won't be any issues."

Mordecai nodded. As he had told me, he had seen this kind of deceit before on his travels. Sailing in these waters often required such trickery. Even so, when the time came to climb into the small boat that would take us to the dock, only Mordecai, Estraya, and I decided to disembark. Hania was still feeling poorly so Benjamin decided to stay with her, and Isadora was leery of venturing into a strange port with the children.

"We might come ashore later, after you brave souls get the lay of the land," Isadora said, holding onto each of her children's hands as they waved with the other.

Chania curved like a crescent around the harbor, its waters sparkling in the sun. Several tavernas, their entrances open to the air, beckoned, but I was eager to stretch my legs.

"Shall we see the town first?" I asked. In all his travels, Mordecai had never been to Chania, so he nodded.

"It's so good to be off the ship, if only for a little while," Estraya said. "What a charming little town."

Beyond the dock, Chania, with its warren of narrow streets and high stone walls, reminded me a little of Toledo. A poorer, more dilapidated version. The tall walls were crumbling in places and an abandoned fortress stood sentinel on the north side of town. The women passing us in the narrow streets wore colorful turbans and long silken tunics, and the men were bareheaded and often bearded. A few passer-byers stared at me and my relatives with curiosity but I sensed no hostility. I suspected the townsfolk were used to travelers stopping at their port to replenish stores or repair their boats.

As we wandered down one narrow street, I saw a woman running in my direction, her arms flailing. She stopped cold at the sight of me and stared, her mouth open in shock. She threw herself at my feet, jabbering in a language I didn't understand.

Baffled, I looked to Mordecai. "What is she saying? What does she want?"

"I don't know. She's talking in a local dialect." Mordecai spoke first in Spanish, then switched to Latin.

The woman looked up and responded in broken Latin.

Mordecai's eyebrows shot up. "I don't believe this. She says you are Pasiphae incarnate. Apparently, this Pasiphae was a famous Queen of Minos and had magical powers of healing. She gave birth to a half-man, half-bull, a creature called the Minotaur. And now this woman says she has been reincarnated in you and sent to help her daughter, who is very sick."

The woman raised her tearstained face and continued talking.

"She asks that you come and heal her child," Mordecai said. "This is crazy. We should get back to the ship."

I understood his concern, but I couldn't walk away from this woman's despair. What would it hurt to examine the ailing child and see if there was anything I could do? Unless, of course, the girl had the putrid and then I would have to keep my distance.

"Tell her I will come and take a look but I can't promise anything and I am certainly no Minoan queen with special powers," I said.

Mordecai frowned. "Are you sure this is a wise idea? We're on a strange island, among strange people; she might be deceiving us."

I patted the dagger in the pocket of my tunic and squared my shoulders. "Why don't you take Estraya back to the ship? I will follow soon."

Mordecai snorted. "You know I can't leave you; your aunt and uncle would never forgive me if anything happened to you."

"I will stay with Rebecca," Estraya said. "I want to help."

Mordecai sighed and spoke to the woman who was still on her knees.

She put her hands together in a prayer of thanks, stood up, and gestured for us to follow her. She led us down the street and through a small courtyard into a house built into the city's outer wall. The woman pointed to a back room and gestured for me to follow her.

I turned to Mordecai and Estraya. "You two should stay here just in case whatever her daughter has is contagious. I will call if I need your help."

I followed the woman into the room and as my eyes adjusted to the dim light saw a little girl lying on a pallet, crying and trying to scratch herself. An older woman sat nearby and spoke in soothing tones to the child. Every so often she would put a hand on the little girl's arms to keep her from scratching her arm. I took a step closer, studying the girl, who was perhaps four or five years old. She had none of the tell-tale signs of the putrid or sweating sickness. I leaned in closer to look at a mottled redness on her arm.

"Mordecai, please come here so you can translate for me," I called. "I think she was bitten by some kind of poisonous insect, maybe a spider."

Mordecai told the mother. The woman gasped and said something I didn't understand. No matter.

"How long has she been like this?" I asked.

The woman told Mordecai the child was fine when she woke up this morning but had gotten sick sometime after breakfast after she went outside to play.

I nodded; the timing concurred with an insect bite. "Please ask her mother to fetch some soap and water, some clean clothes and plenty of salt and be quick about it." Depending on the spider, it might be too late to save her, but I would do what I could.

I rummaged around in my bag for the salve and herbs I always carried with me. The mother rushed back with what I asked for, and I cleaned the wound with soap and water and spread some ointment around the bite. I then sprinkled the salt on a wet cloth and tied the cloth around the bitten area. The girl flinched and tried to move away, but the older woman put a hand on her shoulder and spoke to her soothingly.

"Please tell the mother to keep this cloth on the wound for a couple of hours," I said. "The salt should draw out the venom. If it looks like the swelling is going down, she can pour more salt onto a fresh wet cloth and reapply the bandage. Or she might try peeling and grating a washed potato and then putting a handful of wet potato shreds into a piece of thin cloth and tie that securely around the girl's arm."

Mordecai raised an eyebrow, but repeated what I said. I laid a hand on the girl's forehead; she wasn't feverish, at least not yet. That was a good sign. I put a bit of crushed belladonna into a cup and mixed it with water.

"Tell her mother that if her daughter gets feverish, she should give her some of this belladonna," I said. "I will pray for her recovery."

The woman grasped my hand in gratitude and jabbered something in Latin.

"She says to thank you for your help, that you are indeed a magical healer," Mordecai translated. "I guess we'd better get back to the ship before she finds out differently."

"Very funny." I bowed my head respectfully to the two women and we let ourselves out of the house.

Back on the ship, the story of the spider bite spread quickly. Even the captain came to our table that evening to pay his respects while my family and I were eating fresh fish caught by the sailors. He told us the repairs on the mast were almost complete and the ship would probably be able to sail on the morrow. Then he paused and smiled at me.

"I hear you are a renowned healer," the captain said. "That's good to know."

"Hardly," I demurred. "I have a feeling that little girl would have recovered whether I was there or not."

The captain raised an eyebrow. "You are both modest and beautiful—a winning combination." He called over one of his crew. "Please bring this young lady and her family two bottles from my private collection of Cretan wines."

As he turned to leave, Mordecai asked the captain to join us in savoring the wine. He readily agreed. We sat around the makeshift table on the deck sipping wine and enjoying the twilight.

"Have you heard of this Queen Pasiphae and the beast she supposedly gave birth to?" I asked. "What was its name, Minotaur?"

The captain chuckled. "Ah, this is quite a story. Of course, I have no idea if any of it's true."

"Do tell us," Benjamin said and scraped his chair closer. "By the way, this octopus your men caught is delicious."

"I'm glad to hear it. According to the legend," the captain said, "a beautiful Greek nymph, the daughter of the Sun God and a mortal, married the King of Minos, who ruled over Crete and lived in a fabulous palace known as Knossos. But this nymph, whose name was Pasiphae, was tired of her husband having affairs with all the serving girls.

"So, she . . . ahem . . . made love to one of the King's sacred bulls and gave birth to the Minotaur, half-man, half-beast," the captain continued. "They kept him caged in a labyrinth deep in the palace and every year at harvest time, seven men and seven women from Athens were sacrificed to him. As I remember it, King Minos threatened to have his wife, the nymph-queen who had magical powers, send a plague to Athens if they did not submit to his wishes. The labyrinth was so complicated that no one ever escaped once they were inside. But one year, Theseus, the son of the King of Athens, decided to go to Crete as one of the sacrificial youths. He wanted to kill the Minotaur and be done with this outrageous edict. Theseus was handsome in addition to being brave, and it was just his luck that Ariadne, the daughter of Queen Pasiphae and King Minos, fell in love with him. She told him how to find his way out of the labyrinth should he be able to slay the Minotaur. With her help, Theseus was able to kill the beast and make his way out of the palace. And he took Ariadne away with him."

"How sweet," Estraya said. "Did they marry and live happily ever after?"

"You mean Theseus and Ariadne?" the captain asked. "I'm afraid not. Their ship stopped on the island of Naxos on their way home and Ariadne was captured by the god of wine, Dionysus. Theseus was forced to sail back to Athens without her."

"That's so sad," Estraya said. "Why can't Greek myths ever have a happy ending?"

"Mayhaps because they are like life," Rolston replied. "Life does not always have a happy ending."

"No, it doesn't," I agreed.

Mordecai frowned. "Captain, did the Minotaur and the palace of Knossos really exist? Or is it just a myth?"

The captain chuckled. "Who knows? From what I understand, Knossos may indeed have existed—as the center of some flourishing ancient civilization. A Cretan who sailed with me years ago said the city was destroyed by a giant wave thousands of years ago. As for the Minotaur, your guess is as good as mine."

"How fascinating," I exclaimed. "I hope somebody discovers the remains of this ancient city someday. Maybe they will find evidence of the Minotaur after all."

"Ha!" the captain said. "That would be something."

THE SANTA ROSALIA sailed on the morning tide and five days later, we cruised into Jaffa. Rolston and I stood on the deck as the ship navigated its way into the harbor and I could sense that the pilgrim seemed anxious. I put my hand on his.

"This must bring back memories of the crusade," I said. "Are you sure you want to do this?"

Rolston blinked. "Aye. This is something I must do. I can only hope that walking down the Via Dolorosa—that's where Jesus walked—and offering my prayers will help assuage my guilt."

I nodded in commiseration.

"But I will miss your gentle company and that of your relatives," he said, after a few moments. "Who knows? Mayhaps after I do my penance here, I will come and visit you in Cairo." He looked down, sheepish. "If you don't mind of course."

What was he saying? Could he be interested in me romantically? He must know that wasn't possible, with him being a devout Christian and me a Jewess. And I still hoped that Bernardo would get past his guilt over Rachel's death and make his way to me. But Walt and I could always be friends.

"My family and I would be delighted to see you," I said.

An hour or so later, Rolston waved to me as he climbed into the small boat for the short trip to shore. The other pilgrim was with him, looking pale and gaunt. He had never really recovered from his seasickness during the trip.

I would have loved to disembark and walk around Jaffa and get the measure of the city. but the ship would only be in port for one day. The captain said he needed to make up some time. In the end, we all stayed on board and watched the sailors unloaded the cargo, cases of wine, and olive oil from Spain and Italy, much prized in the Holy Land. The port was alive with men loading and unloading freight, and through the bobbing masts of the ships, I could see an impregnable-looking stone citadel standing tall at one end of the harbor, a red crusader flag flying above the highest rampart, its thick white cross glinting in the sun.

CHAPTER 21

September 1195 AD

THE NEXT MORNING, the *Santa Rosalia* sailed for Egypt. The fair weather held, and early the following day, we reached the bay where the Nile River emptied out into the Mediterranean. We sailed down the wide estuary and arrived at the port of Cairo the following morning.

Desperate to get out of our close-smelling cabin, I soon joined Estraya on the deck. From our vantage point, we saw a massive fortress and mosque with elegant minarets spearing the sky in the center of the city. The captain, who stopped at the railing where we stood, told us that the citadel had been built by Saladin more than a decade ago. It was the seat of government and a central place for worship as well. I asked him who ruled Cairo now that Saladin was dead.

"After Saladin died, one of his sons became Sultan of Egypt while another son rules over Syria. But I understand that Al-Aziz, he's the Egyptian caliph, is trying to take Damascus from his brother." The captain shook his head. "He's power hungry, that one; wants it all for himself."

Estraya pointed at what looked to be a narrow body of water bisecting the city. "What is that?"

It's a canal," he said. "The sultans who ruled a few hundred years ago built these interlocking canals and lakes to take the water when the Nile floods. If they didn't have them, a lot of homes would be flooded. It would be a disaster. Some say that when the Nile floods, Cairo looks just like Venice and you can get from one part of the city to another by boat."

"I see one now, over there," Estraya said, pointing in the distance.

Before we left Toledo, Mordecai had written to a cousin who had moved to Cairo a few years prior to let him know we were coming. Benjamin had done the same with an old friend and neighbor of his who had left for Egypt with his family a decade earlier. Hopefully, we'd be able to locate one of these old acquaintances who could help us find shelter until we found a place of our own.

The captain pointed Mordecai and Benjamin toward the Jewish quarter and the two men disembarked to find a porter with a cart. They were waiting on the quay with the cart and its driver as my aunt and cousins and I arrived by small boat. The port was bustling with people and cargo. Almost all the women wore colorful head scarves, so I drew my own scarf over my head. It helped cut down on the dust that swirled in my eyes as I walked by the donkey-led cart carrying Hania and the children as well as our belongings. Even so, the air was hot and stifling, and I found myself perspiring through my light silk tunic. I hoped we would find Mordecai's cousin soon. But what if he had moved away? The idea of my family and I being stranded in this strange city come nightfall made me uneasy.

We passed by a bustling market where vendors seemed to be hawking everything from herbs and produce to live monkeys. Tart spices like cumin and cinnamon warred with the stench of animal droppings, rotting fish and freshly oiled leather. Mordecai, who had dropped back to walk besides the cart with us, explained that Cairo was the center of the east-west spice trade as well as a market for exotic animals from Africa such as lions, monkeys, zebras, and giraffes, which were often given as gifts to the Sultan and kept in his extensive menageries.

Daniel jumped up from his seat and almost fell off of the cart. Hania grabbed hold of him.

"I want to go and see a lion," Daniel exclaimed.

"Yes, please, Papa," Amanda pleaded.

Mordecai rolled his eyes. "Maybe once we're settled. But not now. Sit down, Daniel, or I will strap you to your seat."

The porter took us through a narrow warren of streets and over several small bridges to the south of the citadel. Most of the houses were wooden and built on top of the next, and seemed similar in size and design to the dwellings in Toledo. We passed a few larger stone houses, no doubt home to wealthier families who could afford the luxury of high walls and outer courtyards.

Mordecai and Benjamin directed the porter to take us first to Mordecai's cousin since he had emigrated only a few years ago. But when we arrived at that address, we discovered that Mordecai's cousin no longer lived there. The house was home to a stranger who had no idea where the previous occupant had gone.

By this time, we were all tired and hungry, so we stopped by the side of the narrow street under the shade of an acacia tree to eat a quick meal of biscuits and cheese. A sense of foreboding gripped me. If we couldn't locate Benjamin's old friend and neighbor, where would we go? I had been too angry and proud to get the address for Bernardo's sister in Egypt before we left Valencia, and we knew no one else in this strange and forbidding city.

It was late afternoon by the time we located the address Benjamin had for his neighbors, which was well to the south of Cairo's main marketplace, and I felt like sinking to the ground, I was so hot and tired. I didn't think I could walk another step under this unrelenting sun. The wooden house we stopped at was larger than the one Mordecai's cousin had once lived in; it rose two stories above high stone walls and looked immaculately kept. I was sure we would be turned away. And then where would we go, how would we find accommodations for the night? It didn't bear thinking about it.

This time, however, we were in luck. The wife of Benjamin's friend, Nahon, was home and she recognized Benjamin and Hania. She invited all of us inside, where we sank gratefully onto pillows strewn around the house's small inner courtyard. The woman, whose name was Mira, asked her daughter-in-law to bring us cool drinks and some tahini, olives and pita. While we waited for the refreshments, Mira told us that Nahon, bless his memory, had died two years ago, of heart collapse. But her son, whom Nahon had brought into his jewelry business, was doing well. They had been able to add a second story to their home and enlarge the courtyard.

"What brings you here?" Mira asked.

Benjamin explained that we had left Toledo because of the anti-Jewish riots there and were hoping to make a new home in Egypt. He introduced us to Mira one by one.

"This is Rebecca, my brother's daughter," he said, when he came to me. "She is a gifted healer and is teaching our Estraya the skill."

Mira scrutinized me, and I felt my face flush under her keen gaze.

"My uncle overstates the case," I said. "I hear you have a truly august healer here in Cairo: Maimonides."

"Yes, Moses ben Maimon. Nahon knew him when we were all growing up in Cordoba," Mira said. "He left with his family when he was around twenty years old. If I recall correctly, they moved to Morocco first. Only after the Almohads executed the Maimons' rabbi and teacher for being a practicing Jew, did they come to Egypt. Maimonides is a very learned scholar."

I thought about how much I would like to learn from this man. Would he grant me an audience? Did Egyptians even recognize women as healers? I had so many queries about this new country, its customs and culture. But now was not the time to probe.

"Is Maimonides still a physician to the court?" I asked.

Mira looked at me sharply.

"A friend from Spain told me that Maimonides was Saladin's physician," I added.

"He was but Saladin is dead," Mira said. "Al-Aziz, his twenty-two-year-old son, rules now and probably has little need of a doctor. But from what I understand, Maimonides is still consulted by the court about medical matters. Ah, here are the refreshments."

Amada and Daniel fell upon the food as if they hadn't eaten in days.

Isadora admonished them with a click of her tongue.

Mira smiled. "Let them eat. They are children."

She turned to Benjamin. "You are welcome to stay with us for a few days until you find accommodations. I can ask my son and daughter-in-law to sleep with their children to give you the two rooms at the back of the house."

Benjamin began to thank her, but she waved him away. "I know you would have done the same for us if the situations were reversed. It is what Nahon would have wanted."

CHAPTER 22

THE NEXT FEW days passed in a blur as we settled into Mira's house and explored Cairo. Within the week, Benjamin and Mordecai had found a house in the Jewish quarter that was big enough to accommodate us. It even had an attached shed that could serve as an apothecary if I decided to take up healing again. I had learned, from talking to Mira and her daughter-in-law, Solena, that women in Cairo were respected as midwives and healers, although they had no official status as physicians. But I still had doubts about the wisdom of setting up shop. What if I was accused of being a witch again?

Before leaving Toledo, Benjamin had written to his trading contacts in Cairo. They went to visit those partners to discuss restarting their business in Cairo. But when we sat down for dinner that evening, both men were unusually quiet.

"So how did your meetings go?" Isadora asked.

Mordecai frowned and exchanged a look with Benjamin, who cleared his throat.

"Well, our partners were not exactly delighted to see us," Mordecai said. "You see, they've been managing our affairs just fine here in Cairo and now that we're here, they fear we don't need them. I tried to assure them that wouldn't happen but . . ." He spread his hands palms up. "I'm afraid we have some negotiating to do."

Hania patted Benjamin's hand. "Well, you're a good negotiator my dear, so I'm sure everything will turn out fine. Mira, this chickpea stew is delicious—how do you make it?"

BY WEEK'S END, we had moved into our new dwelling, outfitting it with bedding and furniture we bought in the Cairo markets. Estraya and I shared one room, Benjamin and Hania another, and Mordecai and Isadora took the largest bedroom for themselves and their children.

Estraya and I finally found time to look around the old shed behind our house. I was delighted to find wooden shelves already built in above a countertop, but the place needed a thorough cleaning if we were going to use it as an apothecary.

"I'm not sure it's wise to start practicing just yet," I said, running a finger through the dust. "I'd really like to talk to a woman healer here to hear about her experience first."

Estraya nodded. "That makes sense. From what I've heard, the Islamic world has a very sophisticated approach to medicine."

"You may be right," I said. "But I'd still like to meet some other healers first. Let's ask Mira and Solena if they know any."

Mira did indeed know of a woman healer, an older Jewess originally from Seville who had come to Cairo years ago with her family. Mira sent her a message and a few days later, received a reply.

The healer was willing to see me the following afternoon. I told Estraya I didn't want to intimidate the woman by having both of us turn up. But the real reason, I had to admit, was more selfish. As much as I loved my cousin, Estraya could be heedless at times and I didn't want to risk alienating this woman whom Mira had spoken so highly of. I wore a veil, as many women in Cairo did, so as not to attract any unwanted attention.

I walked through the sweltering heat of the Jewish quarter, glad of the scarf that kept my eyes partially shielded from the fierce sun. The marketplace was quiet at this hour, a handful of turbaned men hawking their wares to a few veiled shoppers. But most people were inside, napping or resting during the hottest time of the day. By the time I got to the healer's house at the other end of the Jewish quarter, I was sweaty, the folds of my scarf dust-ridden. She lived in a handsome, two-story stone house closer to the citadel.

I was ushered inside by a servant and asked to wait in the entryway, while her mistress finished seeing to a patient. The hall was cool, and I gratefully slid onto a cushion. Not long afterwards, the healer herself walked into the entryway and greeted me. She was tall and almost gaunt, in her late fifties or sixties, and one of her eyes was cloudy, the other a clear piercing brown. I noticed that her hands were wet. She must have just washed them, a sign that she too believed in the importance of cleanliness.

"I am Ledicia," the woman said. "Please come into my sitting room."

Ledicia's sitting room contained a low table with colorful cushions strewn about it. A skillfully woven tapestry hung on one wall showed some turbaned men on horseback hunting gazelles. I stopped to look at it.

"This is beautiful. Is hunting a popular pastime here?" I asked.

"Not really," Ledicia said. "Although I hear our current ruler is very taken with it, when he's not off fighting his brothers."

She lowered herself gracefully onto some cushions and gestured for me to do the same. Two glasses of squeezed lemon juice, water, and sugar sat on the table, and Ledicia picked one up and drank from it, all the while studying me.

"Please help yourself, Rebecca of Toledo," she said. "And now, what can I do for you?"

"I've been a healer for many years, but now I'm having doubts about continuing," I said.

"Why are you having these doubts?" Ledicia asked. I told her of my life in England, how I was almost burned as a witch by a Catholic military order, and how I had helped the king's mistress in Spain to get pregnant, only to see her murdered by the Church.

Ledicia listened with interest, interjecting a question here and there.

"You've led quite a life, Rebecca of Toledo," she said. "I hope you find a more peaceful existence in Cairo. Let me reassure you: women here, indeed, in all of Egypt, are respected as healers and midwives. As long as you are careful and practice good medicine, you shouldn't run into any problems."

I felt lightheaded with relief. We spent the next hour talking about our approach to healing and the medicinal herbs we relied on. Although she looked nothing like her, Ledicia reminded me of Miriam. I felt comfortable in her presence and realized there was a lot I could learn from her.

"One if the biggest threats to our health is the pestilence from the swamps," Ledicia said. "When the water in the canals and lakes recedes in a few weeks' time, people get the fever sickness and many die. I think it either comes from the air in the marshland or from the insects that thrive there."

I leaned forward, enthralled. I had never heard of such a connection before, but it made sense. "How intriguing. Have you shared your theory about insects with any doctors?"

Ledicia snorted. "Most of the doctors here can't conceive of the idea that bugs or the air we breathe might have something to do with illness. The only one who thinks there might be something to this is Maimonides, but after Saladin died, he lost influence at the court. And besides he is so busy writing about rabbinic law and whether there is a God that he doesn't have time to promote good health policies."

I was impressed that Ledicia even knew Maimonides. It didn't surprise me that he would be so open-minded.

"I'm sorry to hear he has lost influence," I said. "I would love to meet this great scholar. I'm sure every healer feels that way."

Ledicia's mouth twisted. "Good luck with that; he is a very busy man. So, have I allayed your concerns?"

"Very much so," I said. "I am grateful you have given me so much of your time."

Ledicia studied me for a long moment. "I am cutting down on my practice—as you can see, my eyesight is not what it used to be. I'd be happy to send some patients your way should you decide to go into practice."

"That is so kind of you," I said, feeling a rush of gratitude. "I am most grateful."

ONE MORNING SOON afterward, Estraya and I visited the marketplace in the Jewish quarter. It was teeming with shoppers, mostly women in colorful head scarves bargaining with swarthy men in white tunics and turbans, who wiped the sweat from their brows as they haggled. We walked slowly amid the stalls, looking for herbs we might need for our practice. Estraya laid a hand on my arm.

"Look, isn't that valerian root?" she asked. "We could never find that in Toledo!"

She rushed over to the stall and started haggling in broken Arabic with the seller. Estraya caught onto new languages much faster than I did. I listened intently, but could only catch a few words here and there. I was suddenly reminded of Bernardo and our outing in the Toledo countryside that glorious spring day. I had to fight the urge to cry right then and there. There was a very good chance that Bernardo would never get past Rachel's death, that I would never see him again.

In the end, we found almost all of the herbs we needed—besides valerian root, we purchased ginseng, chamomile, belladonna, and witch hazel. A good thing, because our practice picked up quickly. Mira and Solena told their friends about me and true to her word, Ledicia sent some patients around. Word spread that I was Ledicia's protégé, and Estraya and I soon found we were busy from early in the morning till late afternoon.

One day, I treated an older Jewish woman with painfully swollen hands. As I was examining her hands, she said, "You should visit Ben Ezra for Simchat Torah." She was referring to the synagogue located in Fustat just south of central Cairo. Fustat had once been the center of Egypt's ruling government but had been burned to the ground almost thirty years ago by its own vizier to keep its wealth out of the hands of invading crusaders. The Crusaders never made it this far down the Nile, but after the fire, the sultan moved his seat of power to Cairo. Fustat, however, was still home to many Jews, including Maimonides, from what I'd heard.

"What is Simchat Torah?" I asked. In England, my father and I rarely went to synagogue—Isaac said he had little use for a God that had allowed his beloved Sarah to die—and after the York massacre, we didn't go at all.

"Simchat Torah is when we celebrate the ending of the yearly cycle of readings from the Torah and the beginning of the new cycle," my patient said. "It's a very festive occasion."

"When is this holiday?" I asked as I spread a healing ointment on the woman's swollen knuckles.

"Ah that feels good. Tomorrow evening," my patient said and smiled slyly. "It might be a good way for you and your family to meet more of the Jewish community here, especially some eligible young men for you and Estraya."

I laughed at the woman's boldness. I was not interested in meeting other men. However, I had to admit I was curious about Judaism, having not had the opportunity to attend services in England or Spain. As for Estraya, well, she was almost seventeen and Hania and Isadora were already making noises about finding possible suitors.

"I'll see if my family is interested in going," I told my patient. "Thanks for letting me know about it."

I broached the idea at dinner that evening, leaving out the part about meeting eligible men. I didn't expect Isadora to come. She had recently announced she was pregnant again and was experiencing some nausea.

"I'll stay home and help Isadora with the children," Hania said.

Estraya smiled at me. "I'll come. I could use an evening out."

Mordecai and Benjamin exchanged looks. One of them would have to come along as a chaperone if Estraya and I were to go.

"I can't go; I am meeting with a possible trading partner tomorrow evening," Mordecai said.

Benjamin sighed. "I guess that means I'm going."

Hania patted his hand. "That's very good of you, dear. You'll enjoy it. How long has it been since you've been inside a shul?"

Benjamin rubbed his ear. "It's been years. After the Almohads took power, the only synagogue left in Cordoba was a secret one, hidden in Don Ezmael's house. But we didn't feel comfortable worshipping there. Hard to believe we can observe openly here." He turned to me. "Are you sure it's safe?"

I shrugged. "So my patients tell me. Several of them go regularly."

THE NEXT EVENING, Benjamin, Estraya, and I set out on foot for Ben Ezra, which we'd been told was about a twenty-minute walk from our house. The temple, which had been built two hundred years ago, was a handsome stone structure with gracefully rounded arches and a domed ceiling. It reminded me of the mosque in the citadel, but a smaller, less ornate version. Clusters of handsomely garbed Cairenes strolled through the columned entrance, mostly men, but here and there I could see women draped in silken tunics with colorful turbans, a few holding the hands of children. As we neared the entrance, I heard someone shout. I turned around to see a group of men clustered around another bearded man, greeting him with deferential acclaim. One of the men in the cluster exclaimed, "Maimonides, it's good to see you!" I stopped short, my heart racing. Was that the famed doctor himself? Maimonides wore a white turban and tunic and had a closely cropped salt and pepper beard. I tapped Estraya on the shoulder.

"I think that's Maimonides, the renowned doctor and scholar. Oh, how I would love to meet him," I whispered.

Estraya's mouth dropped open and Benjamin stared. I was thinking of how I might arrange an introduction when someone jostled me in an attempt to get by.

"We need to get out of these people's way." Beniamin said. "Either that or go inside."

I moved forward and Benjamin and Estraya followed. I comforted myself with the thought that I would have time during the service to think of a way to approach Maimonides. Once inside the synagogue, my cousin and I were directed to the women's gallery upstairs, while Benjamin was pointed toward the main sanctuary reserved for men.

I leaned over the balcony and saw Maimonides being ushered to a seat of honor near the front of the sanctuary. On a raised dais, several men, also dressed in white with tall white hats on and embroidered shawls, were gathered around the pulpit. One of the men chanted Hebrew hymns and another man opened the ark and withdrew a Torah scroll. He handed it to a third man and then took out a second Torah scroll. Both men, holding the scrolls aloft, stepped off the dais followed by the cantor. They paraded the scrolls in a circle around the congregants, swaying and chanting a Hebrew hymn. The congregants soon joined in the chanting and some of them followed the men with the scrolls. Then to my astonishment, the men danced—whirling around the sanctuary in a ragged line of bearded men and boys, all dressed in white. This was obviously a joyous occasion but I had no idea why.

I turned to the older woman beside me. "What is happening?" I asked in Ladino.

"They are celebrating the end of the Torah reading for the year," the woman said. "After the men make seven circuits around the sanctuary, they will read the last portion of Deuteronomy from the first scroll, and then from the second scroll, they will read the first portion of Genesis, the beginning of the Torah."

I stared at her, confused.

The woman chuckled. "You've never been to Simchat Torah, I see. The whole point is to illustrate that the Torah never ends and that we, as Jews, never complete our learning."

I thanked her. That made a lot of sense. I hoped to always keep learning new things about healing. That was why I was so eager to meet Maimonides, but how?

The great man himself hadn't joined the snaking line of men dancing around the Temple. He stood watching the display, hands clasped in front of him, a slight smile on his lips. Finally, the dancing came to an end, the men carrying the scrolls climbed back up on the dais, and everyone sat back down as the rabbi and his helpers began reading from the Torah. I didn't understand Hebrew and couldn't really follow the readings. But I watched the goings on with avid curiosity. At some point, an older man shuffled down the aisle toward the back of the sanctuary; perhaps he had to use the privy chamber.

That gave me an idea.

"I'm going to wait outside for the service to end and see if I can waylay Maimonides then," I whispered to Estraya, who smiled and nodded. I waited until the readers had begun chanting from the second scroll, and then I got up. I excused myself each time I squeezed in front of a congregant and made my way to the narrow gallery staircase.

After using the privy chamber, which was a hole carved out of stone, I walked back to the front of the synagogue. A stocky, bearded man stood at the entrance. He was no doubt keeping an eye out for intruders.

"Excuse me sir, but I need some fresh air," I said. "I thought I'd wait out here for my relatives. Do you have any idea when the service will be over?"

The man frowned, looking at me sternly as if I was a wayward child. "It's almost over. They just finished the Torah service."

I thanked the man and walked over to one of the outside columns. The cooler evening air was refreshing after the stale heat of the synagogue. I leaned against the column and watched the first stars wink into the purple sky. Was Bernardo still in Spain or on one of his trading excursions? Would I ever see him again? I sighed and focused my thoughts on Maimonides. I had heard that he was long married and had one child, a son. He must be in his fifties now. Would he be annoyed if I went up to him and introduced myself? Would I even be able to get that close, given his entourage of adoring acolytes?

Finally, a loud murmur of voices signaled that the service was over. I turned around and positioned myself so I could see the entrance, lit by tapers from inside the synagogue. I didn't have to wait long. Maimonides was walking in the center of another cluster of men, all talking and gesticulating with their hands. As he came toward me, I raised my voice and called to him. I pushed my way toward him.

"Please, I must speak with the doctor," I said. "It's important."

The men gave way and Maimonides himself halted. He raised an eyebrow at my approach.

I swallowed hard, and screwing up my courage, raised my chin. "Dr. Maimonides, your fame has spread far and wide. I am Rebecca Manasses, recently arrived from Toledo, Spain, where everyone has heard of you. I am a healer and would like nothing better than to learn from you."

Maimonides smiled wearily. He was probably used to getting accosted by strangers, but at least he didn't seem put off by my boldness.

"My dear, I'm sure you are an excellent healer but I am too busy these days writing my treatise to take on an apprentice," Maimonides said. "Even if I was still active as a physician, I don't think I would be allowed to bring on a woman, especially in the Sultan's court." He studied me for a moment. "A pity my son Abraham is not old enough to be betrothed. You are a beautiful woman."

Several of his companions snickered.

I tried hard not to show my disappointment.

"If something changes, I will let you know. And now I must go. My wife will never forgive me if I'm late for supper." He leveled his gaze at me. "Be well, Rebecca of Toledo."

I managed to croak out a goodbye before Maimonides inclined his exquisitely turbaned head and swept by me.

Estraya hurried toward me. "What happened? Did Maimonides actually talk to you?"

On our long walk home, I told her and Benjamin all that had transpired.

CHAPTER 23

OCTOBER 1195 AD

A FEW WEEKS later, to my utter astonishment, I received a missive from Maimonides, saying he would like to see me at his home in Fustat. I was excited but apprehensive at the same time. There was no question of refusing his summons. But what could this great man want of me? He had already said he had no need for an apprentice.

On the appointed day, Mordecai agreed to accompany me to Maimonides' home near the Ben Ezra synagogue. As we approached the high walls of his compound, a tall, half-naked black man armed with a spear outside the entrance stopped us. I had seen such imposing Africans guarding the Citadel, but why would Maimonides require such a guard? He was a physician and a scholar; surely, no one would want to harm him.

Mordecai showed the guard the scroll from Maimonides and he waved us inside the compound. Two handsome houses stood next to each other, separated by a central courtyard with a fountain spilling water into a small clear pool that was surrounded by stone benches and jasmine bushes. Another man wearing black robes and a turban rushed out to usher us through a side entrance into one of the buildings. He took us to a small anteroom littered with cushions and bade us wait until Maimonides himself could see us.

As we waited, a servant came in and served us glasses that contained the lemon drink so popular in Cairo. I sipped the concoction gratefully; it was delicious.

"Why do you think Maimonides needs an armed guard outside his residence?" I asked Mordecai.

He scratched his chin. "It might have something to do with his stature. I hear he is considered the Nagid or leader of the Jewish community here. Perchance there are elements in this city who wish him and his family harm. I don't really know."

The same turbaned official came to collect us a little while later. He ushered us into a large room richly appointed with tapestries on the wall and oriental rugs scattered around the floor. Maimonides, dressed in brown silk robes and also wearing a turban, was seated on some cushions, reading a parchment. When we entered, he stood and smiled, appraising us with shrewd brown eyes. He was smaller in stature than I remembered, with a closely cropped salt and pepper beard and mustache.

"Rebecca of Toledo. You are even more beautiful than I remember."

I stared at him, surprised. Was this respected scholar trying to play the coquet with me?

"I also hear you are a skilled midwife and healer. A woman of many talents."

I bowed my head, still a bit annoyed. "Thank you. This is Mordecai, my cousin's husband."

"Good to meet you." Maimonides gestured for us to sit at a small table across from him.

We chatted for a bit—Maimonides was particularly interested in Mordecai's recollections of Córdoba, his childhood home.

Maimonides finally straightened and focused his attention on me. "As you may know, I am one of the young sultan's physicians. He knew of my service to his father, Saladin, and insisted I stay on, even though I mostly play an advisory role these days. Well, just last week, one of the Sultan's favorite concubines, who was pregnant with his child, died in childbirth and the infant along with her. Al-Aziz was furious. I wasn't there but I'm told he flew into a rage and threatened all of his physicians with physical harm if we allowed another one of his, ah, women to die. So, we decided we needed to find a more skilled midwife for his harem."

I narrowed my eyes; surely, he didn't mean for me to put myself in such danger.

"Yes, I know what you're thinking," Maimonides said. "Why would you want to get involved into such a risky situation?"

I nodded. The man was an impressive mind reader, I'd give him that.

"I think if you did us this service, you would not only be well-rewarded but it would enhance your stature in the Jewish and Muslim communities. And I, for one, would consider it a mitzvah."

I felt trapped. I was intrigued by Maimonides' offer but it was undoubtedly dangerous.

"What happened to the harem's midwife, the one who was supposedly taking care of the concubine who died?" I asked.

Maimonides blanched. "She wasn't killed, if that's what you're worried about." He paused. "But she was flogged for dereliction of duty." He hastened to add, "I would make sure that didn't happen to you. From what I understand, this midwife truly didn't know what she was doing."

Maybe, maybe not. I felt pretty sure I would be held accountable should something go wrong. Even so, Maimonides' offer tempted me.

"Please," he said. "It would be a great mitzvah for the Jewish community here."

"I am already very busy and I'm not sure I can spare much time for the Sultan's harem," I said. "I would only agree to this if I have leave to hire another midwife of my own choosing to attend to these women on a regular basis, and I would consult on the more difficult cases."

Maimonides leaned back on his cushions, his mouth twitching. He seemed amused at my temerity. Finally, he sat up and spread his hands wide.

"Whatever you need," he said. "I'm sure I can get the vizier to agree to this."

A FEW DAYS later, I paid another visit to Ledicia, hoping she might know of a good mid-wife who would be interested in working with me on this venture. She gave me two names; I interviewed both women, one Jewish, the other Muslim, and hired the non-Jewish woman, an experienced mid-wife in her forties whose approach to healing seemed more akin to mine. She also spoke Arabic fluently, which I knew would be an asset in the harem.

Estraya, who was as curious as I was to see the inside of a harem, tried to convince me that she should come and help out as well. But I didn't want to expose anyone else in my family to the sultan's wrath should something go wrong. I was willing to take that risk myself, but I would never forgive myself if I put my cousin in harm's way.

Maimonides himself accompanied me to the sultan's palace the first time. As we neared the sprawling compound, I was momentarily blinded by the sun striking off of its white walls. Maimonides explained that the palace had been built of limestone quarried from the nearby Mukattam Hills and its façade surfaced with marble.

At the main entrance, Mery, the Egyptian mid-wife whom I had hired to work with me, was waiting for us. I introduced her to Maimonides, and we approached the entrance. I was nervous. What would happen if they turned us away? But the guards recognized Maimonides and waved us through. We walked through a beautiful courtyard redolent with palm trees, jasmine, and red poppies. Water lilies floated in a sparkling rectangular pool. At the other end of the courtyard, a fat turbaned man with a double chin was waiting for us. It was clear he was a eunuch, a man who had been castrated so he could serve in the sultan's harem.

"This is Mahmoud, he is in charge of the harem," Maimonides said. He introduced Mery and myself.

Mahmoud grunted. "Come with me."

We followed him through a series of spacious high-ceilinged rooms decorated with bright blue and golden yellow tiles, ornate rugs strewn on the floors. Finally, we stopped in front of a closed door guarded by a tall fierce-looking Nubian holding a spear.

"I can go no further," Maimonides said. "Mahmoud will take over from here. Good luck Rebecca and Mery." He bowed to us and walked away.

The Nubian stood aside and we entered the harem. More than a dozen exotic-looking women in colorful silk robes reclined on cushions scattered around an exquisitely tiled room that opened up onto another open courtyard. Some of the women chattered with each other and sipped cold drinks. A few worked with embroidery, one woman played a harp, and one or two others tended to small children who appeared to have free run of the place. Mahmoud clapped his hands and the women all stopped what they were doing and looked at him.

"This is Rebecca and Mery, your new midwives," he said. "They will attend to your needs from now on."

A dozen eyes were assessing me, and one full-figured young woman, her expressive brown eyes lined with kohl and her arms circled with silver bracelets, pointed at me.

"Our Lord and Master might want her to join us here, she is so beautiful," she said, prompting giggles from some of the other women.

Mahmoud ignored her and gestured at a very pregnant young woman with striking red hair who was reclining by herself in one corner of the room.

"Celia, come with us," he said.

Celia frowned and rose slowly, putting a hand on the wall to help herself rise. She was tall and thin, except for her very rounded stomach, and had brilliant blue eyes, the color of topaz, and an aquiline nose. She couldn't have been more than sixteen or seventeen. I stared at her in confusion.

What was this beautiful European woman doing in the sultan's harem? With her red hair and proud bearing, she reminded me a little of Rachel, a younger, more frightened Rachel.

Mahmoud led us to a smaller room off of the courtyard, with a low-lying bed and basin of water. "This is the birthing room. You can examine Celia here."

Celia backed away from the bed, squaring her frame against the wall. I could tell she did not want to be touched, at least not in the presence of the eunuch.

"Thank you, Mahmoud," I said. "May we have some privacy please?"

Mahmoud scowled, making his chins wobble, but he turned and left the room.

"I will be waiting outside for a full report," he said.

After he was gone, I sat on the bed and patted a corner of it.

"Come sit with me," I said in the rudimentary French I had learned from Miriam.

She appeared to understand me and walked to the bed and sat on the edge, looking as though she wanted to flee at any moment.

"Where are you from, child?" I asked.

"How do you know my language?" she asked.

I waved a hand. "It was just a guess. I have lived in England and Spain and learned some French from my mentor. Are you from France?"

"Yes, we lived in Nice, that is, until my father was killed." Celia frowned. "He is the reason I am here."

"Do you want to tell me what happened?" I asked gently.

Celia slumped onto the bed. More than two years ago, she said, her Papa had been killed in a fight over gambling debts, leaving her mother, herself, and two brothers to fend for themselves. Her mother, who came from Genoa, decided they should go and live with her family. But on the way there, their ship was blown off course in in a squall. And soon after that, they were attacked and boarded by Berber pirates who took everyone who couldn't pay a ransom as slaves.

"We didn't have enough money to pay them off, so they were going to take all of us as slaves. I overheard those bastards talking about how with my looks I might fetch a sizable sum at auction. So, as they were deliberating, I climbed up onto the rigging and threatened to jump into the sea unless they let my mother and younger brother go," Celia said, her blue eyes flashing.

I gasped.

"Yes, it was rather reckless of me, but at that point, I felt like I'd rather drown than submit to their barbarity. To my surprise, they agreed to my terms and just took my brother and me as slaves. We were both brought here and sold, my brother to a rich landowner and myself to the sultan's vizier. He in turn gifted me to my Master."

I had heard about such evil doings, but this was the first time I had come face to face with someone who had been enslaved, brought to a foreign land, and forced to submit to the will of a powerful man. My heart cried out for this girl. I moved closer to Celia and took her hand.

"I'm so sorry," I said. "Is there anything I can do to make your life easier?"

"My life is over. I live for the child I am bearing my Lord." Celia said, patting her stomach. "God willing, he will be a healthy boy and the sultan's second son."

I understood that she was expressing a desire to have a boy, not a certainty.

"Inshallah," Mery said. "Shouldn't we get on with it, before, uh, Mahmoud loses patience?"

She was right. "Celia, do you mind if we examine you to see how the baby is doing?"

A FEW WEEKS later, I was summoned to the palace; Celia was experiencing labor pains. I sent a messenger to locate Mery but when I arrived at the palace, she wasn't there yet. I asked to be escorted to the harem, where Mahmoud, who was in a state of barely controlled panic, waited.

"This *mahaziya* is very important to his Majesty," he hissed. "You had better not lose her."

I nodded. I left Mahmoud fidgeting outside the birthing room and went inside alone. Celia was lying in a corner of the room, moaning in pain, a young slave backed up against the wall, looking terrified. I asked her to bring in a basin of warm water and clean clothes. Murmuring soft words of encouragement in Celia's ears, I got her up on the birthing bed and examined her. Her vulva was dilated and the birth pains were coming every five minutes. The baby felt like it was in the right position but Celia had narrow hips and I was worried she might have trouble delivering it.

I walked her around the room and showed her how to breathe when the pains came on.

A little while later, Mery rushed in, apologizing for the delay. She had been attending another patient when the messenger came and hadn't been able to leave right away. Shortly after that, the slave came back in with the supplies I requested. Just as I dismissed her, Celia started screaming and panting in earnest. The baby was coming. I bade her sit on the edge of the bed and Mery put some pillows behind her back. While Mery wiped Celia's brow and murmured to her, I washed my hands quickly in the basin of water, and then squatted in front of Celia. The baby was crowning. It was all happening so quickly I didn't have time to worry about anything else.

Celia let out a shrill scream.

"Push," I said. "Push as hard as you can."

The baby slid out into my hands. I quickly snipped the cord around its stomach and smacked its behind. It let out a furious squeal. Thank God. Under my breath, I muttered the *Birkat HaGomel*, the Jewish prayer of thanks for surviving childbirth. The baby was a little boy, with ten toes and a shock of black hair, no doubt inherited from its father. I gave the child to Mery for cleaning and knelt by Celia's side. She was barely conscious.

"Good job," I whispered. "You have a beautiful baby boy."

Celia fell back exhausted, a wan smile creasing her face.

By the time I left the harem, Celia was sitting back up against some pillows, nursing the baby, and she looked sleepily content. Mery visited her the next day and reported back that mother and child were doing fine. Thus, I was surprised when a messenger came to my apothecary some days later with a missive from Celia. She wanted to see me, something about birthing pain.

Alarmed, I left my patient in Estraya's care and hastened to the sultan's palace. What could be wrong with her?

This time, I was taken through the harem courtyard to Celia's new quarters, which consisted of a large room tastefully furnished with plush rugs, a soft bed and colorful cushions; there was a separate alcove for the baby. Obviously, the vizier had spared no expense for the mother of Al-Aziz's second son. Celia reclined on some cushions while a servant, no doubt another slave, brushed her hair. Yet another young woman lacquered her nails. She smiled when she saw me come in and dismissed the servants and the eunuch who had accompanied me. I was bewildered. She didn't look like she was in any pain. She put a finger to her lips.

"My little Masudi is sleeping," she said in French. "Thank you for coming." She gestured for me to sit down beside her.

As I slid onto the cushion next to her, I asked, "What's wrong, Celia?"

Celia giggled. "There's nothing wrong with me. I'm fine and my Lord has been very generous with me for bearing his son." She swept an arm around the room. "I now have my own quarters and two slaves dedicated to my welfare."

I looked around, still confused.

"It's my brother. He isn't feeling well. The last time I saw him, he had a rash around his"—she looked up to make sure no one else was listening, and then gestured below her abdomen—"organes genitaux."

"Your brother?" I asked, trying to understand why she was talking about her brother. Hadn't he been sold into slavery to someone else?

"Yes, my brother, Pierre. After I was gifted to the sultan and I, ah, pleased him by becoming pregnant, he allowed me to find out where Pierre had been taken and bring him to Cairo. He works now in the sultan's stables." Her eyes misted. "I am not allowed to see him too often, but at least I know he's safe and well-fed."

I was glad to hear her brother lived nearby. I wondered how she was able to see him at all, but knew better than to ask. His proximity must be a comfort to her in this strange land.

"So how can I be of help?" I asked.

"Can you determine what's ailing him? I don't trust the court physicians," she said.

That was not the first time I'd heard that complaint. From what I understood, the physicians reported everything to Mahmoud and the other eunuchs, who then reported all the details to the sultan's vizier. A few months ago, a young concubine from Morocco, barely into adolescence, was removed from the harem and sold off after she told one of the physicians that she was experiencing pain during relations with the sultan. After that happened, the other concubines were understandably reluctant to confide in the physicians. Although Mahmoud often pressed Mery and me for similar details, we gave him as little information as possible.

"I would be willing to see your brother, but how?" I responded. "I don't think he would be allowed in here and I'm not sure he'd have leave to come to my home."

Celia thought for a minute. "No, probably not. But I could have one of the eunuchs bring you to him at the stables. Please. I can pay you."

"I am well compensated for my time here. Don't worry about that. When do you want me to see him?"

"Now?"

I nodded, and she rose along with me and rang a bell tied to a silken chord to summon one of the eunuchs. A eunuch entered the room and bowed low before Celia. It wasn't Mahmoud, but a younger less fleshy man.

"Asbat, please take my healer to the stables," she said. "She is to examine my brother."

Asbat hesitated. "Are you sure this is wise? Perhaps we should ask Mahmoud first."

Celia glared at him. "There is no time for that. My Lord would wish this of you."

Asbat's face colored and he bowed to her again.

She smiled at me and said in French, "Thank you, I am in your debt."

I pressed her hand. "I am glad you are doing well, Celia. And the next time I visit, I hope to see little Masudi."

I followed Asbat as he led the way out of the harem and through a series of hallways that eventually brought us to the back of the palace. We walked across the yard to the sultan's stables, where were housed in a long stone building that looked every bit as imposing as the palace. Inside, limestone columns separated the stalls, and I could see a few horses behind their wooden enclosures. Most of the horses were no doubt with the sultan as he battled his brothers for control of his father's empire. The place was dusty and smelled strongly of horse manure, hay and stale sweat. I was glad I had wound a scarf around my head and the lower part of my face. I waited near the entrance for someone to fetch Pierre.

A few minutes later, a tall, red-headed, and deeply tanned youth who couldn't have been more than nineteen or twenty sauntered up to me. There was no question he was Celia's brother; the likeness was startling. He was clad in a cotton jerkin, short pants and wore dusty sandals. He stopped and appraised me.

"How can someone so young and beautiful be a healer?" he said in French.

"Your sister sent me," I responded in French. "Is there some place more private where we can talk?"

He looked slightly abashed. "We can go into one of the empty stalls. But step carefully; you don't want to get horse dung on your pretty little shoes."

I carefully stepped over the straw inside the stall, wrinkling my nose at the smell of caked manure. Pierre looked around to make sure no one was watching. He pulled down his pants slightly. "I have this rash that won't go away. It's not too itchy, but it bothers me."

I peered closely at the rash, a series of faint bumps against his skin. I had seen something like this before when I went with Miriam on a house call to tend to a laborer in York. I hoped it wasn't what I thought it was.

"What do you mean by it bothers you?" I asked.

Pierre flushed. "The girls at the brothel down by the lake, when they saw it, they wouldn't lie with me anymore."

"Have you noticed any sores on your, ah, genitals?"

Pierre's face darkened. He looked around again and leaned close to me. "Yah, a month or so ago, there was a sore but it healed up fine. But then I got this rash and sometimes I feel dizzy. What's wrong with me?"

It was as I suspected. The poor lad was suffering from what in England we called Whore's Leprosy, or as it was known elsewhere, the Great Pox. I felt immensely sorry for him. There was no easy or sure-fire remedy to this often-fatal ailment. Miriam had mentioned that sometimes a mixture of sarsaparilla root and mercury, given in recurring doses, could stave off its worse effects, but that was an expensive treatment and often produced intolerable side effects. Indeed, she said that repeated applications of mercury had been known to cause damage to the mind that was similar to that found in advanced cases of the pox. I sighed. I decided to be direct.

"Pierre, you have the Great Pox," I said. "That's why the *ghawazi* won't lay with you. In fact, you probably got it from one of them, who in turn got it from another customer. There is no sure-fire remedy and the rash you have, along with your dizzy spells, are an indication that it has progressed."

Pierre stared at me in dismay. "What are you saying, woman? That I can no longer fuck?"

I felt sorry for this young man but I didn't have time for his lewdness. "That's not the worst of it. We don't know when or how, but the Pox can cause disfigurations and steal your ability to think and remember things. It may eventually kill you."

"Arggh." Pierre grunted as if in pain, bent over, and vomited onto some straw. He straightened with a defiant look in his blue-green eyes. "I don't believe you. This can't be happening."

Then he ran out of the stables.

I returned to the harem and asked to see Celia again. She had just finished nursing her baby. When she saw the look on my face, she stiffened and gave him to the young woman hovering nearby.

"I'm sorry, Celia, but your brother is suffering from the Great Pox and I'm not sure it can be treated," I said. "Sometimes the treatment is worse than the disease."

She started crying. "You must do everything you can for him. Please, I can pay whatever it costs."

I patted her arm. "Let me do some research and see what I can come up with. Try not to worry." I looked at little Masudi sleeping peacefully in the slave's arms. "Your baby is very sweet. Take comfort from him and I will let you know what I find."

As I walked back to Fustat, I decided to consult with Maimonides. Surely, he would have more experience with this terrible scourge, being a man and a much more experienced healer than I. He agreed to see me.

"I'm not hopeful either," he said after I explained the situation. "I have seen repeated dosages of mercury mixed with herbs work in some cases, but not in others. And as you know, there is a danger that the patient will die from mercury poisoning before he dies of the pox."

"Yes, so I've been told." I paused. "How would you feel about administering to Pierre? I don't feel comfortable going to the stables by myself and I'd rather not bother the eunuchs. The less they know . . ."

To my great relief, Maimonides agreed to take over Pierre's treatment. As a court physician and a man, it would be easier for him to gain access to the sultan's stables on a regular basis. I thanked him, hoping for the best but fearing the worst.

CHAPTER 24
December 1195 AD

EVERY TIME I visited the harem, Celia kept me abreast of her brother's progress or lack of thereof. Maimonides' treatments had reduced his feelings of dizziness, but he was nauseous a lot of the time, "quell miserable," Celia said. But she continued to pay for the mercury treatments. She would not give up hope, she said.

By mid-December, there was more bad news. Ledicia's predictions about what would happen once the water in the canals receded proved true, and Cairenes began dropping from the fever sickness. I had heeded the healer's advice and warned my relatives about staying away from the marshy canals and lakes. I could do very little for patients with the sickness, other than giving them herbs to bring the fever down, relieve their muscle pain and exhort their families keep them hydrated. Some recovered, but others entered a more toxic phase where the disease attacked their organs and most of these patients died. Ledicia had said the disease was not infectious and that proved true as well, because Estraya and I never became ill.

But one day, Amada, who had been playing with some other children near a canal, accidentally tumbled in. She might have been pushed; her parents never got the real story from her. Hania had been keeping an eye on the children and she rushed down the canal bank and pulled her granddaughter out of the marshy water. A few days later, she came down with a fever, chills, and a headache. Amada also came down with a fever and chills.

The seven-year-old recovered quickly. Her grandmother was not so lucky. Despite my best efforts, Hania became acutely ill.

Benjamin sat by her side, holding her hand as she struggled for breath. She soon slipped into a coma and early one morning, as Benjamin and I dozed by her bedside, she drew her last breath. I startled awake and felt her pulse. I shook my uncle's shoulder.

"She has passed," I told him.

Benjamin cried out and knelt by her body. "Why did I ever agree to come to this cursed land? I have lost my beloved, my heart. I want to die."

I felt horribly guilty and depleted in every muscle in my body. Hania had been so kind and accepting of my father and I when we unexpectedly turned up at her home in Córdoba more than a year ago. And now Hania was gone, having unwittingly forfeited her life to rescue her granddaughter.

I went to wake Isadora and Estraya. They came in and knelt by their mother's side, crying. Isadora intoned the Jewish prayer for death, *Baruch dayan ha'emet*. Then she stood and put a hand on her father's shoulder. He was still prostrate with grief.

"Papa, we need to ready her for burial," Isadora said. "Can you give us a few minutes?"

Benjamin rose unsteadily to his feet, looking drawn and years older. He shuffled out of the room.

Later that afternoon, our garments torn in mourning, we walked beside the cart carrying Benjamin and Hania's body to the Jewish cemetery. It was located on a knoll some distance from us in the ancient city of Fustat. I was surprised to see the cemetery dotted with grandiose mausoleums and many smaller tombs, both stone and wooden.

The cemetery worker who attended us said the dead were not buried underground because of the soil. "It's too sandy and swampy here to put the graves underground." He leered at me. "Course if you got the money, you can build a stone mausoleum all your own." He swept a hand around the cemetery. "We call this the city of the dead and some say the ghosts come out at night and . . ."

Amada's eyes widened in horror. Isadora noticed her daughter's reaction and nudged Mordecai.

He stepped forward. "Can you please take us to our mother's tomb? We'd like to say the burial prayers and get back before it turns dark."

WE ARRIVED AT the wooden edifice where Hania was to be buried, and Mordecai helped his father-in-law out of the cart. Benjamin looked as though he could barely stand. He leaned against the cart, his eyes glassy with grief.

"Do you want to say the Kaddish or do you want me to?" Mordecai asked.

Benjamin waved a limp hand.

Mordecai took that as an assent and began intoning the Kaddish. After he finished, Isadora talked about what a wonderful mother Hania had been. Halfway through a sentence, she choked up and had to stop. Estraya stepped in and said a few words, her arm tight around her older sister. Finally, each of us picked up a handful of dirt and put it on the coffin, which was resting on moveable wooden slats.

As Hania's coffin was slid on the slats into the tomb, I couldn't help but marvel about how ingenious this burial process was. I wondered who the clever person was who had thought up the idea to stack the coffins above ground had been; no doubt he was dead and buried in this very cemetery.

We arrived back at our house as the sun dipped in the sky. My uncle said he wasn't hungry and went to lie down. I hurried out back to wash my face and hands. The trip to the cemetery and back had been hot and dusty. Just as I finished scrubbing my hands, I heard a shriek of joy from Estraya. I almost dropped the soap. What could have occasioned such enthusiasm at a time like this?

Estraya came rushing outside. "You must come. We have a visitor."

"Who?" I asked, mystified.

"You'll see," Estraya said, grinning happily.

I hastened into the house, my heart leaping like a hooked fish.

Bernardo, dusty and looking tired, stood in the middle of the entryway, surrounded by my relatives. He saw me and smiled. "How are you, my dear?"

I stared at him in disbelief. "You came?"

"I came," he said.

I rushed to him and he wrapped his arms around me. "I'm so sorry to hear about your aunt. May she rest in peace and her memory be a blessing."

I looked around. My relatives were all grinning at me.

"Um, can you join us for supper?" I asked. "We don't have anything prepared; we just got back from burying my aunt. I'm afraid it will be a cold meal."

"Actually," Isadora interjected, "Mira left us a warm dish of chicken, olives, and cous cous. Please do join us."

I helped Estraya set the table and we all sat down to eat at the kitchen table. I couldn't help stealing glances at Bernardo. I couldn't believe he had come.

"How was your trip?" Mordecai asked as he helped himself to some chicken and then passed the plate to Bernardo.

"We had fair weather and good winds," Bernardo said. "It only took us three weeks to sail to Jaffa. I did some business there and then found another boat bound for Cairo."

"And here you are," Isadora said. "Welcome. I'm sorry you arrived at such a sad time."

"I am sorry too," Bernardo said. He turned to Mordecai. "Have you and your father-in-law been able to restart your business?"

"It hasn't been easy," Mordecai said, frowning. "My father-in-law's contacts don't want to go in with us. They want the business to themselves. But we've been buying up some goods and we're looking for a partner to bring them back to Spain."

Bernardo raised an eyebrow.

Mordecai exchanged a glance with Isadora. "My wife is expecting and I'd rather stay close until after she gives birth."

"What wonderful news." Bernardo rubbed his chin. "My sister and her husband moved here a few years ago, and he and I work together. I'm sure he knows a few traders who might be able to help. Would you like me to approach them?"

Isadora nodded vigorously and Mordecai chuckled. "I think my wife would like that very much. And so would I."

A little later, as Estraya and I got up to start clearing the table, Isadora put a hand on my arm. "Estraya and I can take care of this. Why don't you and Bernardo get some air?"

As the sun dipped toward the horizon, we strolled through the Jewish quarter until we came to a small park. Even though it was early January, the air was very mild and dry. We found a bench beneath some palm trees, and Bernardo turned to me.

"I want to apologize for the way I behaved in Toledo," he said, his dark brown eyes searching mine. "Can I tell you a story?"

I nodded.

"I always fancied myself in love with Rachel—she was a year older than me and afraid of nothing. We were best friends as children and always getting into one scrape or another. In the back of my mind, I thought we would wind up together. But then Rachel's father pushed her at the king. Before I knew it, Rachel had become King Alfonso's mistress, and I could see she was enamored of him and her new status at court. So, I backed off and drowned my sorrows in travel and building up my business. But then I met you and I fell in love for the first time since I was an adolescent at Rachel's beck and call."

Bernardo paused. I had heard all of this from Bernardo's sister.

"But then she was killed, and I felt like I was drowning, as if I hadn't done enough to save her, as if it was somehow all my fault." Bernardo hung his head. "I just couldn't face you or anyone else. I needed time to sort things out."

I resisted the urge to stroke his cheek. "I understood that. Have you sorted things out?"

Bernardo nodded, his mouth trembling. A fortnight after we left Spain, he said he had visited his father in Valencia and opened his heart to him.

"My father said there was nothing that he or I or anyone else could have done to save Rachel," Bernardo said. "She had chosen to stay in Toledo and stand by her lover and he failed her."

"He certainly did," I said, feeling a surge of anger once again at the king's betrayal.

Bernardo leaned toward me, his eyes glistening with emotion. "My father told me something else. He said that what I felt for Rachel was puppy love and that what I feel for you is the real thing. And as he said it, I realized it was so." He folded his hands over mine. "I love you, Rebecca, and I want to marry you. Will you still have me?"

I searched his face. A hint of anxiety glittered in his eyes, as if he was afraid I would reject him.

I laughed to myself, released a hand from his grip, and swatted him playfully on the shoulder. "Of course, you silly man. I would have you or no one else."

We found each other's lips and were oblivious to anything else, as the deepening twilight enfolded us in its arms.

ACKNOWLEDGEMENTS

I first read *Ivanhoe*, Sir Walter Scott's classic novel, when I was in college and was captivated by the tale of a medieval knight who rescues the Jewish healer Rebecca from being burned alive at the stake. In Scott's 1819 book, Sir Wilfred of Ivanhoe is grievously injured in a tournament in England shortly after he returns from fighting in the crusades, and Rebecca, who happens to be attending the tournament, takes him into her home and heals him. He returns the favor by presenting himself, still wounded, as her champion and rescuing her from an ugly fate. Some forty years later, the character of Rebecca returned to me in a daydream and I began toying with the idea of writing a sequel to Scott's novel. The first thing I did was reread *Ivanhoe* and rediscovered that after her harrowing escape, Rebecca and her father made plans to leave England for Spain, where her father had relatives. I then did a tremendous amount of research about living conditions for Jews in Spain during the twelfth century. In the course of my research, I came upon the fascinating true-life story of Rachel of Esra, the Jewish mistress of King Alfonso VIII (who ruled over Castile and Leon), and realized I had to weave her story into my tale. A number of the events that take place in my novel are historically accurate, such as King Alfonso's loss in 1197 to Yaqub al-Mansur, the Sultan who ruled southern Spain at the time, and the Church's fomenting of anti-Semitic riots in Toledo.

I was already familiar with the story of Maimonides, the famous Jewish physician and philosopher who was born in Spain but left with his family, first for Morocco and then Egypt, where he became a favored physician of the Sultan and achieved fame for his writings about the nature of God. I consulted a number of online sources and books, among them *A Guide for the Perplexed* by Dara Horn, and learned that during the twelfth and thirteenth centuries, the Muslim rulers of Egypt were more tolerant and accepting of Jews than most European monarchs. So, it made sense for Rebecca and her family to seek haven in Egypt after fleeing persecution in Spain.

I would like to thank my good friends, Debbi Solomon, Larry Marion, and Karen Osborn, as well as my son, David Aronlee, for taking the time to read and comment on early drafts of this book; their guidance was incredibly helpful. I am also grateful to Debra Ginsberg for her insightful assistance in polishing the novel. She suggested I read *Ashkenazi Herbalism; Rediscovering the Herbal Traditions of Eastern European Jews* by Deatra Cohen and Adam Siegel, which gave me further insights into the healing practices of Rebecca's time. I would also like to thank the production team at Bedazzled Ink Publishing for their help, including C.A. Casey for her incisive edits and creative cover design, and Elizabeth Gibson for her astute marketing guidance. And many thanks to Kathleen Schmidt, whose dedicated professionalism helped spread the word about my book.

More information can be found at the following online sources:

https://en.wikipedia.org/wiki/Rahel_la_Fermosa
https://www.jewishencyclopedia.com/articles/6085-fermosa
https://www.casadellibro.com/libro-la-historia-de-fermosa-la-amante-de-alfonso-viii/9788461289301/1336401
https://www.britannica.com/biography/Alfonso-VIII

Alison Bass is an award-winning journalist and the author of three critically acclaimed nonfiction books: *Brassy Broad: How one journalist helped pave the way to #MeToo*; *Getting Screwed, Sex Workers and the Law* (2015) and *Side Effects: A Prosecutor, a Whistleblower and a Bestselling Antidepressant on Trial.* (2008). *Side Effects* received the prestigious National Association of Science Writers' Science in Society Award and the film rights to Side Effects have been optioned.

Bass recently retired as Associate Professor of Journalism at West Virginia University. She was a long-time science and medical writer for *The Boston Globe* and a series she wrote for *The Globe* was nominated for a Pulitzer Prize in the Public Service category. Her articles and essays have also appeared in *The Los Angeles Times, Buzzfeed, The Village Voice, Psychology Today,* and numerous other media. She has received a number of journalism awards for her work, including an Alicia Patterson Fellowship and the Top Media Award from the National Mental Health Association. For more on her credentials, please visit her website at www.alison-bass.com.